OUT OF DARKNESS

OUT OF DARKNESS

INVIDIA BOOK 1

Glen R Stansfield

The Man in a Hat
7 St John Street, Creetown, Newton Stewart DG8 7JA

To my wife, Jess, who puts up with a lot.

ACKNOWLEDGMENTS

These are the people that in one way or another made this book possible. My thanks go to the following, and I hope I have not forgotten anyone.

Juliane Retsch, Fleetmon Support Customer Service, for providing an insight into AIS ship tracking.

Sue Noyes, for her unceasing proofreading and editing.

Seumas Gallacher, for his continued encouragement and invaluable advice.

The Bahrain Writers' Circle, for always being there.

And how could I possibly forget Rohini Sunderam and Saira Ranj who seem to have a far more faith in my abilities than I.

CHAPTER ONE

The first Gulf war decided it for him. He loved driving but the thought of being shot at or bombed didn't exactly excite him; and the heat, relentless, shrivelling-the-hair-up-your-nostrils heat. Not to mention all that sand; it got everywhere, food, eyes, mouth and other orifices he didn't care to mention. When it got into your clothes as it inevitably did, then it chafed the skin, especially your groin where it seemed to congregate the most.

How anyone would choose to live in that, he had no idea. To top it all, they expected him to drive wearing an NBC suit. No one knew whether Saddam would use chemical weapons or not and the Army were taking no chances. Your own personal sauna inside a sun-heated oven - lovely.

Driving tank transporters placed him in a good position to get a job when he came out. As soon as potential employers discovered his previous driving experience, they knew they had a competent driver on their hands. Her Majesty generally prefers her equipment to arrive in one piece and the Army trained him well to ensure it did so.

A pity Junction 26 Diner was closed at this time of day. A cuppa would go down a treat right now, and it was getting close to his compulsory rest break. The delay in loading at

CHAPTER ONE

Southampton gave him barely enough time to push on to South Mimms Services for a compulsory fifteen-minute break. Soulless place compared to Junction 26, still, beggars can't be choosers.

He let out a yawn, stretching his neck first to one side, then the other. Neck and shoulders always bore the brunt of driving. He couldn't imagine what it had been like in the old days; no power steering or brakes. Brute strength would be needed to just keep the truck on the road. Those guys must have had necks like tree trunks.

He missed listening to Janice Long and Alex Lester on the After-Midnight show; cost cutting apparently. Now the night program consisted of rehashed daytime radio repeated through the night, but occasionally a real gem would come on and cause him to turn up the volume. He pressed the button on the steering wheel and the sound of 10cc's *I'm Not in Love* filled the cab.

~§~

They were certainly banging out the golden oldies tonight. It was definitely not Money for Nothing in this job and as for chicks, they didn't come free or otherwise.

He glanced in his mirrors then back to the road in front. Instinctively he pressed hard on the brakes, the cab dipping sharply as he did so. The scantily clad young woman caught in the beam of his headlamps waved her arms wildly, signalling him to stop. He was trying but a forty-tonne truck does not stop in a matter of metres. In desperation, he swung the wheel to the right, but he feared it was too late.

This part of the motorway had no hard shoulder. The nearside lane being so close to the crash barrier had given him little time to react.

He felt sick as he looked in his nearside mirror. The woman silhouetted in the headlamps of the following vehicles, lay motionless next to the barrier as the truck shuddered to a halt in a cloud of blue tyre smoke, straddling the first and second lanes of the motorway.

~§~

At the far end of the room, the double doors opened, and two men entered. Michael Strong, looking as good as ever, led the pair. Even as the thought occurred, Helene suppressed it. She was learning to cope and be more circumspect with her relationships. He was strictly 'work' and she intended for it to remain that way. Besides, she already had someone in her sights.

Her attention turned to the second man and her heart dropped; Chief Superintendent Brandon, her nemesis in the Met; the man who told her to find another line of work — that women had no place as detectives, and especially women of colour - only that wasn't quite the way he worded it.

She rolled her eyes and must have let out a low groan causing the man sitting next to her to turn and stare. Brandon caught her eye, grinned and winked at her.

Really? What the hell was going on?

After a brief discussion with Strong, Brandon signalled for Helene to join him. Without a word, he ushered her through the double doors and out of the room. Wondering if her career had ended before it started, she watched Brandon as he closed the doors behind them.

He turned, a smile on his face. She stood defiantly with her arms crossed defensively in front of her. She did not like this man and she had no qualms about showing it, even if it meant she would be seeking employment elsewhere.

'Helene, I owe you an explanation.'

He paused, lowered his head for a moment, then looked up into her eyes.

'And an apology for pushing you so hard in your last post. I recommended you for this position, but I couldn't be sure you would be interested, given your dedication to the Met. You are the best, and we need the best here. The only way I could see to steer you towards this job was by making you uncomfortable in MIT. I really do apologise and hope you can forgive me. If there had been any other way ...'

Helene's eyes narrowed with suspicion.

'So, you are part of this now?'

'I've been part of it since the outset, but I'm still employed by the Met. You probably already know this but before I came to SCD, I was with SO17 and the rest of the departments that followed. I got to meet people in high places, people I wouldn't normally be able to reach, and gained access to some interesting information. So, when this group was first mooted, the powers-that-be knew I could speak to the right people. It will all become clear once you hear what we have to say.'

He gestured towards the doors.

'Perhaps we should go back in and start the briefing. Michael can explain how this is going to work in far more detail than I can. It's his baby and by the way, he is one sharp cookie.'

Helene cocked her head on one side.

'Who exactly are these "powers-that-be," sir?'

Brandon shook his head.

'That, I'm afraid I can't tell you. Just suffice to say you are still in the employ of the UK government, although they will deny it if ever challenged.'

She studied his eyes for a few moments.

'There's something I need to say.'

Brandon gestured for her to continue.

'You are an absolute bastard.' After a pause of several seconds, she added, 'sir.'

Brandon let out a loud laugh.

'I suppose I deserve that and believe you me, you're not the first to say it. I wouldn't expect any less from you, Helene. You always played it straight and said it straight. Those are qualities I very much admire in a person. I really am sorry I had to treat you the way I did, but I desperately wanted you running the ops side of this. So, are we good?'

Helene smiled, a "welcome aboard the flight" smile.

'We'll see.'

Brandon laughed again.

'Not what I expected to hear.'

'And what exactly did you expect to hear after putting me through hell these past few months? "Oh certainly, sir. All is rosy in the garden." That isn't how it works.'

'No. I expected you to say, "fuck you" after what I did, so there's hope after all.'

She couldn't help but giggle at that. Not the response she expected either.

They returned to the room: all eyes turning to watch as she returned to her seat, wondering why she had been singled out for a private chat. As she took her place, she glanced at the others. They would be her responsibility from now on.

Strong took up his position at one of the two remaining seats at the table: Brandon taking the final one to his right. Now with the room's attention back on him, Strong addressed the newly assembled team.

'Ladies and gentlemen, you all know my name by now and my position as the head of this project, which from now on will be known as the Invidia Syndicate. As most of you don't know each other, I will start the introductions with Detective Chief Superintendent Brandon, who is not officially part of the team. He will however provide us with the information on our targets, as well as some key personnel, some of whom are already here.

'Now, as already said, I am head of the project, but operationally you will report to Detective Chief Inspector Helene MacKay.'

Strong held his hand out towards Helene.

'You will notice I addressed her by her former rank in the Met Police. This is because you will all retain the ranks you had achieved in whatever service you came from, although some of you are civilians and will effectively remain so. For the non-civilians, you will show as being on secondment to the National Crime Agency. Your salary, however, will not be the same as your former ranks. This is a specialist team, and your pay will reflect that. I can assure you no one will lose out.

'Helene is in charge because essentially this is police work, and she has the finest clear up rate not only in the Met but in the whole of Europe. Her detecting skills are second to none and trust me, we are going to need that with what we are intending to do.

'Make no mistake, this is a war against crime and the people who undertake criminal activities, a war, which I am sad to say, we are not winning, but that is why we are all here. I will say now, we are not an anti-terrorist unit as such, but if for operational reasons it would be beneficial for us to continue with an operation, rather than hand it over to one of the anti-terrorist groups, then we will do so. That decision will not be ours to make and will come from the highest level. Helene will still carry a warrant card, as will any other members of the group who carried them before; there will be occasions when we must appear to be a branch of the police force.'

Strong took a sip of water before continuing.

'We will have a more informal get-together this evening, when I expect you to become better acquainted with each other, so here's a quick introduction of the rest of you.'

Strong moved clockwise around the table introducing each of the members of the team. An innocuous couple Helene had noted a few moments ago, were introduced as the best undercover operatives at HM Customs and Revenue. The blonde girl to the left of them turned out to be a geek; a computer hacker going by the handle, 0rchid. In common with many hackers, she substituted a numeral for one of the letters in her online identity. She had achieved something most considered to be almost impossible, hacking into the government communications centre, GCHQ. That took Helene totally by surprise and she would need to hear that particular story from the beginning.

Only two members were known to her, one whom she knew on both personal and professional levels; Harry Fielding. He would be responsible for the training of the field operatives. The other, a journalist: Nicky Rolands. Quite why there would be a journalist on the team, she had no idea. The last thing they would want was publicity.

She looked forward to the evening, getting to know the others and hear their stories. The credentials of the assembled personnel made her certain she made the right decision to leave the Met and join the team. This would be her chance to make a difference.

CHAPTER TWO

'Chen Investments. How may I be of assistance?'

An immaculately dressed receptionist smiled as she answered the call. The caller may not be able to see her smile but would almost certainly hear it in her voice. That was company policy; polite, courteous and smiling.

'Certainly sir, I'll put you through.'

Words emblazoned in gold and red on the marble fronted reception desk confirmed the identity of the company. A variety of potted plants dotted the reception area along with several, excessively comfortable and undoubtedly expensive, white-leather sofas. Clients entering these offices had no doubt they were in the presence of a successful business; their investments in the hands of people capable of growing their wealth.

Several corridors snaked out from the central atrium; the curved form only hinting at what lay beyond. Feng Shui lived here and cared not a jot who knew. Each corridor contained a number of offices secreted behind solid wooden doors: no open plan spaces in this company. Anyone doing business with Chen Investments expected their dealings to be private. They were not disappointed. A handful of offices benefitted from access to a private elevator reserved for those clients for whom ultimate discretion was of the utmost importance.

Directly behind the reception desk a final corridor led diagonally away towards the corner of the building; an abundance of artwork and a lack of doorways set it apart from the rest. At the far end of this portal and stationed at a smaller, less ostentatious desk another immaculately presented secretary served as a guardian for the inner sanctum. Behind the solitary solid teak door and occupying a significant portion of the corner of the building lay the office of the founder and CEO of the company, Chen Man-Long.

Through a panoramic window and behind a highly polished walnut desk lay a spectacular view of Victoria Harbour, Kowloon and what used to be Kai Tak Airport, long since turned over to the developers. The magnificent vista and location in Hong Kong Central, the heart of the financial district, were the deciding factors for the occupation of this suite of offices by Chen Investments.

But today, the view held no interest for the man sitting with his head in his hands. He could not suppress the sob; this could not be happening to him. For his entire life in stockbroking his investments had been on the nail. The company he founded, the reason they occupied these offices, his reputation, all built on sound investments; a fabulous home with landscaped garden - an expensive luxury in land-strapped Hong Kong - his own car a Range Rover Autobiography, a BMW M6 convertible for his wife and an S class Mercedes for the driver to take his daughter to one of Hong Kong's finest schools each day, all of this stemmed from his ability to read the markets.

Of course, like most Chinese he wished for a son, a son who would inherit this wealth and carry on the family business but complications in pregnancy put paid to that so Kun remained his only child; a child he loved dearly even though not the son he longed for.

In two-thousand-and-seven, Chen, like many others invested a substantial amount of his own personal wealth in what looked to be a low-risk, relatively high-yield investment, Australian mortgages. Then came the global financial crash.

Funds the world over suffered, mortgage defaults went to a record high and the fund into which he gambled their future and that of several of his prestigious clients became frozen.

That was bad enough, their money locked-up out of reach but the news that reached him this morning, that the investment firm had gone into receivership did not bode well at all. If lucky, they would be offered a few cents on the dollar, but from what he gathered from his contacts in Australia investors would be lucky indeed if they saw a single cent.

He must act fast, take a few chances to build their remaining money into a reasonable nest egg. They still owned the house so that would be safe but unless he took some action soon their lifestyle would plummet and Kun would go to a state school, something he wished to avoid at all costs. His daughter would have the best and one day she would make him proud.

In Chinese culture, one of the worst things that can happen is loss of face; mianzi. The concept of mianzi appears complex to a foreigner and is nuanced in many ways that is difficult to understand for someone who has not grown up with the idea of "face". The Chinese idiom summed it up; men can't live without face; trees can't live without bark.

As with many people when backed into a corner, Chen felt a prickle of fear, one that interfered with his usually methodical and analytical brain. Not only was their future at stake, but more importantly his mianzi. He had never been a gambler but driven by his desire to right the wrongs he had done, he began to scour the market for some of the riskier investments he wouldn't normally touch but desperate times warrant desperate measures.

~§~

This was a part of the job he hated. He could deal with angry motorists, injured passengers and even dead bodies — unless children, that always got to you — but telling someone their loved one would not be coming home, that hurt every time.

Doubly painful this time as a husband and wife had lost their lives in a single vehicle road traffic accident.

The loss of someone close causes immense grief. If this occurs after an illness, the mind and heart at least have time to prepare. The total brutality of loss comes when a loved one goes about their daily lives and something happens to snatch them away before anyone can say goodbye - gone, in an instant, never to return. The chance to tell them of your love, share your day with them, explore their feelings, thoughts and memories, wrenched away with such violence, it feels almost physical.

As a Senior Inspector, Xie Gong Ling would not usually be involved at this level, but when the victims are none other than a prominent Hong Kong businessman and his wife, protocol demands it be handled by a senior officer.

As the driver negotiated his way up the steep and winding roads of the Peak District of Hong Kong, the Inspector reflected on his own position, how it contrasted with the wealthy. Why did money hold such importance in the world? He didn't begrudge anyone getting on in life, he just did not understand why doctors, nurses, firemen and yes, even policemen, were paid so little in comparison to those whose sole purpose in life was to move a set of numbers from one column of a spreadsheet to another, and in doing so, make them bigger.

The poor girl sobbed her heart out as the housemaid tried to comfort her. There is no easy way to break the news that her parents are never coming home. Still, as the daughter of one of Hong Kong's wealthier families she would be well cared for. Money may not buy happiness, but it certainly eased your way in life. For now, she would be looked after by the staff until something more formal could be put in place; enquiries still ongoing as to the next of kin.

The Inspector couldn't help but glance around the property. This room alone probably contained more square footage than the entire floor in his apartment block. He wagered there would be bigger broom cupboards than his apartment. It just goes to show, money can't stop you dying.

He once again offered his condolences to Chen Kun, presented his business card to her and told her to call anytime, day or night, if she needed to know anything. Through the floods of tears, Kun thanked him and he took his leave.

As the police car descended the hill from the Chen household, the Inspector let out a sigh and he caught the driver glancing at him in the mirror.

'I'd forgotten how difficult that is. I need a beer.'

The driver knew the routine, if the Inspector needed a beer then a beer he would have. He put on the lights and siren and made a rapid change in direction, much to the annoyance of the motorist he cut off. The Inspector needed a beer and what was the point in having a police car if you couldn't use all the bells and whistles for such emergencies.

~§~

Kun's Uncle Li questioned the solicitor.

'So, there is nothing, no inheritance, no house, nothing at all?'

'I'm sorry Mr Chen. It seems your brother lost heavily on an investment. He mortgaged the house and used the funds to make further investments. He did take out a life insurance policy for a considerable sum that would be placed in trust for Kun —'

'Ah, so, there is some money, tied up in investments and life insurance?'

'Unfortunately, not. He did not invest wisely. It's all gone. The insurance policy is null and void as the death occurred less than six months into the policy, an unfortunate clause I suspect he overlooked.'

Chen Li paused for a moment.

'Wait a minute, aren't you forgetting something?'

The solicitor raised his eyebrows, waiting for Chen Li's question.

'The company, Chen Investments, he was the CEO. That company is worth millions of dollars.'

Chen Li smiled. He'd found his brother's money at last. The only reason he took on the responsibility of looking after Kun was to get at his brother's money. Chen Man-Long may have ostracised Li when alive, but in death he would give Li a lifestyle he longed for.

'If only that were the case Mr Chen. You brother may well have founded the company and been CEO, but he sold the majority of his shares some time ago. What is left will barely cover the debts. Your brother borrowed heavily to try to recover his position. He gambled and lost. I'm sorry.'

Gambling was something Li knew only too well; his own debts being considerable. He needed this money; he owed a triad and they didn't take too well to people who failed to pay their debts. Li felt the blood drain from his face.

This was typical of his sibling, making sure that nothing came his way even in death, and what's more he was saddled with the man's offspring. Offspring, now there's an idea. She's a pretty girl, young, innocent and educated, just the sort of girl who could make money of her own.

Li didn't speak as he slammed the door on his way out, a plan already formulating in his mind. This may make him debt free after all. Well now, Chen Man-Long, let's see who will have the last laugh.

~§~

The solicitor slowly shook his head as he watched him go. So many times, he had seen relatives distraught not because of the loss of a loved one, but from being told they had been left nothing. What a sad world we live in.

CHAPTER THREE

Anthony Aaron Duncan Hendricks, never wanted for much of anything, and therein lay the problem. Unfortunately for Anthony, his parents seemed far too busy with their careers to pay him much attention; his father on the board of a private bank, a real go-getter, his mother, a high-flyer in the fashion industry.

Anthony, never Tony, understood his social standing even at the tender age of five when his parents sent him to an expensive boarding school, hidden away in the countryside. Despite the contrary opinions of his tutors, Anthony never thought of himself as privileged or advantaged in any way, merely entitled to receive what he demanded.

Rarely did he have much contact with his parents, not even during the school holidays. Often, they would be away, his mother in Rome, New York, or one of the many other fashion centres, his father jet-setting here and there, securing another wealthy customer for the bank. When not at boarding school, he would be looked after by a nanny, or to be precise, a string of nannies; few would put up with his entitled behaviour for long. It was little wonder that in his teenage years, he was unable to bond with anyone, male or female. As far as

Anthony was concerned, the world was there to serve him, perhaps that is why his true soul mate was his cat with whom he had many a long conversation.

Whether it was guilty conscience, or their way of making their only child comfortable in life, no one could say, but whatever Anthony wanted, Anthony received. He learned that money could solve anything, as long as you threw enough of it at the problem. Thus, the die was cast.

Years passed, and he saw the inevitability of his future. Eton, to continue his education, then on to the world of finance, in his father's footsteps. Always, doors would open for him. That was his world and it was a good one.

As Shakespeare once wrote, "All the world's a stage, and all the men and women merely players." Anthony believed the world was indeed a stage; he played the lead, the others merely the supporting cast. There were of course some who admired him and his attitude, saw it as strong character, rather than a flaw, but they were few and far between. Most couldn't stand him, going out of their way to avoid being in his company, yet he rarely noticed. Why would he? What others did with their lives was of no concern to him.

Now, in his late thirties, Anthony had become bored. Never able to maintain a serious relationship, most failing after no more than a few days, he got used to the idea that sex was just another commodity; something to be bought, like a Ferrari or a villa in the south of France. Even though he could afford the finest, he was finding it all a bit tedious. What he wanted was excitement, something to make his juices flow, and there was nothing to be found in his life that raised as much as a spark in him. Of course, it never dawned on him that happiness comes from within. The answer to his boredom did not lie in the outside world, but in his own psyche; something that would never cross his mind.

The real trouble started when one of the girls he'd paid for, refused his request for something a bit kinkier. No one ever said 'no' to him, so he punched her before throwing her out. To his surprise, he found it turned him on. Perhaps this was what he needed; sex on the rough side.

With caution, he investigated the possibility of there being someone who would be willing to serve his needs. To his surprise, he found a considerable number of women who would take part in the sorts of activity he now sought, for a price of course; always at a price, reinforcing the notion that money can buy everything.

Eventually, even that started to bore him, and he began to look for new ways to keep himself entertained. He'd heard about snuff movies, allegedly made during the nineteen-seventies, but was disheartened to find that while rumours abounded, there was little evidence to suggest any real movies were ever made. Of course, videos of executions were to be found, if you searched hard enough on the internet, but that did not satisfy his itch. He wanted women being sexually abused on camera, not executed in a cold fashion.

Unable to find his desired stimulation, his thoughts turned to the possibility of moving from the encounters he now found such a drag, to having the ultimate control over these women; life and death. The thought excited him, controlling a person's destiny and watching a life ebb away until that person no longer existed, leaving behind just an empty shell where they once thrived. How could anyone resist? Becoming a deity with the power of life or death would be the ultimate high.

His thoughts returned to his current problems and how to deal with those, that's when he had his eureka moment, a snuff club. Now he could kill two birds with one stone, so to speak.

As he had no intention of spending even a second in prison, he must ensure that not a scrap of evidence be left anywhere to lead back to him, and for that he would need help. Although he was aware the more people involved, the greater the chance of getting caught, there was no doubt in his mind it would need the efforts of someone with better skills than he to fly this project.

He clenched his fists and shook his hands excitedly as a little giggle escaped from him. He hadn't been this thrilled since his father bought him a battery powered, ride-in Rolls Royce car for his tenth birthday; that lasted a whole year before the boredom set in.

CHAPTER THREE

He must tread carefully, but from what little knowledge he had, the Dark Web was the place to put this together. Without any knowledge of the Dark Web itself, other than it existed, he would need an expert on the internet and it so happened he knew someone who just might fit the bill.

~§~

'I don't know, Anthony. It all seems a bit too risky to me.'

'You've got to admit you like the idea though, don't you?'

Casey Hazelton had known Hendricks for a good number of years, from the time they started together at the same bank as fresh-faced investment bankers. They each discovered a penchant for sniffing out investments which few others would consider, but ultimately turned out to be sound and immensely profitable. Hazelton was the first to leave the bank to pursue that line of work as an independent; Hendricks gave up the corporate banking world for independence, some nine months later. Two years ago, they crossed paths again. Hazelton had been one of Anthony's few admirers, back in those early days at the bank; most of the others shunned Hendricks for being too brash, but Hazelton liked his no-nonsense approach.

It could be said that both had done well for themselves, running their own investment companies. Hendricks, inevitably a little more successful than Hazelton, who didn't have the sort of family background Hendricks enjoyed, and Hazelton lacked that extra inbuilt confidence that comes with hereditary wealth, but nevertheless he was a wealthy man by any standard.

The coffee shop was usually quiet mid-morning; today being no exception. The 'grab a coffee' commuters long since gone, the 'let's do lunch, dahling' set, yet to arrive. In one back corner of the room, the inevitable twenty-something-year-old, wild hair constrained by a pair of electric-pink headphones, stared intently at a laptop screen, fingers occasionally hovering over the keyboard: human raptors in search of alphabetical prey. The latte on the table would more than likely be cold, having performed its duty in allowing the purchaser access to the free WiFi. A group of four occupied a table by the window, each one sending hieroglyphics to a person not present; social media displaying more of its anti-social face. The only other occupants, an elderly couple, both of whom seemed to spend most of their time staring into the distance; perhaps remembering the times when they had something to talk about.

'Well, yes. I must say it does have an attraction. I mean, that's the ultimate control, isn't it? Holding another's life in your hands. Of course, there's just the small matter of becoming the plaything of some hairy docker from Grimsby doing time for theft or something. I'm not cut out for that sort of lifestyle. I wouldn't last thirty seconds inside, and you know it.'

Hendricks threw up his hands in exasperation.

'How many times do I have to tell you? There is not the slightest chance of us getting caught. This Dark Web thingy, as you said, keeps us anonymous. We find the right person to supply the girls and they are not going to shop us are they, dear chap? They want to make money from us, and money is something we have, in spades. They will know a good thing when they see it. What I need from you is the means of getting into this Dark Web, without leaving size ten boot prints all over it. That is why I came to you. You know your way around these electronic gizmos far better than anyone else I know — and I trust you, which is the most important part. Do they still have dockers in Grimsby?'

Hendricks could sense Hazelton was wavering. Rather than push the point, he decided to follow another path.

'Okay, I can see you are not game for this. Forget it. I'll have to see if I can tempt somebody else with the necessary skills, not to mention the cash.'

He watched Hazelton's reaction. As he expected, a flicker of disappointment flashed across his face. Yes! He had him hooked and just like with real fishing, he must take care and not try to land him too early.

'Anyway, enough of this, how are things with you in general, Cas? I heard you landed a pretty big deal the other day; beat me to it by a whisker. I don't know how you managed to do that, not with my abilities.'

He could tell Hazelton wasn't really listening to him; his mind clearly elsewhere. He'd seen that look before, He was thinking, weighing up the options, his analytical brain doing exactly what it did best, analysing.

'Hmmm?'

'Nothing, old chap. Nothing to worry about.'

Hendricks waited.

'It can be done, Anthony, but we will need to buy a few things. A laptop with WiFi, preferably used, so there will be no record of the purchase and a mobile phone with a pay-as-you-go sim. Best get that from one of the market stalls. Then we need to find places with WiFi that don't have CCTV. There is no way we are doing this from your place or mine. I'll need to set up a couple of VPNs and we'll need access to —'

Anthony held up his hands to stop the torrent of words that held no meaning to him. This was the Cas he knew. Mind totally focussed on the problem in hand, working out the potential problems and their solutions, this was why he wanted him on board. Hendricks might know how to play the markets but when it came to the electronic wizardry behind it, he was clueless.

'My dear fellow, I have absolutely no idea what you are talking about, but clearly you do, which is why I wanted you in on this in the first place. Assuming you find these PNV thingies and the other bits and bobs you mentioned, I take it we can set about doing our thing?'

'VPN - it's called a VPN, it stands for Virtual Private Network, we'll use it for —'

Hendricks interrupted him once again.

'It's no use trying to explain it to me, my mind is unable to deal with all this gadgetry, I can barely work a TV remote. No, I'll leave that up to you, but once we are all set up, I'll find us a source of young ladies and some willing members for what will be the world's most exclusive and secretive club. Believe me, our secrecy will make that MI5 lot look like a daytime TV chat show.'

As a member of the Masons, Hendricks knew a thing or two about secrecy, but this little escapade would have to take the meaning to a new level entirely.

~§~

Built in the early part of the nineteenth century, Regent's Canal cut a swathe through the heart of Camden on its somewhat meandering route from the Grand Union Canal to the River Thames at Limehouse. With the advent of the railways, there were many who forecast the demise of the canal system, but had those detractors still been alive today, they would have been stunned to see the activity on the waterways of Britain. Perhaps not the commerce the builders of the web-like canal system had envisaged back in the days of the industrial revolution, but something that few from that era could have predicted. Tourism proved to be the saviour of these feats of engineering, and this part of Camden was no exception. Overlooking the Hampstead Road lock, the only twin lock remaining on the London canal network, Camden Lock Market became a popular destination for tourists and shoppers alike and colourful canal boats traversed the lock on a regular basis.

Taking advantage of the unseasonably good weather for the middle of November, Hazelton occupied a table on the roof terrace of what was once the lock-keeper's cottage, and now home to a Starbucks. The WiFi signal here was strong enough and no one paid attention to yet another person taking advantage of the free connection to the internet. Only, Hazelton had no time for the internet these days. Whenever possible, he visited a public WiFi area to continue working on the joint project with Hendricks; never the same place two days in a row.

The Dark Web became his lurking ground. Hazelton felt they were near to completing the first stage of the venture; several persons having already invested in the project.

'How's it going, old boy?'

Hazelton jumped. He had been so engrossed in the screen he hadn't noticed the approaching figure. Hendricks placed an Americano in front of him, set down his green tea on the opposite side of the table and pulled out a chair.

'You know, psychopaths drink their coffee black, don't you?'

'Yeah? Who says, the Milk Marketing Board?'

'Actually, it came from a study in Austria.'

'The birthplace of Hitler, what a coincidence.'

Hendricks studied him for a moment.

'You seem a little bit on edge there. Is there a problem?'

Hazelton finished the last of his cold coffee before taking a sip from the fresh one.

'Not yet, but there could be. Where are we going to do this Anthony? We have nowhere to go. This isn't something we can do in the Dorchester, is it?'

'You fret too much old boy. As it happens, I've got a house in the country on a six-month lease.'

'Anthony, please tell me you didn't waltz into an agency and rent a house.'

'Of course not, what do you take me for? I've hidden enough assets offshore to know how shell companies work. The lease is for a company in Belize which is owned by one in Bermuda, a subsidiary of one in the Caymans, yadi-yadi-ya. You know how it all works? It's that convoluted they would disappear up their own backsides before they unravelled it, and none of them point to us.'

A little relief crept into Hazelton's mind. Hendricks certainly knew how to hide assets, the process for the lease would be no different. But ...

'What about the keys?'

'Couriered to a virtual office, collected by courier from there to another office, yadi-yadi-ya. Final delivery to a PO Box registered in a fictitious company name and picked up by a kid who earned a twenty to do so. And in case that worries you, it was in Brighton, so hardly likely to find us here, are they?'

Hazelton relaxed. Anthony had been a busy boy and a clever one too.

'So where are we up to, dear chap?'

'We have nine investors already and I have a lead on some assets for you. You did say you wanted to handle that side of things, didn't you? I couldn't believe how many people are in the business of people. Do you know how easy it is to buy another human?'

'Well, thank goodness for that. Otherwise, we would have to go and round up our own, wouldn't we? Yes, let me have the details and I will make the arrangements. On the subject of investors, I think I know of a couple more. I think these may require the personal approach. Not one of us of course, not until they sign up that is, old boy.'

A little prickle of conscience inserted itself into Hazelton's thoughts, a fleeting moment of humanity, only to be driven back into the Freudian *id* by the promise of things to come. Like Hendricks, Hazelton had a morally different view of the world although not quite in the same way; money could pay to satisfy any desire, and everything had a price tag, but unlike Hendricks, he didn't always see that as a good thing.

CHAPTER FOUR

After discovering Kun was not the wealthy young girl he'd imagined, Li traded her to clear his gambling debts and so, at the age of thirteen, she found herself in the seedy underworld of Hong Kong, providing sexual services for anyone with enough dollars to buy time with her. The fall could not be more bitter. What did a thirteen-year-old girl know about sex? Not that her age mattered either to the clients or the triad. There are many in the world that only see a monetary value or a means to an end. Sadly, to them she became both. She withdrew into herself and the clients became reluctant to choose her because of her sullen appearance and lack of enthusiasm. Her earnings diminished, and the triad took the option of cutting their losses by selling her to Xing. Here she found a new friend; Lian Jing.

The two girls clicked from the start, as though they had known each other for years. When not working, they would talk about the day they would leave this place, get married, have children and of all the places they would see. It was these conversations with Jing that kept Kun sane. She hated nothing more than selling her body. Her body, not Xing's. Yet she had to offer it to clients as though it was a biscuit, or a piece of fruit; a cup of tea. It was hers, and hers alone and she should be able to decide what to do with it. As with the triad, Xing found Kun to be earning well below her potential, along with her friend Jing and no amount of cajoling or threats would alter that.

~§~

As businessmen go, Xing Da wasn't the brightest, so when the gweilo asked him if he had any girls for sale, he naturally assumed he meant by the hour, but once the man explained he wanted girls for export, even Xing Da could see a golden opportunity. He was only too happy to oblige; besides, he owed this Westerner a favour, not that he would be parting with his best earners: he didn't owe him that much.

The gweilo wanted young girls who either were or could possibly pass for virgins. Xing Da thought it strange that someone would ask a brothel keeper for girls of this kind. Virgins were in short supply in his game and didn't stay qualified for too long. True virgins would bring top dollar, more than this man would be willing to pay, he was certain. Perhaps that was why he suggested girls who may pass as virgins would be acceptable. Xing told him he would see what he could do. He had two girls in mind who he considered were so lazy, they may as well be virgins.

Although prostitution is a perfectly legal activity in Hong Kong, running a brothel or having more than one working girl on the premises is not. To get around this, most girls worked from an apartment and seemingly no one controlled them or lived off their earnings. Of course, almost everyone was aware the majority of women working this way worked for someone else. Independents didn't enjoy the same level of protection as the other girls. On the other hand, they didn't have to hand over their hard-earned cash to someone else nor did they have to suffer beatings many of them suffered if their earnings fell below expectations.

As pimps go, Xing Da was one of the better pimps. He allowed the girls a certain amount of freedom, never abused them and paid them a decent wage, but there were a handful who still didn't seem to like the idea of working for a living. How hard could it be? Lie there while some pudgy, overweight, middle-aged gweilo has his thirty seconds of ecstasy, send him on his way and then almost a full hour off before the next client. Pity some counted their miseries carefully and accepted their blessings without much thought.

Besides the two of his own, he would find some more from his — friends would perhaps be too strong a word — associates, yes, that would be more fitting. Ten girls in all, destined for some high-class operation in the UK it would seem. The same gweilo asked him about transportation and it just so happened he had a cousin in the shipping industry who knew a man who knew a man, etcetera. Well, isn't that what cousins are for? Xing Da was able to offer a complete package of girls and transport for a bargain price. They would need to be taken off the ship before it arrived at Tilbury with its mixed cargo of timber and containers, but once they left these shores that would no longer be his concern.

The gweilo said he had the perfect solution for removing them at the other end so a deal was struck. Xing got rid of his two least productive girls, his associates did the same, his cousin earned a healthy backhander as did the Captain of the ship. Everyone, even the gweilo was happy so what could be wrong with that? As for the girls, they should be happy too. Xing heard that gold paved the streets of London, what more could a girl want, eh?

CHAPTER FIVE

He worked damned hard to make his business a success. It was not the result of some random chance of being in the right place at the right time. It was the result of ensuring he was in the right place, and in the right business. He didn't believe in luck when it came to business matters. Work hard, play hard, and never take your eye off the ball; that was the key to success and it certainly worked for him.

Starting with nothing but a market stall, he built his company into a small empire covering numerous industries, both legacy and new economy. He didn't believe the hype about traditional businesses being dead, nor did he believe that technology was the only place to be. His granny once taught him that putting all your eggs in one basket was a fool's game.

Now, in his mid-forties, he was comfortably well-off, lived an excellent lifestyle, a loving wife, two adorable children, several holidays a year; in short, everything he had ever hoped for and more — but ...

And therein lay the problem, the But. He had no idea what it was that was missing but something was and try as he might, he was unable to put his finger on it. Still, there were plenty of distractions in his life and tonight was one of those.

CHAPTER FIVE

The Business Association Spring Charity Masquerade Ball was the sort of event from which his teenage self would have run a mile. In those days he could never have imagined he would have danced at all, let alone attend a ball. Yet, this was one of the highlights of the year, spending time with his wife, sipping champagne and dancing the night away. This is how life should be, he'd earned it — they'd earned it. There wasn't a shred of doubt in his mind that his success stemmed from the immense support his wife gave him. Her faith in his ability to do the right thing made sure he did the right thing.

He waited for his wife in the hall of their seventeenth century mansion house, checking his watch for the umpteenth time. They were not late and he curbed his impatience to be on the way. She would come down all in good time.

As manor houses go, this was on the small side but still substantial and of course far more than they needed. Armani suits, the house and a chauffeur driven Mercedes Maybach were all part of the reward for success as far as he was concerned.

His wife descended the staircase and as usual his heart did a little flip. He would never understand what she had seen in the spotty twenty-something year old working a market stall, but she had. Still not over the stage of going red in the face when a member of the opposite sex so much as looked in his direction, she had been the one to make the running. How grateful he was that she had done so.

Now in their twentieth year of marriage, he still retained that same feeling of euphoria whenever he saw her, as he had when they met on their first date. Being a successful businessman, he'd had offers but never once had he so much as looked at another woman. That wasn't the missing part of his life, of that he was certain.

'You look stunning.'

'You don't scrub up bad yourself, kind sir.'

They both laughed. Ever since the first date when he blurted out those words and she responded in kind, they kept up this ritual on every occasion they dressed up to go out. He still meant it, and even to this day he felt he was punching well above his weight.

After they settled into the luxurious leather seats of the car, she reached out to hold his hand.

'Any business to do tonight?'

'Tonight, I'm all yours.'

She smiled.

'Oh good, because I am not wearing anything at all under this dress.'

He glanced up sharply at the rear-view mirror to see if his driver overheard the confession, but as usual he gazed straight ahead, the picture of discretion.

~§~

There are masquerade balls, and then there are Masquerade Balls. This would be up there with the best of them. The committee had outdone themselves on this occasion. The Hotel Café Royal in London's Regent Street proved to be an inspired setting to hold the event. Looking around the Louis XVI style Pompadour Ballroom with its elaborately decorated ceiling, fluted pilasters, and gilt framed mirrored panels, he could almost imagine himself in eighteenth century France. Given his current wealth, it was perhaps good fortune he didn't live in those times, he would almost certainly have been selected to meet Madame Guillotine during the revolution.

Fresh off the floor from a lively foxtrot, he felt in need of a break.

'I think I'll go on the terrace for a cigar. Care to join me?'

She shook her head.

'I don't think so. I'm going to get another glass of champagne.'

At the far end of the ballroom, a set of double doors led onto the covered terrace. On the right, a view of the narrow Air Street, which passed through the arch beneath the terrace to join Regent Street, which was the view to the left. Here could be seen one half of the elegant architecture of the pair of curved buildings lining the street; the alter ego being the one housing amongst its many occupants, the Hotel Café Royal.

He chose to gaze down on the bustling Regent Street and marvel at how busy it remained, even at this hour.

He drew long and slow on his Oliva cigar. He didn't smoke many, but found the Cubans were not for him, preferring these Nicaraguan cigars.

'Please don't look round, and don't say a word. Just nod your head slowly if you wish to continue.'

Something about the voice stopped him from responding to his initial instinct to turn. He inclined his head almost imperceptibly, but obviously enough to satisfy the speaker.

'Very good. Glad to see you can be discreet. Just how we like it. We have been observing you for some time.'

He made to speak but the voice cut him off.

'All will be explained another day, for now it is sufficient for you to know we think you are ready for the next step; to have ultimate control. You will be among some powerful people who can do things you wouldn't dream of. All we need to know at this time is if you are interested. Please nod your head again if you agree.'

Again, the slight movement.

'Good. You must never mention this to anyone, not even your wife. You will be hearing from us in due course. Please don't look back until you have finished your cigar.'

He wasn't sure why he hadn't turned, but now he was intrigued, especially the part about being amongst powerful people. Perhaps this was the missing piece of the jigsaw in his life. The question was, who were the "we" the voice referred to?

CHAPTER SIX

The container door clattered open, sunlight and salty air penetrated bringing relief to the dark, dank and frankly smelly conditions. It took the girls a few moments to adjust to the light streaming in. A deckhand entered carrying a box; this would be the daily meal, a term Kun considered to be somewhat optimistic in its promise. A meagre amount of food normally consisting of a bowl of rice, some tired vegetables and if lucky a small amount of meat, enough to keep them alive and no more. Kun suspected the meat and vegetables were leftovers from crew mealtimes, at least the rice appeared to be freshly cooked.

Now Jing and Kun were locked in this container with others, their time together in the brothel seemed to be one of the happier moments in their lives. Here they were at the mercy of the crew and on their way to God only knew what. Whatever it was, Kun knew it couldn't be good. As far as she knew, no one started a better life by being transported in a shipping container.

Two weeks had passed since they first entered this box. At first, they hadn't understood what was happening; moved at night and then hustled into a dark, stuffy metal box. The movement gave the game away. A swinging sensation followed by a short period of intense activity around them; clanging, banging, yelling. Soon after the yelling stopped, a throbbing vibration reached their feet followed sometime later by movement, constant movement. They were on board a ship; destination and arrival time, a mystery to them. One of the girls tried to question their captors, a blow to the kidneys her reward. A lesson for them all to stay quiet and above all avoid eye contact.

They soon learned which of the seamen to trust and which to fear. This one had roving eyes, an appropriate phrase for someone as walleyed as he, and on occasion his hands would join his eyes in exploring their bodies for a few brief seconds; oily, rough hands and then the stench of his breath in their faces as he had his moment of gratification. Whenever he entered the container, the girls would huddle together at the back; safety in numbers.

He placed the box at the door; a temptation, but none of them moved. Being pawed by this vile man was in no way compensated for by the sort of meals they got fed; not even dinner at the Ritz would do that. He grabbed one and dragged her to the door. She let out a scream which he silenced with the back of his hand; he sought more than a quick fumble this time, his intentions as clear as the day outside. The container door slammed shut again and the bolts rattled home.

~§~

Hamadryad, in Greek and Roman mythology, was a nymph who lived in the trees and died when the tree died. An odd name to give a ship which would often be found carrying a large number of dead trees as part of its cargo. Although most of these came from sustainable sources, the owners were not averse to plying a less than legitimate trade between Papua New Guinea and China, carrying timber illegally obtained from the rain forests.

In charge of this truck of the seas, a former merchant seaman from the Soviet Union, Kapitanskij Rodion Petrovich

Burkov, Rodya to his friends which meant most people called him Kapitanskij. The Kapitanskij was one of those men who had no visible neck, his shoulders seemed to merge into his skull. Although no one had ever seen him work out, he sported biceps as big as some men's thighs. Standing only 167cm in his socks, he had the appearance of someone under the effect of a strong gravitational pull. A completely shaven head rounded off the appearance of a bouncer at a less than reputable nightclub but that is where the similarity ended. Burkov was an intelligent man. After the fall of the Soviet Union, he found his opportunities limited. Although he wished to continue amassing his wealth in the motherland, he had the wrong contacts; men who no longer curried favour with the men in power. He could no longer rely on paid protection for his many smuggling rackets. So, he moved his services to Shanghai; after all it worked for John Wayne in the movies.

If it could be said his employers were not too bothered about the odd bit of illicit cargo, then the Kapitanskij didn't have a care in the world, not even when the cargo turned out to be human and on the way to a wealthy buyer. What did he care as long as they were no trouble and he got paid? Just another cargo on the way to an unknown buyer and none of his business. He planned to retire in Thailand and bed a different girl every day, that's what women were for wasn't it? What more could a man ask for? Well, as long as they could cook too. As long as he made enough money to fulfil his dream, he didn't care about anything else. He reached for the bottle on his desk and poured himself another glass of Scotch, a cheap blended Chinese counterfeit; expensive malts would be wasted on a man who had been known to pour vodka on his morning cereal; intelligent he may be, sophisticated he was not. He leant back in his chair, immersed himself in Tchaikovsky's Violin Concerto and mulled over the journey ahead.

Hong Kong to Tilbury was a routine run for the Kapitanskij; the biggest danger coming from the Somali pirates in the Gulf of Aden. At least the little devils hadn't taken a large ship since 2012, mostly put off by the regular naval patrols in the area, but quite why the authorities had not done more to eradicate the parasites he had no idea. If he had his way the navy would not be discouraging the pirates, but chasing after them, blasting them out of the water and wiping them off the face of the earth. The Kapitanskij did not have his own navy, so he did the next best thing and kept an unofficial and well-hidden arsenal onboard. None of this namby-pamby water cannon crap for him; no one would take his ship without a fight, but so far, the weapons remained unused.

The annoying sound of the phone clamoured for attention, bringing him out of his reverie.

'Da?'

Burkov listened without interrupting the caller, before responding.

'Have him meet me at the taffrail, no one else. He can tell me what happened. All other hands to be below deck or for'ard. I must have complete privacy.'

He hung up before the other party answered, satisfied his orders would be carried out. No one ever questioned his authority. Burkov sighed, downed the last of the whisky from his glass and put on his captain's jacket. Some days a captain's work was never done.

~§~

Golden rays flirted with the scattered cumulus clouds, tempting them to an affair with the setting sun. Waves rolled, lethargic and uncaring; a sea at peace with the world. The Indian Ocean could be a beautiful place.

The walleyed man stood defiantly at the taffrail. What did it matter what he had done? These girls were whores, everyone knew that. He had only helped himself to what was on offer anyway. He brought them food; they ought to be grateful to him.

He didn't come this far aft very often. His duties confined him to below deck most of the time, with an occasional trip to the container to feed the harlots. Even though he had been summoned here by none other than the Kapitanskij, he relished this opportunity to breathe in the salt-laden air.

Surely the Kapitanskij would understand his position; he was a seaman like himself after all. Spending months at sea with no female company, not even the sight of one most months, it was only to be expected that when a bunch of women who sold their bodies came on board, some of the crew would find the temptation a little too much. She wasn't hurt or damaged in any way, so what was the harm?

Still filling his lungs and watching the wake of the ship, he recoiled when a hand clapped him on the shoulder.

He swung round to the smiling face of the Kapitanskij, immaculately dressed as usual in his captain's uniform. The man had never seen him dressed any other way. He was relieved to see the smile, clearly, he understood, otherwise he would be angry.

'Kapitanskij, I ...'

Burkov held up his hand to cut him off, before putting his arm around the man.

'My friend, I have heard all I need to hear. I understand your desires of course, but you must understand my point of view too. I would not expect you to mess with the trees when we carry them, cut yourself a block of wood for instance, nor would I expect to see you riding around the deck on one of the motorcycles we are carrying. As for the females, I don't care what happens to them when they are unloaded, but they are part of the cargo and as such they must not be meddled with. You see my point, my friend?'

The man dropped his head.

'Sorry, Kapitanskij. It won't happen again. I promise.'

Burkov looked down and noticed his bootlace was loose. He squatted down to tend to it.

'No, my friend. It won't.'

He grabbed the man's ankles and in one swift movement pulled his legs high, pivoting the man over the taffrail, letting him drop off the stern of the ship into the foaming wake. As the man's legs swung up, one foot caught the Captain's hat, the wind did the rest and it followed the sailor over the rail.

Burkov watched the man bobbing in the sea, thrashing to stay afloat. Few of the sailors could swim, but that would not matter here, many species of sharks inhabited this ocean. The man would either drown or feed the sharks, probably both. His eyes moved to the hat. That was the real tragedy; those hats cost a lot of money.

~§~

Attuned to the motion and sounds of the ship, Kun felt the vibrations change beneath her feet. She didn't know for sure what it meant but she suspected the ship was slowing. It wasn't the first time, so she thought little of it.

The clatter of the door latch being released startled her. The brightness of the deck lights had them all shielding their eyes. Although not as bright as the usual daylight streaming in, it took some time to get accustomed to any light when kept locked in the almost total darkness of a shipping container.

This was a change of routine; food only came during the day. Kun could make out the silhouette of the man who now stood with his back to them. It was not the one who molested them, thank goodness. She hadn't seen him for some time. Perhaps he had been allocated other duties.

The door remained open, but no one moved. Harsh treatment at the beginning of the journey had taught them to do nothing until told, and then do it immediately. Not understanding the language the men spoke was no excuse, but a smack round the head each time they got it wrong soon led them to understanding gestures and tone of voice.

The man ignored them for a few minutes. What sounded like orders being shouted reached Kun from a distance. She guessed the ship must be quite large because these voices sounded to be far away, but of course that could be the effect of being inside the container.

Now the man was shouting at them; the words meant nothing, but it was clear he wanted them to come out. Kun felt a pang of fear. How strange that a twenty-by-eight-foot box could give such a feeling of safety. Despite understanding that fear came from the unknown, part of Kun became terrified they would be thrown into the sea. The other part reasoned that they could have done that any time, why would they keep and feed them if that was their fate?

Scared or not, she took in the fresh air, it was a welcome relief from the stifling conditions in the container. Despite the fact they were allowed to wash every day, the toilet was merely a bucket and with ten people confined in such a small space, the air soon becomes quite ripe.

For a moment, Kun thought her fears were being realised when she saw the others in front of her going through a gap in the rail at the edge of the deck, then she understood they were being sent down a ladder on the side of the ship.

As she got to the top, she could see a smaller boat keeping station alongside the ship. The ladder, in fact more of a metal grid staircase, ended in a platform alongside the back of the other vessel which was bobbing around in the wake at the side of the cargo ship.

When the first of her companions reached the platform, she was lifted over the side by a man waiting. He held her out from the platform and as the smaller boat rose up on the swell, another man caught her, swung her round on the deck and then ushered her forward into the cabin. When Kun's turn came, as she moved forward towards the small cabin, she managed to catch a glimpse of the ship they were leaving. She couldn't see a name anywhere, but she did see the funnel which was lit. She had seen the half red and half white star before. She didn't know the name of the company, but she had definitely seen it in Hong Kong. That information might be useful someday.

Now they were all on board, they huddled together in the cabin. One of the crew members put his finger to his lips in the universal gesture to stay quiet as the boat picked up speed and moved away from the cargo ship. Kun would have loved to have seen the name of the ship, but from their position on the floor in the cabin she couldn't see outside. Not that it would have made much difference. It was still dark, and that part of the ship wasn't lit.

She turned her attention to the boat they were now in. This style she knew. It was designed for fishing trips. She and her father had once been on one out of Hong Kong. The large open deck at the back allowed several people to fish at once, while the cabin gave cover on the journey to and from the fishing grounds. This was not an ocean-going boat which meant they were not too far away from land.

The crew were all dressed the same; entirely in black, including the woolly hats they all wore. It reminded Kun of the villains in the movies she had seen. They always seemed to wear black. When she was younger, she asked her father, if all the bad guys dressed that way, why couldn't the police just arrest anyone who walked around dressed from head to toe in black clothes. He'd answered that it wasn't that simple, but to her at the time it wasn't complicated at all.

This boat moved around a lot more and some of them began to feel ill. One of the guards pointed to a door at the front of the cabin and soon several of the young ladies were taking it in turns to bring up their only meal of the day. Once that had been lost, they continued with dry retching. Kun had never suffered any form of travel sickness and was glad she didn't have to take a turn in the cramped toilet.

After a while, the steady hum of the engines made her feel sleepy, so she settled into a corner, wrapped her arms around herself and closed her eyes.

~§~

On the very eastern edge of Tower Hamlets, close to the banks of the River Lea, this warehouse had once been the home of a packing and shipping company. A large open space, two storeys high, spread the entire length of the interior, punctuated throughout by girder columns supporting the roof beams; a corrugated panelled roof containing several rows of skylights capped it off. Along the walls, brightly painted swirls of colour formed into letters and shapes; the brick canvas of the graffiti artists' urban gallery. Pools of water gathered where rain dripped through broken skylights; shards of glass scattering what little light filtered through the roof, turning puddles into liquid kaleidoscopes – circles of unexpected beauty in a derelict landscape.

Wet tyre tracks snaked from the entrance, ending at a black Bentley Mulsanne. Parked nearby, a white Transit van; one incongruous in the industrial setting, the other not so much. In a movie, the villain is expected to drive a fancy car. In the real world, it is still expected they will drive a fancy car. Parking one in an abandoned warehouse while negotiating an illegal transaction was a cliché too far; but cliché fitted Charlie Palmer like a glove. He dressed like a villain and acted like a villain. In short, Charlie Palmer was the nastiest piece of clichéd movie style villainy in the whole of London.

'What did I tell you? Did I not make myself clear? Virgins, they must be virgins. My clients are not interested in used goods. They don't want to go where every Tom, Dick and Harry has already been. They want pure, untouched, unsullied young girls — and what did you bring me? Old hags, that's what.'

Don Golding felt Palmer was being a little unfair with that last remark. Not one of these girls was a day over seventeen. Admittedly, they came from several brothels in Hong Kong and could hardly be classed as virgins, but he got them at a knockdown price. He didn't know Palmer would have them checked. He'd been sure he would be able to pass them off as fourteen-year-olds; they all looked younger than their age.

The girls huddled together, naked and scared in the back of the van; clearly not understanding a word being said but fully understanding the tone behind it. This man was not happy; that much was apparent. Subjected to an intimate medical examination, and the probing hands of the angry man, the girls sought comfort in the proximity of the others. Even though mostly strangers to each other before their journey started, solace is often found when you are with your own kind.

'You don't want them then, Charlie?'

Palmer let out a sigh and turned to him, 'I thought I had already made that clear, my son. My clients want virgins, when they are done with them, we can put them to work in my other — ah — places, but I'm not paying top-dollar for used goods. These are high mileage. You're on your own.'

Palmer turned on his heels.

'The best I can do is have a friend call you, my son. He might want them. His clients are not as — particular as mine.'

Palmer settled into the back of the car and his driver closed the door.

Golding watched until the taillights of the Bentley disappeared at the far end of the building.

Bugger.

The best he could hope for now would be to recoup some of the money he forked out shipping the girls from Hong Kong. Still, that was the risk of supplying commodities, especially live ones, and that's all the girls were to him. He didn't see them as fellow humans, only items to be traded, just as all the other illicit cargo he shipped into the UK; guns, drugs, tobacco, people; he didn't care what it was, as long as he made a bob or two profit, that was all that mattered.

He motioned to the girls to get dressed then closed the sliding door on the van. He would have to find somewhere to stash the goods for a few days, until he disposed of them, one way or another.

~§~

Charlie settled back into the beige leather seat of the Bentley. Well, that went better than he hoped. He'd known Golding would try to palm him off with sub-standard goods. What Golding didn't know was it was exactly what Palmer hoped would happen. Now, via an acquaintance, he would get hold of them at a knock-down price and Golding couldn't do a thing about it even if he knew what was happening. He would be desperate to get them off his hands. Better still, Charlie's hands would be clean. You'd have to get up early to put one over on old Charlie Palmer.

'Brian, Charlie here — Yeah not too bad thanks, how's the missus? — Yeah, don't we all mate, don't we all. Listen. I want you to pick up some goods for me, for a little project I have on the go. I'll see you all right of course — Yeah, not over the phone — Where? — Terrific, my son. See you there.'

~§~

Well, that was a total disaster. Getting them straight from the ship into the van, then moving them wherever Palmer wanted them delivered, that had always been the plan. Golding did not want to be the one found harbouring illegal immigrants, especially young girls. These would be classed as children and no way was he going inside for this. He'd heard what they do to prisoners convicted of child offences. Although he had no interest in youngsters of either sex, he didn't want to be classed as a nonce.

He would have to find some way of passing them on if Palmer's friend didn't come up with the goods. There must be someone else looking for a bunch of Asian girls. A lot of the massage parlours offered 'new girls' every week. He didn't ordinarily deal with the Chinese; that could be worse for him than going inside as a child molester, but if this deal went south, he may have no choice. That would have to be his contingency plan.

He could feel the panic rising. Why now? Everything he'd done, every operation he'd planned had gone relatively smoothly. Never so much as a sniff of the law, never a deal called off. He spent many hours planning his operations, and this one had been no exception. Then, the first deal he attempts with Palmer and it goes belly-up. He should have known better than to try and pull the wool over Charlie Palmer's eyes. He'd been a fool and it had come back to bite him in the arse. Palmer had a reputation and not a particularly good one at that. What made him think he could con the man?

His first problem now was where to take them but then in a moment of inspiration he remembered a shabby empty house he had available for let. People were so fussy these days and they wanted bright kitchens and brightly painted walls. Golding on the other hand wanted maximum income for minimum outlay; when the charity, Shelter, talked about rogue landlords, they could use Golding as their poster boy.

Not only was the house empty, it had a nice basement with a single door for access. Once locked in there would be no way out for them. All they needed to do would be put the fear of God into them and they would stay quiet.

Three days passed since their experience in the warehouse. As experiences go, that was up there with having to sell her body for sex. Standing naked in front of all those men ogling her, then the supposed medical examination confirming what they must have known already; she couldn't possibly be a virgin. In any case, there is no such thing as a reliable virginity test, even she knew that, how come these gweilo didn't?

The nasty looking man showed anger; her English was good enough to know that, but even had she not understood all of the words, his tone was enough to show his feelings; the man who brought them here, clearly disappointed as he ushered them back into the van and indicated to them to get dressed.

They remained in the van for a number of hours before being taken to another location. In darkness they alighted, stumbled along a dimly lit alleyway before being ushered into what appeared to be an abandoned house. After descending a narrow flight of stairs, they found themselves in a darkened room. Without a word from their two guards the door closed behind them; the sound of a bolt being drawn home was followed by the receding footsteps of the two men as they climbed the stairs.

The following day, a tiny broken window high up on one wall, allowed a glimmer of light into the room; easily doubled, had someone bothered to clean it. Paint peeling from the walls, confirmed what their bodies already knew, the room held a dampness that seeped into everything within reach. Kun guessed it to be a basement and from the muffled sounds that penetrated the room, somewhere near a river or the sea. Not a fast-flowing body of water, but one that carried ships. Sometimes she heard their horns; a familiar sound to a resident of Hong Kong. No one had dared call out during the night and no one dared now. Who knew where the guards were, and more importantly, what they would do if they heard them shouting?

Kun had noted the British number plate on the angry man's car in the warehouse. Her father brought her to the UK whenever he visited, and she became familiar with the British licence plates; besides, the GB was something of a giveaway: a pity part of it had been obscured by the two men, that might also come in handy later when she escaped. Something inside her told her that was her only course of action. The worst that could happen would be getting killed when she tried and as she feared that would be their ultimate fate, she felt she had nothing to lose.

She remembered that after they transferred from the small boat to the van, the first part of the journey had been uninterrupted, but after that they stopped frequently and the sound of traffic filtered through the sides of the van. At the very least they must be in a town; something told Kun it was London and the nearby river, the Thames.

Now, wearing only their underwear, their clothes having been taken when they arrived at the house, they found themselves being bundled back into a different van and on the move again, with only a blanket each to keep them warm. Kun guessed they travelled between thirty minutes and an hour; her watch stolen by one of the crew on the cargo ship. Darkness at their destination suggested they were no longer in a built-up area and Kun suspected the place to be somewhere on the outskirts of the city. Trees whispered, and the call of a distant owl floated in with the breeze, strengthening her belief of a countryside location.

Up to now, Kun kept her suspicions to herself; not even sharing it with her friend and none of the other girls expressed an idea or any interest in where they might be. Both the transfer from the big ship to the boat, as well as to and from the house, took place after dark; their exposure to the outside world kept to a minimum. Exactly what to do with this new information she couldn't imagine, for now anyway, but if she could get away, the British police would be the first people to contact.

Rough hands dragged them out of the van and forced them into a narrow entrance where a few steps led down to a dark opening. They were pushed into some sort of chamber and once inside, the darkness closed in. A door slammed shut behind them, the sound of a lock being snapped into place and something being dragged, reached Kun's ears. Few people ever experience true darkness, but underground is one of the places where it can be found. The girls whispered to each other and reached out for the reassuring touch of another human.

The change in location signalled an increase in danger. Although conditions in the basement had been far from ideal, it was preferable to being in what appeared to be a hole in the ground. On the way here, the girls chattered about being moved to a high-class brothel, but Kun couldn't think of a single place where prostitutes lived in what appeared to be a pit — high class or not.

This turn of events foretold of a downturn in their fortunes, she was sure. Not for the first time in this whole sorry experience, Kun feared for her life and she began working on a plan to escape. Her father would have been pleased to know the money spent on her education was money well spent.

CHAPTER SEVEN

The gyratory dance of the phone on the polished oak desk, buzzing for attention like a demanding child, distracted him from his thoughts. Of course, that's what they were; children, demanding attention, day in day out; never leaving us in peace for one moment. Although phones can be switched off, children will only require our attention until they no longer need us. A phone will always need us and will wait until switched on again before once more clamouring for attention. We once thought we were masters of technology but technology now has us as slaves.

He glanced at the screen; which one would it be today? Usually it was his wife, only rarely did one of the children call during the day, after all, they would be in school. He frowned. Number withheld. This was his personal phone, he gave this number out to no one, not even his secretary.

'Hello.'

'Are you ready for the next step in your life?'

This was not the same voice he heard at the ball; more refined, lower pitched, almost booming in its delivery.

'How the hell did you get this number?'

'We have some clever people working for us, but that is not important. What is important is do you want to take this further? It will cost, but the price is small compared to what you get in return.'

'I think you already know the answer to that, or you would not have approached me in the first place.'

The line went quiet and he wasn't sure if the caller had hung up, then the voice spoke again.

'I am impressed. You did not ask the price. You must want this.'

He didn't know whether to say anything about wanting something but not knowing what. In the end he decided against a full confession and settled for;

'I want more.'

'Very well. The next call you get will tell you where to be and when to be there. There will be a ceremony to welcome you, and once again may I remind you about the need for secrecy? Not a word of this must get out for obvious reasons.'

Before he could ask his next question, the caller hung up. All he must do now was wait for the call. He felt the thrill of anticipation; the first for many years.

~§~

Three weeks ago, this group were completely unknown to him, yet now he was about to take part in his initiation ceremony; an invitation out of the blue and from a source he would never have imagined being anything other than whiter-than-white. The business world could be a strange environment at times, but this opportunity, far too good to miss. Besides, his curiosity piqued, he wondered if they were what they professed to be, and would they do what they said they could?

He suspected the ceremony would involve something along these lines; the hood expected, the bound hands something of a surprise, especially as he would be required to prove his worth sexually in the presence of others, that part inevitable.

He felt his excitement rising, the blood flowing to his nether regions. He never thought he could be so aroused while standing naked in front of a group of men, not his thing at all, but it wasn't their presence making him this way; the anticipation of things to come being the driving force.

A warmth encircled him, the warmth of a mouth, teasing, stimulating, exciting. Then gone as quickly as it arrived, and he realised he now wore a condom - clever. Hands guided him to the floor, on his back. Now he understood the binding as someone pulled his hands behind his head. The woman, he assumed and indeed hoped it was a woman, lowered herself onto him. Her movements started slowly, sliding up and down with a gentleness that caused him to want more. Someone started a handclap, taken up by a few of the others; the tempo although slow at first, began to increase, and the woman moved in unison. Damn, she moved well.

An object was thrust into his hands; hands wrapped around his to keep it there. He didn't care what it was, his mind concentrating on another part of his body entirely. He arched his back slightly in anticipation of the final pleasure. As he did so, he found his hands being propelled forward, violently striking the woman on top of him. She let out a muffled scream and stopped her rhythmic movement. Again, and again, his hands were thrust forward then pulled away and he felt something warm and slippery trickling between his fingers. This time the adrenaline did not come from anticipation, but from fear. The total lack of control that caused his initial arousal, now created a panic never experienced before.

Even in the dimly lit room, he blinked in the light as someone roughly pulled the hood from his head. Bewildered, he looked at his hands, red with blood. He focussed beyond them to a young girl, no more than a teenager and clearly Asian. Two men held her upright on his body, one with his hands encircling her neck and the other grasping her wrists. The knife in his own hands dripped her life onto him.

A flash from a camera temporarily blinded him. As his sight recovered, he saw the circle of men, hooded and in various stages of undress. Some played with themselves, others merely watched. He dropped the knife turned to one side and threw up; violent, gut-wrenching spasms. He fought to breathe, as though the air lacked oxygen, his mind fought to make sense of it all. It wasn't supposed to be like this; an initiation, nothing more. His vision narrowed; the area of light reduced to a tunnel before completely disappearing as he passed out.

~§~

A voice tickled at his consciousness, competing with the sound of his heartbeat and the blood rushing through his veins. He slowly regained control of his body, opened his eyes and sought out the speaker.

'Welcome back. We thought you had left us for a moment. Congratulations, your initiation is complete, and you are now a fully-fledged member of the Guild. Of course, you must never speak of this to anyone.'

The speaker held up the bloody knife. The full realisation of his position hit home when he noticed the speaker wore surgical gloves, as did the men still holding the body of the girl. His prints alone would be on the weapon, his DNA on the girl and knife. What had he done?

'As much as we trust you not to betray us, this will be kept as insurance. We choose our members carefully, but we must also protect the group. Congratulations on your membership and welcome to a new world.'

~§~

The silver Mercedes SLK pulled into the bus stop, the driver switched off the lights and stopped the engine. His hands remained on the wheel and he stared straight ahead. After being hooded for a second time and driven to where he had been instructed to leave his car, he had been on autopilot when he drove off, and now he needed to take stock.

The initial shock had begun to wear off. A mixture of horror, fear and something else he couldn't quite put his finger on, swirled around in his head, like a dust devil in his mind. Nothing would stay long enough for him to bring into focus. He had killed someone, a young girl, a child almost. Yes, a child. He killed her. Not exactly what he'd expected when he received the invitation to join the group. Not for one moment did he dream they would go as far as to actually kill someone.

Only, they hadn't. He killed her, and they had the evidence.

He would be fine if he stayed quiet, that much the speaker made clear, but he didn't know that he could. He must, or he would go to prison, or worse, they would kill him. What about his family?

Perhaps this was all a bad dream. He would wake up tomorrow and nothing would have happened. Except, it happened, it was no dream, he murdered someone.

Maybe they faked it. Yes! Fake blood and an actress. Of course, he knew the truth, the girl really died right on top of him and while he was inside her; caused by the knife he held in his hands and repeatedly plunged into her. It didn't matter that they made it happen; his hands controlled by someone else. It would be his fingerprints and his DNA on the knife.

The dust devil continued to swirl in his thoughts, rotating ever faster, out of control. He didn't know what to do; what could he do?

The knock on the window startled him.

Jesus no, a police officer. How had they found out so soon? He wound down the window.

'Good evening, sir. Are you okay?'

'Ah — umm — Yes, you just startled me that's all.'

'I meant before that, sir. You've been staring out of your windscreen for the past five minutes. You clearly didn't notice us pull in behind you.'

'I — I felt a little unwell, so I — umm — thought it best to pull over for a while.'

'Have you had a drink at all tonight, sir?'

'Ah, no. I haven't officer. I don't drink and drive at all.'

His mind screamed at him, 'tell him the truth, you don't drink and drive, but you don't mind murdering young women.'

CHAPTER SEVEN

The officer studied him for a moment.

'Do you need someone to come and pick you up, sir?'

'No, no. I'll be fine. I'll stretch my legs and get a bit of fresh air, then I'll be on my way. It's — I just learned about the death of a close friend, that's all.'

'I see, sir, I'm sorry to hear that. Well, if you are sure, mind how you go.'

He watched the taillights of the police car until it disappeared from view.

Fuck, fuck, FUCK. What had he done?

~§~

'There he goes.'

From their vantage point in the Steakhouse car park, the two officers watched the Mercedes negotiate Wake Arms Roundabout and take the third exit to continue along the A104. Once the car drove out of sight, the police car pulled out of the car park and followed at a discreet distance.

'Something's not right, I tell you. I couldn't smell alcohol, but something about him didn't sit right. You know how it is.'

'Well, I can't fault his driving, so I don't think he's under the influence.'

'Aye, you may be right, but I'm going to log a report, just in case. You never know, he might be a murderer or something.'

CHAPTER EIGHT

Three girls taken over three days - or nights. Keeping track of time wasn't easy. The only relief from this dark, dank, disgusting place came when their captors led them up the concrete steps, allowed them to wash in cold water and relieve themselves behind a bush. Kun believed this to be every night but who could tell?

She took in as much of their surroundings as possible in the short time they stayed on the surface. Occasionally she heard cars being driven nearby and a constant dull noise in the background, perhaps from a major highway further afield. Aside from this very little reached her ears.

Yesterday, Jing was taken by one of the men. Kun tried to keep her, but the guard hit her knocking her to the floor. Now, she had no friend here, no one to talk to. The guards warned them not to make a sound while locked away and fearing the worst the girls complied.

She had no choice; she must escape somehow; how being the million-Hong Kong-dollar question. The guards attached leads to collars around their necks before they left the pit and only removed them when they returned.

Perhaps she could slip off the collar and get away when she went to the toilet though she doubted that would be possible. She must think of something, she would not die in this hellhole.

Something niggled at the back of her mind, a pattern altered, a change in routine. Kun struggled to recall what was different this time. She went over everything step by step, carefully considering all that happened to make tonight different to the other nights.

As hard as she tried, she couldn't put her finger on it. Like the elusive word on the tip of the tongue, the thought skittered and floated around her head, flitting away as she tried to grasp hold.

Dejected, she slumped to the floor in the darkness and thought back to happier times in Hong Kong; where things went wrong was only too apparent, but the Why remained as equally elusive as the change in routine she tried to recall.

The lock. That was it, or rather, it wasn't. They forgot the lock the last time they closed the door. She remembered the usual dragging sound, but as for the lock, she was certain someone forgot to use it.

Kun's mind sprang into action. Rather than act on impulse, she worked on a plan. She believed they were in a forest somewhere and that at least one road passed nearby with what she believed to be a major highway some distance away. She would open the door carefully and look around for any signs of their captors; assuming she saw no one, she would work her way quietly through the trees.

She planned to move towards the source of the background noise. Traffic meant people, lots of them, and people meant safety if they were the right people.

One of the others sensed her movement towards the door.

'What are you doing?'

'I'm going to go for help.'

'How will you get out?'

Kun explained her thoughts.

'No. You will be killed. We will all be killed. They will be angry.'

'We are dead anyway if we stay here. The others have not returned. What do you think has happened to them? Come with me.'

A whispered discussion followed.

'We will not come. Go if you want, but we will take our chances here. You don't know the others are dead.'

Kun remained silent, recognising the futility of arguing with those whose minds are closed.

Working her way around the wall, she soon found the entrance. Putting her hands against the door she pushed. It moved easily for the first few centimetres, then stopped. Something blocked its path, something solid; that would be the dragging sound they heard each night.

She turned around and squatting down she put her back against the door. Using the strength in her legs to provide the force, Kun pushed once more. She was rewarded with a further movement then the door steadfastly refused to budge, but this time Kun had just enough space to squeeze her upper body through.

She wriggled through the narrow gap and clambered over the object blocking the door. She caught her first unsupervised view of the outside world.

She never thought she would be grateful for being cooped up in such a dark place, but her eyes were fully accustomed to a lack of light and she could see quite clearly. She looked around her. Not a soul in sight, nor any sounds coming from nearby, only the steady hum of the traffic in the distance.

She crouched next to the entrance for a couple of minutes, listening and looking for any sign that a guard remained nearby, something she thought unlikely as surely they would have responded to the noise she made getting out, but she would take no chances.

Satisfied no one lurked in the bushes, Kun made her move. She would go towards the background noise; she would find people there for certain. At first, she moved cautiously, in case her captors were nearby, but she gained confidence as she moved further away.

CHAPTER EIGHT

Kun found the ambient light to be more than adequate and made good progress. At one point she came across a surfaced two-lane road. She squatted at the roadside listening for anything that would suggest humans, but there was no sign of another living being.

A fear of being caught told her to press on towards the ever-increasing noise of the traffic. She now guessed it to be one of the many motorways surrounding London. She found a small track which appeared to head in the right direction, and she felt she was now far enough away from her prison to move in the open space.

Finally, she saw lights through the trees; moving lights from a multitude of cars and trucks. She increased her pace, only to find a final barrier between herself and the road.

Parallel to the carriageway, a six-foot-tall fence, topped off with barbed wire, stretched away in each direction. Kun examined the deer fence and decided it was something she could scale with ease if she was careful swinging over the barbed wire.

Her small feet fitted easily into the mesh and climbed the fence, dropping down the other side without mishap. A few more metres and she would be able to flag down a vehicle on the fast-moving road.

~§~

'How many?'

'Only one. We still have the rest.'

He closed his eyes, allowing his thoughts to settle. There was bad news and then there was disastrous news. This had the potential to be catastrophic.

'Dispose of the rest.'

'Now hold on a minute, I'm just the shepherd. I didn't sign up to be the slaughter—'

'You will do exactly as you are told. This is your mess and it's up to you to clean it up. You are already an accessory and with a little bit of creative work, you could be the prime suspect. Dispose of them – carefully. When you have done that, you make sure the place has no evidence – both places. I don't care how you do it as long as there is no link back to us. Do I make myself clear?'

The last sentence delivered in such a manner that left the caller in no doubt as to the consequences of his failure.

'And when you have done that, you see if you can find the one who is missing. Someone must have seen something.'

He hung up without waiting for a reply.

Some days were better than others, this most certainly was not up there with the best.

~§~

A forest had been on this site since Neolithic times. From the seventeenth century it took on the name of Epping Forest; Wanstead Flats formed the southernmost tip. Every morning, rain, hail or shine, he would drive the three miles from his home, turn off the road into the main parking area and prepare himself for the morning walk.

As far back as he could remember, there had been a dog in his life, and always a Golden Retriever.

Darlight Harriet, Hettie for short, sat in the back of the car, patiently waiting for him to open the tailgate. Even then she waited for the go-ahead to jump down, wagging her tail expectantly.

His dogs were obedient to a fault, and yet he never raised a voice or hand during training. He knew how to treat a dog, how to get the best from them.

'Come on, girl.'

Hettie jumped out, showing an enthusiasm almost unique to dogs and sat waiting for the lead to be clipped to her collar. Even though she wouldn't wander he wouldn't let her off until away from the car park and on the path; some people didn't understand dogs at all. They were not his sort of people.

His walk would be just over a mile, Hettie's considerably longer chasing after her rubber bone; she was a retriever after all.

A quarter of the way through their stroll he tossed her bone along the path, watching it bounce into the grass alongside. When she reached where the toy landed Hettie froze. Her nose went up in the air, nostrils quivering. She let out a yelp and bounded across the low undergrowth to the edge of a small copse.

'Hettie, back — Hettie!'

That was a first. She never ignored him. She stood at the edge of the undergrowth and a low growl reached his ears. The fur on her back stood in a ridge. He'd never seen her like this before.

'What is it, girl?'

She didn't move a muscle, her gaze fixed steadily ahead staring at the ground a few feet away.

He picked his way through the grass, skirting around the gorse before stepping forward to see what had caught her attention. At first, he couldn't quite make out what protruded from the soil then the horror hit him full in the stomach.

~§~

Helene wondered what was so important that required Strong to summon her to his office this early and on a Sunday. Training was on schedule, the team, while not being quite yet a team, still performed as well as any group of individuals could in the short time they had known each other; in brief, everything in the garden was rosy.

She understood that may not necessarily be the case once the team were under pressure, and to be frank, she was no longer sure about herself. All those months suffering under her former boss took their toll; her confidence, not shattered, but certainly damaged. Then to top it all, she finds him involved with Invidia which did nothing to improve the matter, even though he apologised and explained it all away; the words still stung.

Strong's office, she remembered, boasted an impressive view over Hampstead Heath and the city; the advantage of being on the top floor. She suspected admiring the view would not appear on the agenda today. She knocked on the large oak door, more fitting for a stately home than a crime unit. Working in a pleasant environment made such a difference.

'Come in.'

She stepped into the room and went immediately on the defensive. Brandon occupied one of the two wing-backed chairs, Strong occupied the other. He gestured towards the sofa.

'Please, Helene, take a seat.'

Helene sat with her arms folded across her chest, knees together and pointing away from Brandon. Even a casual observer might comment there was no love lost between them. If Brandon noticed, he gave no indication.

'I know it's still early days, Helene' — Strong's voice was soft and sometimes hard to catch; completely at odds with his role as director of Invidia and having the ear of whichever PM happened to be in power at the time.

— 'but how do you think the team are coming along?'

'They're good, sir. One or two of the civilians are feeling a little at sea at the moment, which is only to be expected when dropped into what is effectively a police environment, but they'll get there. There's no one I would say isn't worthy of a place on my team.'

Strong glanced at Brandon.

'You said *your* team. That in itself is a good sign.'

'I'd say the same in the Met too. I take responsibility for what they do, so yes, that does make it *my* team.'

'Do you think they are ready?'

Helene unaware she had shifted her body to face slightly away from Brandon, had to turn her head to answer his question.

'Ready for what — sir?'

'Ready for their first task.'

'I know I said they are coming along, but I didn't say they'd arrived. They still need time to gel as a team. They are getting there, but I hardly think we should be putting them to the test so soon.'

Brandon leant forward.

'I don't think we have a choice.'

'With all due respect, sir, I understood this to be my team not yours, and I say they aren't ready.'

He leant back in his chair and looked over to Strong.

'I told you.'

Helene's hackles rose.

'What did you tell him? I wasn't good enough, I couldn't pull it off, it isn't a woman's work?'

If anything, Strong spoke softer still this time.

'Please, show a little respect to the Chief Superintendent.'

'I will show respect when he earns it; you weren't on the receiving end of his barbs and having had time to think about his apology and his reasons, they're bullshit. I don't think they address the full story, do you?'

'Told you she was a fiery one.'

Helene glared at Brandon and an uncomfortable silence drifted through the air like smoke in a nineteen-sixties jazz club.

'I knew what was going on and it was with my blessing.'

Helene's turned her attention to Strong who held up his hands.

'The Chief Super painted such a marvellous picture of you and your work, I told him to make sure you accepted my offer at all costs, so if anyone is to blame, it's me.'

'Helene, I told you at the first Invidia meeting and I'm telling you again, you're a damn fine officer, the best I've seen. I hurt you and I am truly sorry but we need you to focus on the future and not the past, so please, let's put this behind us and let's get on with the task in hand.'

'You needn't think buttering me up like that is going to get you off the hook that easily, sir. We still have a long way to go before that happens.'

'I understand, in the meantime can we move on?'

Helen took a deep breath and signalled her agreement.

Brandon handed her a manilla folder.

Conditioned by many years of practice getting the maximum information in the minimum possible time, Helene quickly scanned each sheet and photograph before moving on to the next. When she reached the end, she looked quizzically at Brandon.

He handed her a single photograph.

'This morning, Wanstead Flats.'

He gestured to the other photographs.

'There's been an ongoing investigation since the middle of last year. You even took part in one of them. We still have no suspects, still no viable leads and, this is the bit concerning us all, the one time we got a vehicle description, not once did it show on any video footage, traffic cams, security cameras, you name it. The witness was adamant, the footage says otherwise.'

'You think someone tampered with it?'

'Undoubtedly, and in a very clever way because the time and date stamps were correct. Someone had to know where the investigation was leading and that someone has to be in the Met.'

'So, you want us to take over? A new unit, one that doesn't exist.'

'Exactly.'

'No.'

'Oh, come on, Helene. You said yourself they were as good as ready.'

'I said they were good and will be ready, but not now. If they screw this up, how do you think that will go down? They need more time to practice in their own departments and as a unit.'

'Will they?'

'What?'

'Screw it up.'

'I don't think so —'

'Then so be it. Bring them in and get them started on this as soon as possible.'

Helene shrugged in resignation.

'I have a request.'

'Go ahead.'

Brandon raised his eyebrows at the name but then gave a solitary nod.

CHAPTER NINE

Unintelligible sounds pricked at her mind; snatches of conversations whispered by ghosts hiding in the perpetual darkness.

Kun drifted in the dark, floating, spinning, trying to focus on something concrete. The incessant beeping had no place in this world, yet seemed to be all around; irritating, annoying, unnecessary; needles in her head. The darkness flickered and fluttered, edging away slowly at first before rushing headlong into full flight, chased by the light seeking it out in the darkest recesses, then casting it into oblivion.

She became aware of the pain, more pain than she had ever known. The pain from her body, intense and widespread; that from her eyes, dagger-like, as the light flooded into dilated pupils. She tried to move, her brain sent the necessary signals, but the body refused to comply. Her pupils awoke to her distress, regulating the light to a mere torrent, the lens doing its best to produce a focussed image, but all she saw was whiteness with no form. Her muscles began to respond to her commands, some twitching and disobeying like a two-year-old in a tantrum but finally, her head turned to one side to determine the cause of the irritating noise. A darker area emerged in her field of vision and her brain scrabbled to make sense of the jumble of shapes and shadows her eyes transmitted.

She located the source of the sound, a box of some kind, close to her. Kun stared at the object, her brain trying to untangle the image and keep it in focus. After several seconds, she succeeded in the latter, but the former eluded her. She did not understand what it was, or why it would be there. Then it dawned on her, she did not know where 'here' was, and even worse, who she was, or how she came to be here. With rising terror, she realised she had no memory of anything at all, as though she was taking her first breaths as a newborn.

Darkness returned on the counter-offensive, battling the light for control of her. Although the light fought valiantly, defeat became inevitable. Once more Kun retreated into her dark world.

Although more grassland than forest, Wanstead Flats were not without trees and the grave had been discovered behind a small copse; not the first bodies to be found in Epping Forest by any means and almost certainly not the last. Even though houses surrounded the heathland on all sides, the wide-open space allowed for a great deal of seclusion. Despite being frequented by dog walkers, joggers, bird watchers, amorous teenagers and the like, it remained an eminently suitable location to dispose of someone in the dead of night, bringing a whole new meaning to the phrase.

The sight of a crime scene tape greeted the visitors attempting to enter the main car park. Tomorrow, the crime could be front page news, but for today only a few stood and stared, hoping to catch a glimpse of something grisly.

A special constable kept guard in front of the car park entrance waving away anyone who attempted to enter; some arguing before complying, but all finding themselves looking for an alternative place for the day's recreation. Colleagues would be fulfilling the same role at each entry point to the park. Wanstead Flats was now an active crime scene. 'Police' tape marked a path to a white crime scene tent, barely visible in the distance. A regular constable, armed with a clipboard, stood at the entrance to the path.

Another car turned towards the car park entrance and the constable began his well-practiced gestures. A quick flash of warrant cards and the constable stepped to one side allowing the car to pass and take its place amongst the growing community of marked and unmarked police vehicles. Two figures emerged, extracted paper crime scene suits from the boot of the car and quickly donned them before stepping briskly towards the path. The constable checked their credentials before noting their details on his clipboard; every person entering recorded in the log. Trace evidence at the scene that couldn't be attributed to the investigators may belong to the perpetrator. The crime scene suits reduced the possibility of contamination.

After a brief discussion, the constable gestured towards a man standing beside the open tailgate of an estate car, the only vehicle that didn't belong to the emergency services. In the back of the car lay a dog. One of the white-suited figures broke away and walked towards the man, arousing the interest of the dog but not to the point where it could be bothered to sit up, preferring to casually sniff the air and point its ears towards the newcomer.

The second person continued towards the tent where the process of verification and logging was repeated.

Once inside, the purpose of the tent became clear. A freshly dug pit lay in the centre. Strong floodlights illuminated the horror within. The newcomer noted several partially covered bodies of what appeared to be young girls; recently buried, judging from the lack of decomposition. The bright pink "Hello Kitty" underwear on one of the victims jarred with the nature of the scene. Such items should not be seen in these circumstances. Such circumstances should not be seen at all.

'What we got, Doc?'

Pathologist, Dr James Melbourne turned his head and raised an eyebrow. Even whilst clad in the utilitarian paper coveralls, face masked and hood pulled tightly around her face, he clearly recognised DCI Helene MacKay.

'I thought you moved on, Helene?'

Helene smiled behind her mask.

'Hello James. I'm guessing a mass grave is going to fall on my desk sooner or later, so here I am. Anyway, what are you doing here? This is a bit out of your area.'

'Special request from high up, apparently. Running the case? I thought you left the Met?'

'I did, James. I'm now loosely connected to the National Crime Agency.'

'Loosely?'

This was the first case for her new team and although he was not yet aware of it, she intended to recruit James.

'I could tell you, but then I'd have to kill you.'

One eyebrow moved up his forehead again.

'Oh?'

'Oh, don't worry James, I need you too much for me to do that.'

She smiled again.

'So?'

She nodded her head towards the victims.

'As pushy as ever, eh? Okay. Nine IC5 females, as far as I can tell for now. The top six are recent. I'm still processing the top two and they appear to be still in rigor, if the other four are the same the deaths are probably contemporaneous. The bottom three are in a slightly more advanced stage of decomposition suggesting they almost certainly didn't die at the same time as the others, although probably no more than a few days apart. Until we move them, I can't see them all clearly, but of the ones I can, they have ligature marks on the neck, some have signs of restraints around the wrists and ankles. I can see some stab wounds too on one of the lower ones. There is evidence of animal activity on the uppermost one, a fox I suspect, which is probably why the grave was discovered in the first place. Whoever did this must have been in a rush or underestimated how much space nine humans require.'

Helene grimaced. Not her first murder scene, but her first mass grave; poor souls. What did they do to deserve this? What did anybody do to deserve murder? She reflected on that for a moment. Some people probably did deserve to die, but not these; not the innocents.

'You said in a rush, buried at the same time then?'

'I would say so.'

'In that case, this isn't the murder scene'.

'Highly unlikely.'

'I suppose it's too early to suggest a sexual motive?'

James nodded. 'You know I'm not going to determine that until I get them back, but from the way they are dressed ... '

'Yeah, I know, but you can't blame a girl for trying. I'll be back in a minute.'

Helene stepped out of the tent and stood for a few minutes taking in the scene.

She watched as her new sergeant made her way from interviewing the dog walker to join her at the crime scene. Sergeant Ruth Cannon missed the first meeting but was now fully briefed on the workings of the group. She seemed as keen as Helene to take on the villains on a more equal footing and came highly recommended; the latest recruit from Chief Superintendent Brandon. Despite their differences, he did seem to have an eye for the right people. It was always a challenge to break a new officer into your way of thinking, but Ruth would fit in just fine.

'Ruth, scout around and see if you can find a way into the park close to here. You might start by seeing if you find any tyre tracks nearby.'

The park was closed to public vehicles, but service vehicles had access. Following the tracks would not be an easy task, nor would any they found necessarily belong to the perpetrator's vehicle.

'Yes, boss.'

As she left, James shouted from inside.

'Helene, get an ambulance, quick.'

CHAPTER NINE

Helene hurried back into the tent to see James looking slightly ashen faced.

'One of them is still alive.'

As a pathologist, James rarely dealt with the living, and certainly not when they were already buried.

Helene summoned an ambulance on her radio as James tended to the victim. Somehow, she survived the strangulation and burial but not unexpectedly, was in a bad way. Whether she would recover was open to debate.

'I think that confirms your rush theory, James. Whoever did this must have been in a hurry to dispose of them.'

Ruth made her way to the nearby path, as good a place as any to begin; mostly flattened grass with patches of bare earth dotted along its length. Each stretch of damp earth held the inevitable motorcycle and bicycle tracks. Local youths often ran unlicensed dirt bikes on the Flats and many mountain bikers used the area.

She followed the path until she came to a track clearly used by four wheeled vehicles. This probably ran around the perimeter of the park. Moving to her left, she inspected the next bare patch and was rewarded with several vehicle prints. One pair stood out, fresh in the light mud. Ruth was no tyre expert, but these appeared identical to her, running slightly offset to each other. Either the vehicle passed this way twice or reversed. She retraced her steps to the path then followed the track in the opposite direction to find another patch of earth. Bingo! No fresh prints in that one; the vehicle hadn't come this way.

As she returned to the previous tracks, she kept an eye out for marks in the grass leading to the crime scene. At the back of the copse she saw the grass flattened in two parallel lines, undoubtedly caused by a vehicle, but she would leave the examination of that area to crime scene techs.

She followed the trail until it came to a turning leading to an access gate. More of the same tyre tracks led directly to it.

Ruth followed. A brass lock secured the gate; whoever made these tracks must have a key. Footprints in the mud on both sides, showed where someone had alighted from the vehicle.

Possibly these had nothing to do with the murders, maybe this vehicle belonged to a park keeper, but Ruth's instincts told her she was looking at a prime piece of evidence.

As she turned to go back to Helene at the tent, something made her inspect the lock once more.

'Oh, you clever buggers. The boss lady is going to love you,' she thought, as she hurried back. Not a bad start to her new career.

~§~

'Ladies: Gentlemen.'

The thud of a manila folder landing on the table attracted their attention.

'Our first case.'

She held up her hands to head off the chorus of objections from around the table and raised her voice to be heard over the noise.

'I know, I know. You are all training on your own aspects of our work and we've not had chance to pull everything together yet and you need many more weeks before we can go operational. Those were my exact words when this was handed to me and I was told what I'm going to tell you. This case means we'll be doing all that on the hoof.'

Helene waited for the noise to die down before opening the meeting.

'For those of you unfamiliar with police investigations, a briefing will be carried out each morning to bring the team up to date with any progress, and during the day if any major developments occur. If you are out in the field, a briefing communication will be issued; if you are operating undercover, this will only be if information relevant to your continued safety comes to light. During these briefings, you are free to voice an opinion, idea, or even black humour. You might think this is outlandish, but sometimes this provides us with the one piece of the jigsaw that allows us to put together the rest. One observation on my final case with the Met allowed us to find the person responsible for a series of murders last year.'

Helene paused and glanced in the direction of one of the team members. Yes, they found the person responsible, what she left out was that person sat amongst them, right here at the table, as part of the team. A fact she would never divulge to the others.

For a moment, she reflected on the contrast of holding a briefing in a spacious oak-panelled room, rather than the often cramped and chaotic rooms at the local nick. Why couldn't better conditions be provided for all the officers who worked their bollocks off trying to put together a case?

A small jolt passed through her body; the realisation that this was it. She now controlled the entire team. Any cock-ups would be her responsibility, and hers alone. Although running a police MIT carried similar responsibilities, often things outside her remit created hold-ups, or resulted in cases being thrown out. With the exception of the Crown Prosecution Service, and in one way they did have their own CPS, the team contained personnel recruited for all those specialised elements, tasked with catching the criminals who evaded the clutches of the more conventional law enforcement bodies; a self-contained unit with all the necessary skills and equipment to operate autonomously. Almost. She still required a pathologist; a work in progress for now, but she would get her man, of that she was certain.

She looked at the faces waiting expectantly for her to continue.

'Early this morning, a dog walker discovered the bodies of eight young IC5 women on Wanstead Flats. A ninth victim was still alive, having been buried along with the other eight. Initial indications are that death occurred at different times for three of the victims, but all within a week of each other, and not at that location. It's thought the bodies were buried contemporaneously and in something of a hurry. Some of the victims showed signs of strangulation and some suffered stab wounds, but we'll know more when we receive the post-mortem results; the PMs will start tomorrow. Our crime techs are still working the scene and have recovered several sets of tyre prints from close by. The grave was believed to be no more than twenty-four hours old when it was discovered, a belief supported by one victim still being alive at the time of discovery. It's early days of course, so information is a bit scarce now. Super sleuth Ruth' — Helene gestured towards the sergeant, then realised she'd probably saddled her with a nickname that wouldn't go away; it could be worse — 'picked up the tracks before the crime techs and traced them to an access gate where she found the lock forced and glued back together. The techs are working that one too.'

'Err, IC5?'

Helene turned towards one of the civilian members of the team, the computer hacker known by the name Jack Sparrow, real name Chris.

'Yes. Sorry, I forgot some of you are not familiar with these terms. IC refers to the Identity Code which allows us to classify people according to their ethnic appearance. In this case, the 5 refers to Chinese, Japanese or other Southeast Asian origin. When I get a chance, I'll put together a glossary of police terms, so you can all get used to them.'

'Isn't this a police matter?'

'Normally I would agree, Smoke' —

Helene addressed Customs Officer Daniel Spencer by the nickname he adopted for his last undercover case. He spent a year working under that name as a Hells Angel, along with his wife Katrina, who took the name Gypsy. Somehow the names stuck.

— 'but this is the second such case in less than six months, and a few individual cases in the past year seemed a little bit odd. We failed to ID the body in a case I worked on last year, nor did we make any progress. No reports of a MISPER matching the ..., sorry, Missing Person, matching the description, IC5 female, approximately sixteen-years old. That isn't all that uncommon, but when tied in with other, almost identical cases, then it's a whole new scenario. The individuals were IC5, all found in empty flats or houses. Nothing linked the owners of the buildings and all showed signs of forced entry. Forensic examinations of the scenes found nothing common between them. To be exact, they found very little at all and we suspect polythene sheets were used. Blood at the scene was minimal but lividity suggested the buildings to be the likely primary crime scene in most cases. That blood had to go somewhere. All victims showed evidence of the same MO – modus operandi. COD, sorry again, cause of death, exsanguination caused by stab wounds to the chest, signs of a ligature of some sort around the neck and wrists, and evidence of recent sexual activity, although no body fluids present. We thought we had a serial killer on our hands.'

'How come we haven't heard about these?'

'We kept it quiet, Nicky. Organised crime was suspected once we linked the murders, so we asked for and received the co-operation of the press.'

She smiled at the reporter, Nicky Rolands, and continued, 'I suspect your editor didn't let on, sorry.'

'Oh, no need to be sorry. I doubt my editor has a clue himself, otherwise he would plaster it all over the front page. He couldn't keep a goldfish, let alone a secret.'

Helene smiled again, then continued.

'The mass grave changed our perspective. If this is a serial killer then, the size of the escalation is almost unheard of. The general consensus is this is the work of a gang or gangs. Our initial thoughts were that perhaps this was something to do with sex trafficking and these were working girls who had outlived their usefulness. But they were still young and attractive, so that seems unlikely. One theory was that rival gangs were having a turf war and wiping out the opposition's assets but none of our reliable sources heard anything about such activity. As sick as this sounds, we believe that a person, or persons, are paying for the pleasure of killing, and an individual, or possibly a syndicate, is supplying the victims, no doubt for a hefty price.'

A murmur went around the table. Some members of the team led relatively sheltered lives before being recruited. The idea of killing for sexual purposes, well beyond their normal day to day lives.

Smoke spoke up again.

'Even if it is organised, surely the SC&O would have jurisdiction. Were all the victims found within the Greater London boundary?'

As Smoke suggested, a crime of this nature within Greater London area would normally come under the control of the Metropolitan Police Specialist Crime and Operations Division, in particular the Homicide and Serious Crime Command, which ran the Murder Investigation Teams. Helene's previous role was as senior officer in one of the MIT units prior to her recruitment to Invidia.

She nodded.

'In normal circumstances, I would agree, and investigations have been ongoing in SC&O since last year. There are no firm leads as yet, but three names are in the frame as possibles. The ethical considerations in gathering evidence are a little less problematical to us.'

Despite her having trust in her team, she was not about to let them know of a possible leak within the Met and the prime reason for Invidia being handed the case.

'As police officers, we are mindful of section 78 of PACE. We couldn't set up a sting operation where we enticed someone to commit an offence who would not otherwise have committed that offence' — she broke off. — 'Sorry, Smoke, this is for the benefit of the others. I'm sure your knowledge of PACE is as good as, if not better than mine.'

She continued. 'Section 78 allows the courts to exclude any evidence gathered this way, if they feel it was entrapment. We may go to court but if we do it will be a court of our choosing, and I can't elaborate any further on that. Because we don't exist, we can operate a little differently to other agencies, and we don't necessarily need to worry about that restriction being placed upon us. Our methods will be to gather evidence in any way we can. If we bring in suspects we will hopefully gain a confession, but that will be done by using the evidence we have gathered. We will not resort to obtaining confessions under duress. No one will wear an orange suit and hood.'

She saw that everyone in the room understood the reference.

'What happens after that is up to those upstairs to determine. If the suspect thinks cooperation is the lesser of two evils, he will go to court in the normal way and serve his time, and if he doesn't, well, that is not our decision to make, but suffice to say, access to other judicial methods is available to us.

'Because we must start somewhere, we will target a few of the names suspected of being involved in human trafficking, but I should warn you now, these are only the three most likely possibles from the evidence gathered so far. The list is long. Moving people is a lucrative business.

'We'll show interest in a similar scenario to what we suspect is happening here; ask the suspects to provide us with a number of women for a client of ours with peculiar tastes. As some of our colleagues across the water say, "let's shake the trees and see what falls out." Once we nab the suppliers, we can go after the rest.'

Once again, Smoke spoke up.

'I'm sensing an undercover op coming up here, boss.'

Despite her request for everyone to call her Helene, keeping the unit on an informal footing, everyone insisted on calling her 'boss', even the civilians. Whether they got together and decided to do this, or it was something the civvies picked up from the others, she couldn't say for sure. It showed the beginnings of the unit working together as a team, and she couldn't ask more than that.

'You sensed correctly, Jedi.'

Helene drifted back to one of her final briefings in the Met where her Detective Sergeant earned the name of Jedi from his uncanny abilities. Pity he hadn't shared her views on what they were doing here. Although she never asked him outright and didn't drop the slightest hint about the team, he made it clear where he stood if they couldn't catch a criminal within the confines of the law. She gave an inward smile and carried on.

'You and Gypsy will be in the market for young girls for your high-class operation. A private operation for rich clients will, I'm sure, entice someone to rise to the bait. Our problem will be if all three suspects rise, but my gut feeling is that once they hear the specifics, the job will be a little too extreme for most of the organised groups and individuals. I think we are looking at a small but highly selective gang or perhaps an individual. This doesn't smell like your average criminal operation. The IT and Documents teams are working on your background. Once that's done, and you're happy with your new personas, we'll set everything in motion.'

'Err, boss?'

She turned to Harry.

'Am I right in thinking you won't need us for a few days on this one, if at all? Cos, if it's all right with you, I'd like to take the lads somewhere nice and remote for a little extra training.'

'Not too remote, Harry. I need contact with you at least once a day for the briefing, and if things do go pear-shaped, I want you back here, pronto.'

'Aye, no problem. Likely I'll be in the pub; the lads are the ones who'll be staying out.'

'Have you no shame?'

'What do you think?'

She couldn't help but laugh at his self-assuredness. Harry knew his business and his place in the world.

'Any questions?'

She looked around the room; lots of eager faces and one or two anxious ones looked back at her. This was their first case and as she had told Brandon and Strong, many members of the team were still finding their feet, and for some police work fell well outside their area of expertise, leaving them slightly apprehensive. Helene's responsibility would be to put them at ease and help them slot into the team with the minimum of stress. As nobody had anything to ask at this point, she concluded the meeting.

'Go catch me a killer.'

~§~

Dartmoor can appear bleak and lifeless even during the day. At night, for those with a vivid imagination, all manner of things may be lurking in the dark. In reality, the most dangerous thing to be encountered, aside from humans, is adders. Contrary to popular belief, adders do not lie in wait ready to bite the nearest unsuspecting human but will if disturbed or cornered. Mostly, they just slide away and stay out of sight.

Harry's men were well aware of the dangers of snakes, the adder being amongst the milder end of the venomous creatures they encountered in their careers; not all of them non-human. But snakes would be the least of their concern today; their brief from Harry perfectly clear, 'defend' this hill; Harry would attempt to infiltrate and they had to spot him. They all thought him mad. How on earth could one man infiltrate a group of four, in the middle of moorland, on top of a mound with three-hundred-and-sixty-degree visibility, and in broad daylight?

The four men hunkered down in positions chosen to give the maximum coverage of the terrain around them and with the minimum of exposure to themselves. Helmet radios ensured they kept contact, even when not in sight of each other. The exercise would start at 10 a.m. and finish at 4 p.m. Within that period Harry would make his attempt.

As trained professionals, they took the task seriously, despite the general agreement it was an exercise in futility and part of Harry's process of showing them he was in charge; something entirely unnecessary. From the start, they were all aware of Harry's 'presence'. Something about the man didn't so much whisper danger, as shout from the rooftops, yet somehow, in a very quiet way. Everything about Harry was measured and even; the perfect example of someone who knew how to blend in wherever he was. Even though he was somewhere in his sixties, he remained quite cagey about his actual age, he kept up with them on all the physical exercises; a fact they respected very highly indeed. Not only did they respect his physical prowess but also that of his mind. Here was a man who knew his onions, despite the fact some twenty-five years had passed since he last served. So why did he think he needed to stamp his authority on them with this futile exercise? Blend into a human situation he may well be able to do but no one could move across this terrain without at least one of them knowing about it.

The four men; Brian Martins, Bartholomew Fitzsimmons, Terrence Godfrey and David Lightfoot, otherwise known as House, Fitz, Private and Twinkle Toes, all had distinguished careers in the special forces, more specifically the SBS, Harry's former unit, which is why they were handpicked from the squad. Harry bonded well only with people he respected, members of his 'pack.' The higher powers who put together the team were aware of this and ensured that at least the members Harry would work with closely, would be on the same wavelength as him.

'One, clear.'

'Two, clear.'

'Three, clear.'

'Four, clear and bored out of my skull. Told you he was just pulling our plonkers.'

A chuckle came over the radio.

'You think?'

'One, identify.'

'Chief plonker puller here, One. Now if you gentlemen would care to stand up, turn yourselves around, and look to the centre of this piece of real estate ...'

From various locations on the hill, small grassy mounds began to move and rise from the ground, each one turning towards the centre of the hill, where an equally grassy mound, in the form of Harry, stood holding his weapon in the ready position.

'What the fu ...?'

'How the hell did you ...?'

With their helmets removed, a general discussion ensued as to how Harry got into position and the possibility that he never left in the first place.

'You all saw me leave, gentlemen. I can't have been here all the time.'

Fitz asked the question the others wanted to.

'How long have you been here?'

'Here? An hour. On the hill? Three-and-a-half.'

'Nah, not believing that, Harry. You couldn't have been here that long.'

Harry chuckled and pointed to their packs.

'Gentlemen, please examine your backpacks and you'll find I've left you a little present.'

They scrambled to remove their packs and examine the contents.

'Well, I'll be buggered.'

Twinkle Toes pulled out a Creme Egg, as did each of the others.

'I thought you might like a treat after being up here this long.'

Harry held up his hand.

'And before you say I put them in your packs before leaving base, why do you think I had you check your kit when we got here? They weren't there then, were they?'

House squatted on his haunches looking up at Harry and shaking his head.

'So, you're saying you've been on this hill for three-and-a-half hours, and in that time, you've planted four eggs in four packs without us even knowing you were here?'

'Aye, laddie, I am. Welcome to my world.'

CHAPTER TEN

She lay on the bed staring at the ceiling. Not the first time she'd been in this position in recent months, especially after the breakup and the problems at the Met. On those other occasions her thoughts were almost always the same; how come so many men know so little about the female body?

Her therapist said her behaviour was complex; a three-way battle. The need to feel good by sexual gratification, the need to be loved and wanted and an overwhelming desire to punish those who left her still wanting at the end of the night; the seemingly endless string of one night stands always ended by her totally ignoring their calls and texts.

That in itself created a vicious cycle, attempting to achieve the feel-good factor then falling into despair but trying it all again the following night. The therapist likened her behaviour to that of some serial killers; commit the deed, feel empowered, come down from the high into depression, then repeat the cycle once more; an endless cycle of ups and downs. Helene pointed out a flaw in her observation in that the men she brought home rarely gave her the high in the first place. Damn woman had an answer for that too. Seems you can't win an argument with a psychologist.

Despite having a couple of one-night stands since, one solitary person did make her feel good, wanted, loved and damn it, he was married. So, she did what she thought would be the right thing, threw herself into her work, sought therapy, and up until today, pushed him to the back of her mind. And therein lay one of the reasons why sleep eluded her. Dr James Melbourne.

Tomorrow she would attend the post-mortem as senior investigating officer to keep the chain of continuity for any evidence uncovered; essential to the justice system and even though this may never reach a court, she intended to have the same rock-solid chain for Invidia. Tomorrow, she would tell him how she felt.

The other reason sleep eluded her lay in her own confidence. The constant berating from Brandon took its toll. Whatever reasons are given after the event, the human psyche reacts badly to belittlement, having efforts dismissed, being singled out for blame. So, despite knowing she achieved a result on a difficult case and learning that Brandon had an ulterior motive, she still lacked the confidence she once had.

Tomorrow the enquiry would kick off for real and Helene had sole charge of the way it ran; not just the investigation but the whole operation from labs, to IT, to field agents to pathology, etcetera. Invidia operations lay squarely on her shoulders and for the first time, that immense responsibility made its presence truly known.

Sleep was not going to come easily. She looked at the business card next to the phone. 'Call me anytime, day or night.' One of the first steps in repairing the mind is knowing when to ask for help. She picked up the phone and dialled.

~§~

Helene had spent many hours here, none of which she would describe as being her happiest but they would have been much worse were it not for the company. She entered the nondescript single-storey red-brick building, standing behind an equally nondescript two-storey red-brick building in Poplar

Street, Tower Hamlets: The Mortuary and Coroners Court. Occasionally she sent another member of her team, but as a Senior Investigating Officer for one of the Metropolitan Police Force Murder Investigation Teams, she attended many a post-mortem here to establish continuity of evidence, for presentation in court later, if necessary. It was true you became a little hardened to the whole process, though remaining detached became difficult when children were involved.

Today was different; she no longer worked directly for the Met Police, but she was here to attend another post-mortem, several in fact; the Asian girls found on Wanstead Flats. She had a secondary reason for a visit; to attempt to recruit Dr James Melbourne into her team and into her life. Her mind flitted back again to Detective Sergeant 'Jedi' Barnes and his favourite quote from Yoda in Star Wars; 'Do or do not, there is no try.' She would recruit her man, for both jobs.

She'd lost count of the number of times she'd entered this office, almost always to take part in the examination of the earthly remains of yet another poor unfortunate. Not all would turn out to be murders, of course. Even though this case involved what appeared to be several murders, an eager anticipation filled her heart but not for the procedure she was about to witness. She hadn't realised how much she wanted this man in her life until she was sure she might never see him again.

During her own recruitment interview for Invidia, Helene's lack of steady relationships was mentioned as both a positive and negative factor; the negative coming from a multitude of one-night stands. Invidia members may be called on to spend extended periods away from home, possibly undercover, with the obvious detrimental effect on a long-term relationship. A husband-and-wife team already existed within the group, Daniel and Katrina, aka Smoke and Gypsy, and after much discussion with her boss, Michael Strong, they agreed that as long as any relationship did not interfere with the work, then any future relationships between team members would be acceptable.

Apart from her personal interest in recruiting James, she wanted him on board because he was the finest pathologist she had worked alongside. Having an in-house pathologist would reduce the reliance on outside agencies for their work; vital to maintain their invisibility.

'Good morning, James. I hope I'm not disturbing you.'

He looked up from the papers in his hands, smiled and came from behind his desk to give her a hug.

'Helene, lovely to see you again.'

Helene pulled back slightly, her head to one side.

'Do you really mean that?'

He frowned.

'Of course, I do, why wouldn't I?'

Helene answered by kissing him hard on the mouth.

'Wow, I think you missed me, Helene.'

Helene nodded slowly.

'We need to talk, about lots of things; two in particular. But first there's a post-mortem or two to do, I believe?'

'Well, yes, but when you said this was your case, I didn't realise you would be the SIO. I thought you were management now.'

Helene caught hold of his hand.

'I am, but I am still the SIO.'

She laughed at the bemused look on his face.

'Actually, I the one who asked for you to be the attending pathologist at Wanstead.'

'I'm impressed at your new-found influence.'

'That's one of the things I need to talk to you about, but first, shall we?'

Helene indicated the way to the post-mortem examination room.

James bowed from the waist with his arm outstretched.

'After you, m'lady.'

'Yes, I am, and don't you forget it.'

Seeing James made her come alive again. When in his presence she had a sense of calm and certainty as well as the giggly effervescence of pubescent teenage girl on her first serious date; a contradiction which she could not explain. He made her feel alive in a swirl of colourful emotions she found intoxicating; he was the missing part of her she hadn't been aware was missing.

She hoped he would be interested in both the job offer and her, and that her sudden disappearance, so soon after that ill-judged one-night stand with him, hadn't caused any lasting animosity; judging by his reaction to her kiss, she didn't believe that would be the case. But she had her doubts. Apart from that one night, when they had both been under a lot of stress and slightly worse for wear with drink, James showed no real outward signs of his feeling towards her at all only the merest hint of more hidden away. Perhaps her desire caused her to see hope when there was none to be had at all. She would find out soon enough.

She needed James Melbourne in her life, and now, after recently hearing of his separation from his wife, she hoped this would be the right time to make a move and that he felt the same about her.

~§~

'A bloody ghost he is, boss. Can't be done I tell you, but he did it anyway. Bloody ghost.'

Helene was getting the story of Harry and the boys on Dartmoor. She'd been moving through the team having coffee before they started the morning briefing. This was the first time with the full team since Harry and his boys returned from their training exercise.

She already had experience of how good Harry was at blending in, but her instincts told her there was more to this than meets the eye, and she made a note to ask him after the meeting.

Helene called the briefing to order and brought everyone up to date with the progress so far, which amounted to very little apart from the elimination of one of the names; already detained in one of Her Majesty's prisons, on remand for surprise, surprise, human trafficking. But one of the other names returned some interesting results.

'Vincent David Howard, DOB twenty-third September, nineteen-sixty-nine, is known to run a string of high-class girls catering for extremely wealthy clients. He visited Hong Kong late last year. He has no record of violence, but money changes people and as such he is now our prime person of interest. Home office records indicate he returned to the UK some seven weeks before the discovery of the first grave. Assuming the girls were smuggled in by sea somehow, and I think in this case that's a relatively fair assumption, then we are looking at a sea time of around four weeks. Allowing time at each end for getting them on and off the ship, we are in the right time frame. Orchid, although I'd rather use her proper name, Emma, is currently digging into his financial transactions. We may be putting two and two together and getting oranges, but this is the best we have to go on for now.'

She turned at Smoke and Gypsy.

'How are the new personas coming along?'

'I think we're good to go, boss.'

Smoke glanced at Gypsy for confirmation and got a nod.

'Yep, good to go.'

'In that case, let's see if we can set up a meeting with Howard and take it from there. Any questions?'

'If I were him, I'd change at least one of my first names.'

'Why's that, Brian?'

'I just think the initials VD can't be good advertising for the business he's in.'

Helene let the howls of laughter die down. She couldn't argue with that.

'Any more comments or questions?'

This time none were forthcoming.

'Smoke, Gypsy. See you in my office in five. Harry, you got a minute?'

Harry nodded, and they waited until the briefing room emptied.

'Okay, spill the beans.'

Harry frowned.

'You know what I mean. You're good, I know that from personal experience, but you aren't a ghost.'

He laughed.

'Ssshh. Don't you go destroying my reputation. I've had to work hard for that you know.'

Helene tilted her head to the side and raised her eyebrows.

'Which bit don't you believe?'

'The eggs.'

'Ah. Well that one's easy. Sleight of hand.'

'Explain.'

'It's true, I did ask them to check their packs before I left, but then I distracted them. As we clustered around to look at a map, they didn't notice that the 'we', didn't include me. Five seconds, that's all I needed: Four eggs, four packs.'

She smiled and shook her head.

'You're incorrigible, Harry.'

'No, boss. I'm a ghost, remember?'

Armed with their new identities, Smoke and Gypsy set about tracking down Howard. Ask anyone what the hardest part in any undercover operation would be, the answer would likely be getting an introduction, especially one that avoided arousing suspicion. People like Howard remained on the outside of a prison cell not by being lucky, but by being suspicious of everything; by nature, they remained wary of strangers. Arranging an introduction often took some time, as proven by Smoke and Gypsy's last case for the HMRC.

The year they worked undercover as Hells Angels, served as a way to gain an introduction to their target; a drug distributor. Not the street corner seller variety, but a bulk buyer who then sold to the £10-a-bag merchants via his own distribution network; never handling the drugs himself. Through one of the dealers, Smoke finally persuaded him to meet on the pretence of having four kilos of quality gear to move on, with the possibility of more if the deal worked out. Lured by the promise of large profits, the buyer took the bait and set up a meeting with Smoke, which the HMRC subsequently raided; two years in the planning and one in execution. All that time and effort spent only for the case to be cast aside by the CPS on the grounds of insufficient evidence.

That was then. Now they were in a new job, working to a new set of rules, but they would use the same tried and tested methods to work undercover. For this operation, they would start by putting the word on the street; someone in the market for some high-class, zero mileage goods.

No longer disguised as Hells Angels, the pair appeared as well-dressed business people, the type clearly with money, as borne out by the Aston Martin Vantage now parked outside one of the well-known haunts for the higher-class working ladies. Many of them operated as independents, preferring to look after their own safety, employ their own protection and pocket a higher return than those who worked for an agency or employer. These girls preferred not to seek the 'quickie' clientele, but the long weekend in Paris or extended business trip types. An hourly rate didn't feature in their profiles because they didn't work by the hour. Of the others frequenting the place, a few were reputed to work for a certain Mr Howard. After visiting several other establishments, creating a trail of enquiries, Smoke and Gypsy entered the nightclub. It didn't pay to approach your target directly in this game. Anyone worth their salt in this business would ask around before speaking to someone with whom they had no prior dealing, and Invidia considered Howard to be a cagey adversary. He would be certain to check and would be slightly less suspicious of their motives once he discovered this club was not the first and only place on their agenda.

Should they manage to arrange a meeting with the somewhat shy Mr Howard, the first order of the day would be to establish their credentials as high-class operators, and this is where the IT and Documents department came up trumps with their identities.

They would take on the identities of a couple involved in a number of rackets in the Manchester area; the real couple, the male member of which turned out to be conveniently named Daniel, currently enjoyed the hospitality of the Invidia

Team in a safe house in the Lancashire Pennines. Remote, moorland farmhouses proved to be far more versatile than perhaps the original builders envisaged, especially when holding someone without charge; a concept of course frowned upon by members of the legal fraternity and civil rights groups.

Any Met Police officers who may be associated with Mr Howard in some way, especially those with access to the PNC and perhaps owed him a "favour", would find Mr and Mrs Smith to be a real couple, with a real reputation, and any of Howard's Manchester associates would only be able to report a recent and sudden absence of the Smiths; whereabouts unknown.

The fact that Smoke and Gypsy bore a remarkable likeness to Mr and Mrs Smith did not occur by chance. ITDOCS scoured the PNC and other databases to find the closest physical match to the undercover couple. Short of coming face to face with someone personally acquainted with the Manchester duo, the operation ought to run smoothly.

Gypsy sat alone at the bar, still relatively quiet this early in the evening; in the corner, Smoke chatted with two of the working girls, establishing his credentials as an employer.

'Hi hon. What are you doing here?'

Gypsy turned to face the tall, leggy, platinum blonde addressing her. She allowed her gaze to wander from the top of the long and immaculate silky hair, via the professionally applied make-up, through the perfectly manicured nails, down the impossibly long legs, all the way to the Jimmy Choo shoes.

'Not the same reason as you, I suspect.'

The blonde placed one hand on her hip.

'Meaning?'

'Save yourself the hassle, love, I'm not competition. My partner and I are looking for girls.'

Gypsy's slight Manchester accent would be convincing enough for any Southerner, and most Northerners would assume she was either trying to hide it or had left the city some years ago.

'Is that your partner, the hunk you came in with?'

'Nothing gets by you does it? Yes, it is.'

The woman tossed her hair which rippled and shimmered in the light.

'Well, if you are looking to play, I may be interested. He'll certainly have no luck with those two.'

'Down girl. We're in the same business, but he and I are more, shall we say, in a management capacity.'

'You run an agency?'

'Not in the way you think. We satisfy the requirements of wealthy clients, with what you might call specific tastes.'

'And I don't qualify?'

Gypsy laughed, and the woman jerked her head back sharply.

'Sorry, I don't mean to offend, but you are at least ten years too old, not anywhere east enough, Essex doesn't count, and I suspect you may have seen one or two dicks in your life.'

The woman studied Gypsy then let out a giggle.

'I like you. You're direct. Let me tell you, most of the men I meet are dicks, but that's another story. I take it you are talking Asian and young?'

It was Gypsy's turn to be surprised.

'You know of some?'

The woman shook her head and took another sip of her cocktail.

'No, but you're not the first to ask. Word went around at the end of last year that someone was in the market for young Asians. I don't know who, or even if they got them, but I know a man who might, or maybe who knows who to talk to. I'm assuming you mean virgins, right? Any other specific tastes in mind?'

'The tastes I can't tell you, that's between us and our clients, but you're right about the virgins.'

'Same as the others wanted. Sad isn't it? All this experience and some men only want to be the first in the queue. Personally, give me someone who knows what he is doing, any day, not that most of them do; couldn't find a g-spot with a satnav. Give me your number and I'll see what he says. He might be able to help. This sort of thing isn't his normal line, but he might be able to point you in the right direction.'

'Does he have a name, this man?'

The blonde smiled.

'And have you go direct to him? No, darling, I'm on commission. You come through me. I'll tell you his first name, and that's all. If he is interested, Dave will give you a call.'

Gypsy handed over a plain white business card with the name Daniel Smith and a mobile phone number.

'He's called Dave? Well, that narrows things down to a few million then.' Gypsy tapped the number on the card with an equally manicured fingernail.

'That's my partner.'

The blonde held up the card between her fingers.

'And will you change your mind about playing?'

Gypsy shook her head.

'That will never change, darling. We only have time for each other. The rest is purely business.'

'Pity.'

Gypsy cast her eyes over her again.

'But if I ever start batting for the other team, I know where to come.'

The woman smiled and slipped the card into her clutch bag, genuine Gucci, Gypsy suspected. This woman earned good money and didn't mind spending it on the good things in life.

CHAPTER ELEVEN

The tapping on the glass door caused Helene to look up; Smoke, inevitably with Gypsy in tow. Never had she seen a couple so devoted to each other. Perhaps her and James would be the same, once she plucked up the courage to speak to him. Despite the recent opportunity, she still hadn't broached the subject. Professing undying love at a post-mortem seemed a little off somehow, and not the most romantic way to tell him her feelings. At least the kiss planted the seed. Now all she needed to do would be keep it watered and watch it flourish and grow. Now, more than ever, she wanted to be with him for the rest of her life.

Helene beckoned to the couple to enter and raised a questioning eyebrow.

'Howard's taken the bait. Wants to meet to discuss our requirements; somewhere public, a place of his choosing, and'—

Smoke glanced at Gypsy.

— 'he wants me to come alone. I think our Mr Howard is one very cautious man.'

Gypsy grimaced, that topic clearly discussed already. Gypsy's face spoke of her disapproval.

'So it seems. Did he say where?'

'Not yet, and it will be short notice. Howard appears to take his security seriously and doesn't want anyone to set up surveillance in advance. I will be checked for a wire, I'm sure. It wouldn't be the first time. Probably a sweep from someone nearby.'

Helene frowned.

'I'm not entirely comfortable with you going in cold. If there's enough time we'll set up a mobile surveillance. We own some pretty high-tech equipment that both of our former masters could only dream of getting their hands on. As soon as you know where, I want to know. If we can arrange for back up in time, we will.'

'I appreciate that, but if we do have someone inside, they need to use a mobile not a radio.'

Helene gave him a look.

'Sorry, boss, I'm teaching granny to suck eggs. Anyway' — Smoke rubbed his chin.

— 'I don't think it's our man. Bearing in mind the business he's in, something about his whole manner makes me believe he's running as clean a racket as he can. Not that I agree with what he's doing, of course, but I think he looks after his girls. The ones we've seen are not the trafficked kind.'

Gypsy intervened.

'The one I spoke to the other night seemed more than happy in her work. She's in the business by choice, and making good money too, judging by the designer gear; genuine as far as I could tell.'

Helene pondered for a moment.

'Okay, you may be right, but currently he's the only lead, so we stick with what we have. We need a way into this case somewhere. If things don't pan out, we'll regroup and see what else we can come up with. In the meantime, I want to know as soon as you hear where he wants to meet, and don't take any risks.'

Smoke nodded his agreement.

Once the pair left the office, Helene put a call through to Strong.

'The laser microphone, how good is it?'

'Pretty damned good. As long the target is in line of sight and there's something we can reflect off, we can pick up anything above a whisper.'

'How long to set up?'

'What's this about, Helene?'

She briefed Strong about the possible meeting and her hopes to set up surveillance at short notice.

'I'll get the team together now, ready to go. Takes about ten minutes to set up. A window is ideally what we would like to bounce off, but anything in their proximity that can reflect and vibrate should give us a good signal.'

Armed with that knowledge, Helene awaited Smoke's call.

~§~

Helene answered the call on the first ring.

'MacKay.'

'RS Hispaniola, Thames, one hour.'

She responded to this information by giving Smoke a mini briefing. He listened carefully then prepared himself. Although Gypsy would not take part in the meeting, Smoke assumed his arrival would be monitored by someone on Howard's payroll. Gypsy would drive the Aston to the rendezvous and drop him off. The car and her clothing ought to convince any observer these two were not the average couple in the street.

Fifty minutes later, with a squeal of tyres, to the accompaniment of angry car horns and a solitary cycle bell, Gypsy swung the Aston onto the lowered kerb separating Victoria Embankment from Transport for London's latest brainchild, the East-West Cycle Superhighway.

A lycra-clad, middle-aged cyclist muttered a few choice words in the direction of the Aston as he swerved around the passenger door, then continued his journey in the direction of Waterloo Bridge.

Smoke waited until the cyclist passed then stepped out of the car, straightened his cuffs, sidestepped the bunch of joggers going the opposite way to the cyclist and crossed to the entrance of the Hispaniola.

So much for the cycle highway he thought, noting the joggers outnumbered the cyclists by ten to one. The brief Helene gave included instructions to sit at a table on the river side of the boat, next to a window if possible, but if Howard wanted to meet on the upper deck that would be covered too. As long as the table was in sight of the south bank of the river, the techs reckoned they could work with it, but Smoke must use a pint glass, and for the most part leave it untouched in a prominent place on the table.

Smoke's career included several undercover assignments, but here he felt like a rookie just out of training. As dangerous as those investigations sometimes were, this had a far more cloak and dagger feel. The familiar thrill of anticipation hit him, as always when an assignment kicked off, and he stopped for a moment to find his bearings. This was a good sign; complacency could be a killer in this line of work.

Twenty minutes before Gypsy incurred the wrath of the cyclist, an Environment Agency Incident Command Unit van parked on the south bank of the Thames, alongside the railings separating the Queen's Walk from the river and close to the railway bridge leading to Charing Cross station. No one paid any attention as two men clad in white overalls, exited the front of the vehicle, went around the back and removed a set of portable barriers from inside. Swiftly erecting them and completely encircling the van, they took one last look around before climbing back inside, this time through the sliding side door.

The R.S. Hispaniola, formerly known as the MV Maid of Ashton when owned by The Caledonian Steam Packet Company, had previously operated as a ferry on the Holy Loch route. She even carried royalty in her time, when Princess Margaret sailed on her down the River Clyde. She moved to the Thames in 1983, where she was renamed. Now she spent her time as a floating restaurant and function venue, permanently moored in the shadow of Hungerford Bridge; the same bridge near to which the Environment Agency van parked earlier on the opposite bank. Her role today, albeit a small one, would be as part of the ongoing investigations of Invidia.

Inside the van, the two technicians wasted no time in setting up the equipment. Environment Agency vehicles tend to attract little interest from the public and often carry an array of equipment on the roof. In addition to a satellite communications dish, this one sported a laser microphone, but how many casual observers would be able to identify such a thing, or even be aware of their existence? Only an extremely keen eye would spot the signs on the side of the van were of the magnetic variety. Signs such as this were not unknown for vehicles on a temporary lease to a company, but not usually on one carrying such specialist equipment on the roof.

Any kind of van provided the perfect place from which to conduct undercover work. Rarely did anyone notice, let alone question the myriad of working vehicles parked around the country. To ensure the maximum anonymity, and depending on location, a variety of other signage existed at the Invidia headquarters, including BBC outside broadcast unit, Scottish - Southern Electric, and of course, police.

The first technician swung the laser towards the Hispaniola and selected a target. Once designated, computer software would maintain the alignment of the transmitter and receiver on whatever the technicians chose. As long as the laser remained in direct line of sight of the target, the signal would continue. As a test run, they decided to eavesdrop on a conversation by targeting the smallest object that would still allow them to hear clearly, a shandy glass between two young ladies sitting at a table on the forward deck.

'... so, he said, "How about I come back to your place for a nightcap." Well, I'd had a few and he was really rather hot, so I said, "Why not?" Well, no sooner we'd got through the door than my knickers were around my ankles, and he was ramming me hard against the wall. I'm telling you, babes, I was gushing. I never got a wink of sleep that night.'

The two techs looked at each other and grinned.

'Never a dull moment, eh?'

'We should make this a business, you know. Record a few of these and write the next Fifty Shades of Grey.'

'Are you kidding? We can do better than that. '

'Foxtrot One arriving.'

The radio announced Smoke's arrival. One of Harry's men, seated at the bar, sipping a pint and seemly engrossed in his mobile phone, previously established Tango One, Howard, to be on board already. The technicians didn't acknowledge the transmission, the less radio chatter, the better.

At least this time the wait would not be a long one; something the surveillance techs had grown accustomed to over the years.

~§~

Smoke entered the bar area and scanned the area. Although he'd seen Howard's picture in the briefing, he was not supposed know what he looked like, after all, they never met before today. His gaze swept the room, completely ignoring Howard, who sat at one of the window tables. Smoke moved to the bar, avoiding eye contact with Harry's man, only feet away from him, and ordered himself a pint of Guinness. He made a show of looking at his watch then looking around. There would be no doubt to any observer, he was expecting to meet someone.

After several minutes, Howard rose from the table and made his way over to the bar. Smoke once again looked at his watch, his impatience evident.

'Waiting for someone?'

Smoke turned to face the man addressing him.

'Uh, yes.'

His gaze swept the room once more.

'Not good when people are late. A friend?'

He returned his attention to Howard.

'No. I've not met them before.'
'Oh, a blind date.'
Smoke smiled.
'A business meeting.'
His eyes moved back to scanning the room.
'You wouldn't by any chance be Daniel, would you?'
Smoke looked back at Howard.
'Mr Howard?'
The man smiled and held out his hand.
'I am indeed. Shall we go on deck and take in a little sunshine while we talk.'

Smoke sighed inwardly. Sit by one of the big windows if at all possible, Helene had said, now Howard had moved away from the window to go on deck. He couldn't very well push the issue, so he acquiesced.
'Certainly.'
'After you.'
Howard held out his arm to indicate Smoke should take the lead. At least that was a break.

On the upper deck, he turned to the port side of the ship to search for a place on the river side of the vessel. Only one appeared unoccupied, although a collection of glasses remained uncleared. The table forward of theirs he noted to be occupied by two young ladies; the one aft, a young couple gazing into each other's eyes and holding hands. He felt both couples would be less inclined to listen to the two businessmen than perhaps some of the occupants of the other tables, not that he had much choice in the matter if they were to take up a position on the river side. Still, he would choose his words carefully.

Howard opened the conversation once they were seated.
'So, what can I do for you, Daniel?'
Smoke carefully placed his pint in front of him before replying, as if deliberating on how to broach the subject.

Howard listened carefully as Smoke explained his clients' need for unused goods and the utmost discretion, especially given some of his clients' tastes. Tastes that while he couldn't disclose them, he hinted they were perhaps a little extreme.

He wondered if Howard or any of his associates could fulfil such a need.

When he finished, Howard studied his face. When he spoke, his voice remained quiet and measured but Smoke saw an anger in his eyes.

'I'm sorry, Daniel. I can't do business with you. I employ staff directly in my own business and for each and every one, I make sure they are legitimate. They come to me because I look after them, and they are paid exceedingly well and I maintain a high standard. My low turnover of staff and high number of repeat clients demonstrate this. I have no intention of putting any of my gir —, err, people in that sort of situation. I don't know what you were expecting of me and quite frankly I'm disgusted by anyone who would consider the sort of activity you are suggesting. Your clients will have to look elsewhere. Good day to you.'

He left the table without glancing back.

Smoke raised his eyebrows. That told him, good and proper. He settled back in his chair to drink his Guinness. The techs wouldn't need the glass now, so he might as well enjoy the drink.

His instincts proved to be spot on. Howard was not the type of guy to sell his granny, even if the deal was right. Considering his trade, he proved to be surprisingly ethical. Smoke found his respect growing for the man. He may be involved in an illegal activity, but he retained a certain amount of integrity, that much was clear.

The good news was that was one suspect less, the bad news, this put them back to square one. Someone was supplying girls and they still had no clue as to who.

~§~

One of the two techs in the van shrugged his shoulders. Clearly nothing valuable would come from that conversation. Their man received a brush off, and in no uncertain terms.

He swung the microphone back to a glass on the adjacent table.

'... I'm telling you, he hammered away for a good hour. I thought I'd never walk again.'

No sense in wasting the whole day. This was better than watching any porn movie.

CHAPTER TWELVE

This time the pain wasn't quite so bad. The ghostly voices still floated around her. Once again, the light pursued the darkness, parrying and thrusting, until forced to flee completely. This time she understood her surroundings, a hospital.

Memories came flooding back in a flurry of images, sounds and emotions; her parents' death, her ghastly uncle, the various massage parlours. She remembered a sea journey in a large metal box, and the horrible man who first brought their food. A brief time in the basement of a building, then days in darkness. Finally, she recalled her escape. She trembled as she saw the headlights and she re-lived the fear of the moment, but after that, only darkness and the sounds of the ever-present ghosts: until now. Now she understood it all.

Police. She must tell the police everything. There may be time to save the others.

'Welcome back.'

Kun turned her head to locate the source of the voice. Her eyes came to rest on a nurse looking down at her. The nurse smiled, took hold of Kun's hand and gently squeezed.

'You have had us worried.'

Kun spoke.

In times of stress her native Cantonese took precedence.

The nurse patted the back of Kun's hand.

'It's fine. You don't have to worry about a thing.'

'She is not worried. She is asking for the police.'

Kun lifted her head slightly to seek out the owner of the second voice; a young Asian nurse, writing something in a folder on the top of a trolley.

She realised her mistake and repeated her request in English.

'Police, I must have police.'

The nurse smiled again.

'Oh, don't you worry yourself, I'm sure they'll be along as soon as we tell them you're awake. They've been waiting to ask you some questions.'

'No. You don't understand. Now, I need them now.' Kun frowned. 'How long have I been here?'

The nurse patted her hand again.

'Almost a week. You had us a little worried for a while.'

Kun's head sank back on the pillow. A week! How many of the others would be dead by now? All of them? A tear rolled down one cheek. She tried to save them and but for the accident she might have succeeded.

The sobbing came quietly at first, small, gentle heaves of sadness rising as the face of each of the girls came back to her; when the face of Jing appeared, she let out an uncontrollable cry of anguish.

~§~

The door to Helene's office flew open, and Ruth knocked as she dashed into the room.

Helene raised her eyebrows.

'That normally happens the other way around, Ruth. I take it this is urgent?'

'Yes, boss.'

'Breathe, Ruth, breathe. I don't want to have to resuscitate you.'

Ruth stopped to take a deep breath, and then a second.

'Just received a message from Edmonton nick. There's an Asian girl, Chinese to be exact, in North Middlesex University Hospital. She was in an accident on the M25 a week ago, hit by a truck and has been in a coma ever since, until Saturday that is. Edmonton thought we might be interested.'

Helene raised her eyebrows. She knew not to interrupt when someone had a story to tell and was rushing to get it out. Better to let things flow naturally.

'Well, the first thing she said was she needed to speak to a police officer. Edmonton eventually managed to despatch a Sergeant and PCSO to take a statement. The PCSO remembered some intel I'd sent and was bright enough to recognise this for what it was. He alerted the Sergeant, who followed up. The girl claims she and the others were shipped from Hong Kong in a container and sold to someone in London. She thinks they were kept in an underground chamber of some sort, and only let out at night. Each night, one of them would be taken away, and they never came back. She escaped when they forgot to put a lock back on the door and made her way through the woods to the M25. Unfortunately, she didn't judge the speed of the truck too well. Lucky to be alive.'

'Where was the accident? What about the driver?'

'The north edge of Epping Forest; made her way out of the forest directly to the motorway. This next bit is the good part, boss. She reckons she can identify some of the men involved since she arrived here. The driver wasn't injured, nor at fault'

'Yes!'

Helene clenched the air in the universal gesture of success.

'This may be the break we need. I take it she isn't well enough to come to us. Get yourself over to Edmonton, pick up a copy of the statement and then pay her a visit if she is well enough to talk. We have more intel than Edmonton so we may be able to ask questions they wouldn't necessarily think to ask. Whatever she can remember. Oh, and take a couple of Harry's men with you. If she's caught up in this, she'll need a guard.'

As Ruth went through the door, Helene called out after her.

'They were wrong about you.'

Ruth popped her head back around the door frame with a quizzical expression on her face.

'Boss?'

'They told me you were good. They were wrong. You're bloody brilliant.'

A broad grin spread across Ruth's face.

'Thanks, boss.'

Helene hoped this was the break they needed to nail the bastards who did this. If so, a certain Sergeant and his PCSO would be finding themselves on the receiving end of several pints.

~§~

'You are all probably aware by now that the meeting with Howard was a washout. Smoke and Gypsy's instincts appear to have been vindicated and for now, Howard is no longer a person of interest.'

A few groans rose from around the table. There was nothing worse than pursuing a promising line of enquiry, only for it to reach a dead end. Helene held up her hands and the noise died down.

'We were also hopeful that the sole survivor from the crime scene at Wanstead would be able to help us with our enquiries, but unfortunately she is still on life support and hasn't regained consciousness. Doctors are not sure she ever will. What most of you don't know, and the reason for briefing, is that we now have a significant lead because there appears to be a second survivor.'

The murmurs started again and then settled as Helene continued.

'Several days ago, a young Chinese girl from Hong Kong, Chen Kun, was involved in an RTC with a truck on the M25 near Waltham Abbey. She was dressed only in underwear. On Saturday, she woke from a coma and asked for a police officer. Thanks to our Theresa and her cuts, none were available until this morning. A very bright PCSO, whom I will

lavish with a massive kiss, several in fact, if ever I meet him'
—

This brought a round of 'oohs' from the office.
'What if it's a her?'
Helene rolled her eyes and moved on.
— 'remembered reading a report in his station about the bodies on Wanstead Flats. He alerted his sergeant and the nick got in touch with us. Ruth went to interview the girl and we struck gold. She's a little hazy on the time frame but thinks she was shipped from Hong Kong with nine other young ladies, and by young, I mean young; none of them over the age of seventeen, most considerably younger. She said a few days before she escaped, they had been moved to a new location, where they received minimal food and water and a few blankets to keep them warm. Over a three-day period, three of the girls were taken away. None returned. We have three bodies with an approximate time of death a day or two before the others five. Those three were the stab victims. The others were asphyxiated.'

Helene turned away for a moment and cleared her throat. She didn't want them to see the tears forming.

'So, we know they left Hong Kong and we have an approximate departure date, to within a day or two.'

'Do we have any clues on the method of entry into the UK, boss?'

'Near the end of the journey they transferred from a container cargo ship, their primary transport to the UK, to a smaller and faster boat. Once onshore, they were bundled into a van and taken to some sort of disused building. By then it was daylight. They were given a medical examination; she believes this was checking their virginity.'

She shook her head and muttered something inaudible to the rest as she checked her notes.

'After the examination, apparently one of the men got very angry and drove off in a fancy car. The car was black, and the van was white; no index numbers or makes other than she believes the van was possibly a Ford and the car almost certainly a Rolls or Bentley.'

'Terrific. A white Ford van. That'll be a doddle to find, boss.'

Helene acknowledged the observation from Twinkle Toes with a shaken look of resignation.

'Oh, it gets worse, another white van after that and then a blue one. Whether they were passed along a chain or not, she's not sure. So, we don't know if they all had the same owner or we are looking for multiple persons. We need to locate any of the vehicles, the Rolls or Bentley should be easier, but we need one of those vans. Where this meeting took place, any of the locations where they were kept, the route into the country, are all lines of enquiry. Any one of those should crack this wide open. Easy-peasy.'

'What about this last place she mentioned?'

'Yes, we have some pretty specific information. She never left the wooded area when she escaped, before reaching the motorway, apart from crossing what from her description appears to be a B road. They were kept in a small building of some sort. She thought possibly some sort of underground room as no light came in at all. The room had some sort of wall in the middle, but they could still move all the way around the edge. A storeroom of some sort maybe? That description doesn't make any sense to me — a wall in the middle?'

'Pillbox.'

Helene turned to Nicky.

'Go on?'

'You say this was on the Waltham Abbey stretch, yes?'

Helene nodded.

'East or west of the town?'

'East.'

'Makes sense. The M25 skirts the north edge of Epping Forest there. During WWII, invasion was a real threat, so the government built defensive rings around London. The outer defensive ring ran through that region. The place is littered with pillboxes, anti-tank traps, gun emplacements, you name it, it's probably in the forest. From her description, I would suggest she's describing a pillbox.'

Helene scanned the report.

'She says the walls felt rough.'

Nicky emphasised his words by jabbing the air with his pencil.

'I'll stake a month's wages they were in a pillbox.'

Helene looked at him quizzically.

'How do you …? Forget I said that, you're a reporter.'

Nicky grinned at her.

'In one, boss.'

'Right. We are going to split into two teams. I think until we have a location at least, trying to find the vehicles is a washout. Team one will concentrate on trying to find the final location and take it from there. Trace evidence such as tyre tracks that can lead us to the vehicle, or at least tie it to the burial place may still be out there. Look for disused buildings, barns, outbuildings, whatever you can find in a two-mile arc from the accident scene' — she glanced at Nicky — 'including a WWII pillbox. Nicky, you can assist on that.'

'Oh, that I can. I just happen to have an overlay of all the locations on Google Earth. Shouldn't take us long to find the right one. Many have fallen into disrepair, although there are groups that preserve them. This one will probably have a new door. Stick out like a sore thumb.'

'Brilliant. Okay, the other team is going to Hong Kong to attempt to pick up the trail from that end. Kun has given us intel on her last employer. This away team will shake the Chinese trees. Now, two guesses who is going on the Hong Kong trip?'

That brought a number of catcalls. Helene couldn't help but smile. The team had gelled and accepted her enough to show their feelings without fear.

She stuck her tongue out at them.

'Rank has its privileges, and one of those privileges is I can choose who goes with me. I'll be taking Emma and Harry.'

Harry looked up, startled at the news.

'You sure, boss?'

'Yes, a little birdy told me that you were once an Arab. This time you will be wealthy.'

CHAPTER TWELVE

None of the others around the table had a clue what Helene was referring to, but Harry knew his boss must have had access to his SBS files. How the hell she'd managed that, he had no idea, but his admiration for her went up another couple of notches.

CHAPTER THIRTEEN

Emma had flown once before, yet this was to be her first landing. On the previous flight, she exited the aircraft at 11,000ft, attached to the chest of a skydiver; one of her adrenalin junkie experiences. She hadn't managed many of that kind, but she took them whenever she could afford them, although she preferred to spend most of her spare income on computer equipment.

Her first landing would also be her first time out of the country. Apparently, a trip to the Isle of Wight doesn't count as going overseas. This proved to be a little problematic as she didn't have a passport. Helene told her she would arrange to have one issued through Michael Strong, but Emma suggested a quicker way.

Four hours later, she took the short walk from Victoria tube station to collect her brand-new passport from the HM Passport Office in Eccleston Square. What was the point of being one of the top hackers in the world if you couldn't put it to good use now and again?

The business class flight on the Emirates A380 to Dubai was a vastly different experience to her first ever flight in the cramped cabin of the single engine aircraft used for her tandem jump. That didn't even have seats, let alone ones that converted into a lie flat bed. The arrival was somewhat different too; disembarking on the airbridge in the company of Helene, not strapped to the chest of Kevin from Essex. Still, jumping out of planes was an adrenalin rush, and that she enjoyed.

Emma was fascinated by Dubai Airport. She had been impressed with Heathrow, but now she had a new favourite airport on her list of two. Immigration formalities were swift and simple. Although a flight to Hong Kong departed in a little over eight hours, Helene elected to keep them in Dubai for two nights to allow Harry to get back into using his Arabic tongue. The wait at baggage reclaim turned out to be brief, and before she knew it, they were in the chauffeur driven BMW on the short drive to the hotel at Festival City. Harry was already waiting, having taken a flight the previous day.

~§~

'Please enjoy your stay with us and if there is anything we can do to make your stay more pleasurable, do not hesitate to ask. Your luggage will be taken to your rooms. Mr Khalid is waiting for you on the terrace.'

The receptionist pointed the way to the Vista Bar and Terrace.

Emma frowned and Helene gave her a wink, which left her even more puzzled. Where did this Khalid fella fit in; she wasn't expecting to meet anyone other than Harry.

As they wandered out onto the terrace, Emma looked around to see if she could see any sign of Harry and she wondered who this Khalid chap was that Helene seemed to be eager to meet. Perhaps it was something Harry arranged.

She noticed several men in the bar dressed in traditional Arab robes and sipping coffee, something she didn't expect to see in a place that served alcohol. Then again, she had no real understanding of Islam other than it existed. She made a mental note to find out more once they got back to the UK.

Helene stopped and turned to Emma.

'Wait here a moment. I need to go back to reception. I forgot to ask them something.'

Before Emma could reply Helene strode back the way she came.

'As-salām 'alaykum, my little flower.'

It took a moment for Emma to realise that the Arab gentleman seated at the table next to where she stood was addressing her.

She suffered a moment of panic; this was all outside her comfort zone. What was Helene thinking leaving her in a bar full of strangers, in a strange land.

'I'm sorry but I think ...'

The audio scratch pad kicked in. The first part she didn't understand but the second bit, that was English. My little flower? Harry called her that on account of her hacker handle, 0rchid.

She narrowed her eyes, unsure whether she would be committing some unforgiveable transgression if she was mistaken.

'Harry?'

'Mr Khalid, my little flower. You must address me as Mr Khalid from now on. I'm your wealthy boss, remember that.'

'Even though I know it's you, I don't — It's amazing. You look totally different. How did you — and what you said at the beginning, that was Arabic, yes?'

'It kept me alive, many years ago, in another life. My father was from Bahrain, a country not far from here and although I'm sure you will recognise, I'm a Northerner, as in the English north, I'm also fluent in Gulf Arabic. We spoke both languages at home, my father made sure of that, and it's stood me in good stead.'

A grinning Helene joined them.

'You were right, she had no idea.'

Emma turned to Helene.

'You knew?'

'Of course, Emma. It was my idea. If you didn't recognise him, then I'm sure there's little chance anyone in Hong Kong will either.'

'Are we expecting someone might?'

'You never know, Emma. We have no idea who is involved in this, either the buyers or the suppliers. It could be someone Harry has come across before and as for myself, I'll not be present at any of the meetings in case it's someone I've nicked in the past. You will be Mr Khalid's personal assistant. Besides, I'll be talking to one of my contacts at the HKPF.'

Emma gave her a quizzical look.

'Hong Kong Police Force.'

'Ah. Of course you have contacts there, you have contacts everywhere. It wouldn't surprise me to find out you are acquainted with the odd alien or two.'

Helene laughed.

'I did meet Sigourney Weaver once if that counts.'

'Stop it. As if I'm not jealous enough of you already.'

Emma gave her a playful push on the shoulder.

Helene wondered what she meant by that remark and made a note to follow it up with Emma later. She turned to Harry.

'Right, Mr Khalid. I believe we have a briefing to do. Would it be appropriate for us to join you in your suite?'

'To avoid any suspicion of impropriety, I booked a meeting room.'

'Good thinking, Mr Khalid. Lead on.'

As they walked from the Terrace, Emma fell in step with Helene.

'He gets a suite and we get just a room?'

'He's a wealthy gentleman, my dear. Besides, you haven't seen your room yet. My advice is to not open the curtains until you have turned off the lights, and then just take a look across the creek to the city. In the morning, with a bit of luck it will be misty. Then you will see an amazing sight.'

Emma looked questioningly.

'I'm not telling; you just have to see for yourself.'

~§~

The briefing had been fairly short, but intense. There was a lot to take in, and Emma had to do a little bit of work the next day in Dubai, the work she lived for - hacking.

When she got to her room, she remembered Helene's words as she opened the door, located the key card power slot she'd been told about, and the lights came on. After several attempts at switching various lights on and off, she finally found the master switch which plunged the room into darkness. She navigated her way across the bedroom, a difficult task in a dark and unfamiliar room. Cracking her shin on the coffee table, resulted in a few choice words of Anglo-Saxon, but finally she managed to locate the window and drew back the curtains.

Oh — wow. Just WOW.

Across from her room, the skyline of downtown Dubai appeared in the distance. What a sight, and there, looking like something out of a sci-fi movie, stood the famous Burj Khalifa, the tallest building in the city and indeed the world, but about to be overtaken by the Jeddah Tower in Saudi Arabia, or so she had been told by Harry. Now she saw what Helene meant. She'd always imagined the Middle East to be rolling sand dunes, interspersed with palm encircled oases. She never imagined a skyline that could put London to shame. That illusion had been put to rest on the way from the airport, but this, yes, this was something else. Helene had promised her a trip to the fountains in the shadow of the Burj Khalifa the following night. Emma couldn't wait.

Mesmerised, she stared at the view for a full ten minutes before the day's events caught up with her. She closed the curtains again, and switched on the bedside lamp, once she'd finally located the switch. This was more like the life she wanted. Who'd have thought it, eh? The little orphan girl from Tower Hamlets, facing a long, if not boring career in banking ahead of her, and now suddenly, she was jet-setting around the world in pursuit of criminals. If she read this in a book, she wouldn't believe it.

She thought sleep would come easily but it didn't. Until now she had been caught up in the whirlwind of excitement, the passport, flight, a new and strange culture but doubt began to edge its way into her mind; an invasion of ivy on the brickwork of her soul.

Hello little orphan girl. Yes you, the one living the high life. You don't belong here among these people. You don't deserve this. Your place is not sipping a gin and tonic in a room full of Armani, Dior, Gucci and Rolex. Your place is with the Primark and Sports Direct crowd, struggling to pay the rent and drinking WKD and mixers.

She had no idea where the last part came from, she'd never had a WKD in her life. She realised a long time ago, the only true home for her lay in the world of Tron, a land of electrons, bytes and data packets. A land which few had a true grasp of its intricacies and nuances, but that was her world. Who was she trying to kid being here? What if she couldn't do this, what if she wasn't capable of delivering what Helene expected?

A tornado of thoughts circled, picking at her mind and casting pieces into distant and dark recesses. Her despair deepened until finally the overwhelming assault of the day's events flitted away like a kite on the wind, and a dreamless sleep descended.

~§~

Hong Kong's Chek Lap Kok Airport was a bit of a disappointment. Emma had heard so much about the old Kai Tak Airport and its unusual approach through the skyscrapers, she felt a bit let down that the new airport was almost forty kilometres from the hotel and Hong Kong Central.

For Emma this was becoming a journey of firsts; the hotel's chauffeur driven Rolls Royce Phantom being the latest. Helene, Mr Khalid and herself, settled into the plush leather seats and discussed the forthcoming business meetings, entirely for the benefit of the chauffeur. The more they could keep up the pretence, the better. The cover story must remain rock solid.

When Helene briefed them in Dubai, she indicated she had no idea if the export of girls was solely the work of Kun's old boss, or if he was part of a syndicate. The fact that Kun believed Xing Da was not connected, didn't mean that he wasn't, and was one of the reasons for Helene's upcoming visit to the HKPF headquarters. The only facts of which Helene had been sure was that Kun's Uncle Li had disposed of her to one of the syndicates, who then passed her on to Xing Da. Either way she didn't want to raise any suspicions until they had an inkling of who was involved and could act accordingly. In the meantime, a number of legitimate business meetings had been arranged for the export of various goods to the UAE, none of which would come to fruition, but anyone checking on Mr Khalid's business credentials would find them to be of the highest order. The company website told of a long history of successful trading around the world, and should anyone be that clever, they would find a history of archived pages going back several years; Emma having worked her magic yet again.

If Emma had been impressed with the view over Dubai Creek, then the vista from her hotel room overlooking Victoria Harbour was out of this world. What had blown her mind was the hotel element of the building didn't start until they reached the hundred-and-third floor of the building. The tallest building in the UK, the Shard in London, only sported eighty-seven floors. She couldn't wrap her mind around that. Who builds a hotel on top of a skyscraper? She'd seen places like this featured in glossy magazines, but this was not something she imagined in her wildest dreams was in her future. What a tough choice it had been between this and prison; the future she thought was likely. To think, had it not been for a little devious gameplay by their current masters, she never would have been caught. She left no trace, triggered no alarms, but she'd been caught nonetheless, by a betrayal, someone she trusted but she since learned had little choice in that betrayal and in fact worked for the same outfit as she was now.

She looked around the room again, she couldn't imagine what Harry — Mr Khalid's suite must look like. This was plush in the extreme. She would never look at her pokey little flat in the same way again. Anyway, enough of the dreaming.

Time to get to work. Today the doubts remained hidden. She would enter her world, a land where she was Queen; where she knew her subjects better than she knew herself. Doubts were for the real world and that alone.

Miss Smith had a room booked and paid for in advance. Neither of those facts were true, but as far as the hotel's computer system was concerned, they were and she would shortly be checking in and would be issued with a key, a key Emma was about to create from the spare card she asked for.

'I'm always killing these key cards with my cell phone,' she explained to the receptionist on checking in. Before Dubai, Emma had never stayed anywhere that issued a key card; her usual accommodation was either a tent, or if she really splashed out, she might manage a night in a B&B. However, Helene reassured her that a sure-fire way to kill a hotel key card was to put it next to a mobile phone.

Whilst in Dubai she had hacked into the Hong Kong hotel's reservation system, a task she found far more difficult than she'd anticipated. Not something the average hacker would manage, but she wasn't average. Emma inserted her spare key card into the encoder, recently delivered to her room by Helene, and quickly encoded the key for Miss Smith's room.

Now, all she needed to do when working her way into any of the systems in Hong Kong was to go to Miss Smith's room and work from there. Although the chances of a traceback were highly unlikely, anyone who did manage it, would find the trail went cold at the non-existent person in room 11314.

It would seem that Helene was really Jane Bond, knowing how to cover Emma's trail and hide her in plain sight. She certainly paid attention to detail.

~§~

It came as something of a surprise to Nicky that the number of pillboxes in the area of interest was far less than he'd imagined. Yes, the Outer London Defence Ring certainly did run through the area, but in that part of Epping Forest, it consisted almost entirely of an anti-tank ditch. In fact, according to the Pillbox Study Group, which their website states is a society "Committed to The Study & Preservation Of 20th Century United Kingdom & International Pillboxes & Anti-Invasion Defences", and whose overlay he was using on Google Earth, the number of pillboxes in the search area was precisely, one. Nicky loved these groups. Search engines were fine for obtaining basic information about a particular subject, as indeed was Wikipedia, but when you wanted specialist information you couldn't beat specialist groups, and those with specific knowledge and a passion for something.

Nicky still preferred the old-fashioned ways, a trip to the local library in preference to a computer, causing many of his former colleagues to describe him as a dinosaur, but even he had to admit there were times when the 'good ol' internet' was the place to be. Much of being a reporter was knowing where to look, and with over thirty years as a journalist under his belt, there were not many places Nicky didn't know where he could find the information he needed.

But right now, he wished he hadn't bet a month's wages on a pillbox being the place where the girls were held. Sometimes his certainty got him into trouble. On the other hand, he could well be right. The only way to find out was to take a look.

That is why he now found himself trekking through the northern part of Epping Forest accompanied by Jason, another member of the team recruited from Her Majesty's Constabulary, a former detective from the Lancashire Constabulary.

After five minutes of tripping over branches and stumbling into shallow ditches, they finally managed to locate the pillbox. They circled it at a distance looking for the entrance. They had circumnavigated just over halfway when Jason stopped Nicky and pointed. The nearby ground had clearly been disturbed recently by a number of people.

Carefully avoiding the disturbed ground, they continued to circle the structure.

'The girl mentioned in a statement that something blocked the door. I think we may have found it.'

Nicky pointed to an old washing machine lying on its side.

'Strikes me as odd. Why would someone come this deep into the woods dragging a washing machine unless they needed it for something? Even so, why a washing machine. Sticks out a mile out here. It's not the sort of thing you keep in the back of a van just in case you need to barricade a door is it?'

'And there's a new door, just as you said there would be. We better get the crime techs down here right away.'

'I think my month's salary is looking pretty safe right now.

He sighed as he looked at the caller ID on his phone. What now?

'Hello.'

'I thought I told you to dispose of them carefully.'

'I did. They're buried, and like you said, I made sure there was no evidence.'

'And just exactly how did you do that?'

'We removed everything the girls used and doused the places in bleach.'

'And that removed all the evidence?'

'Yeah, of course it did.'

'Please tell me, in that tiny little brain of yours, how you think that tidying up a little and spraying bleach removes the evidence. Have you never watched a CSI programme? A little bit of spring cleaning is not going to work is it? A little birdy told me your boots and tyre prints are as we speak, being analysed by forensics. Fibres and DNA collected from a pillbox have gone for analysis and that eight bodies are in the mortuary, one in the hospital, albeit in a bad way. Now they have the girls' DNA, they are going to link them to this pillbox, and the footprints and tyre tracks will tie that to you. What the fuck made you think burying the bodies near a path on Wanstead Flats was a good idea?'

'I didn't want to be driving too far in the middle of the night with bodies in my van. What if I'd been stopped? Anyway, how did you find out about the DNA and shit?'

'That is none of your business. We had a plan to dispose of them. Why didn't you follow the plan?'

'I thought —'

'No, you didn't think, you panicked. That's the problem. This is a clusterfuck. There's an evidence trail as wide as the M25 and it leads right to your doorstep. So, this is what you are going to do. Round up everyone's footwear and have a damned good bonfire. Make sure you do this nowhere near the pillbox or the house. Once you have done that, I suggest you dispose of the van, somewhere it will never be found, because if they get the VIN and find just one shred of evidence inside linking it to the girls, you my friend are sunk. Get it crushed, drive it off a cliff somewhere, I don't care, but whatever you do, make sure no one can recover any evidence from it. I just thank my lucky stars there are enough breaks in the chain between me and you or I would be having to consider a hasty retreat from these shores. As it is, that won't be necessary.

'Once you've done all that, you will report back to me. After that you won't attempt to contact me again. This number will no longer be in use. If I need you again, which given this mess, I seriously doubt, I will contact you. Do I make myself clear?'

~§~

After giving his instructions and hanging up, he made a second call. This wasn't his personal phone, but a cheap Nokia picked up from the market and using a recently purchased pay-as-you-go sim card. Replacing the sim cards regularly made life very difficult for law enforcement. Even if they managed to trace a number, it would vanish as quickly as it appeared. But better still, he was aware of every move they made and although he knew the informant, the informant did not know him, not even a first name.

'This is *One*. Tonight's meeting has been cancelled and will not be rescheduled for some time. There has been a shift in the market, one which wasn't foreseen.'

'I have to say, that is a major disappointment, but I will defer to your judgment. I'll pass on your message.'

In a cell structure reminiscent of the French resistance, each small group remained unaware of the identities or contact information of the others, or at least that was the theory. At their meetings, it was inevitable that some would know others from another group, hooded or not, or at the very least, suspect their identity. Theirs was a relatively small world after all, not open to every Tom, Dick or Harry.

Only *One* knew how to contact the group leaders, none of whom knew his identity. This latest setback was just that, nothing more and nothing less. They would lay low until the investigation stalled and then they could resume their operations once again.

During the brief discussion, he walked randomly, the way all callers do when using a mobile, until he reached the wall of the terrace overlooking the Thames. He casually leaned against it as if admiring the view and when the call finished, he dropped the phone into the river.

The chimes of Big Ben rang out. He would have to dash to the committee meeting. Why on earth people could not follow a simple set of instructions remained beyond his understanding but was something he had learned to expect from the plebs of this world.

CHAPTER FOURTEEN

Ruth Cannon had an idea. Kun told her that she was certain the ship they were on did not call at another port on the way to the UK. That narrowed down the search considerably, and with that information, she approached the Maritime Coastguard Agency with the intention of tracking all vessels coming directly from Hong Kong, and with a departure date within the timeframe Kun believed they left Hong Kong.

In her statement, Kun said that when they had been transferred to the smaller vessel, they had only been onboard for what she thought was little over an hour. The boat landed them on some sort of breakwater or jetty and she remembered it was very quiet and dark, their footsteps seemingly loud on the wooden boards. They were bundled into the back of a van and told to be quiet. As soon as they were all in, the van set off and drove for a few minutes before stopping for what she thought was a similar length of time they were on the small boat. She could hear the occasional car passing nearby but traffic wasn't heavy. Once they set off again, they went straight to the warehouse where the angry man had been. Although she only had rough timings, Ruth believed the transfer had taken place somewhere in the Thames estuary and the land transfer, possibly on the north bank of the Thames somewhere. That would put the warehouse somewhere in the East End of London. Well, that was a help, the East End was littered with disused warehouses, although a substantial number had been converted to apartments or demolished to make way for new buildings.

That contained a bit of good news for the detectives. Unless the vessel turned back, it was likely that the container ship had continued to one of the three London container ports. Ruth believed it an unlikely scenario the ship had turned around. Manoeuvres such as that tended to draw unnecessary attention from the authorities. Narrowing down the port of arrival would reduce the number of Hong Kong arrivals they had to consider.

She was pondering this when she recalled a discussion with a woman she met on holiday the previous year. She worked for a company that did vessel tracking and kept records of movements including the actual tracks. She only vaguely remembered the details, something about ship transponders. If only she could remember her name; she may be able to help. A quick search on the internet came up with AIS, Automatic Identification System. That was it, now she needed to remember her name and find the company she worked for. She remembered it was a German company, so she tried AIS Germany as her search term, that didn't produce the desired results, so she added Historical to the search term. That was it, Fleetmon, that was the company and as soon as she saw that name it triggered her memory of the woman's name too; Juliane. She hoped she still worked for Fleetmon and that there was only one Juliane as she didn't recall ever knowing her surname. Even so, it would be worth a call. She dialled the contact number on the website.

Half an hour later, Ruth had a list of ships sailing directly from Hong Kong to the three London ports over the last six months and it was a much smaller list than she had imagined. Most ships sailed from port to port, picking up and dropping off containers on the way, so taking Kun's statement into account, she dismissed those. Then she correlated the data with the date of the current case. Only two ships matched. Only one of the previous cases occurred within the six months of data she had, but that eliminated one of the remaining ships. That hadn't been to the UK at any time in the six weeks prior to the discovery of those bodies.

'Oh, ya beauty, Ruth.'

One name tying in with two cases was good, but still not enough; she needed something a bit more concrete.

Another phone call to Juliane and she had what she needed. On each occasion over the past eighteen months, when according to Helene bodies had been discovered, the Hamadryad, a Shanghai registered mixed cargo ship, had docked at Tilbury shortly before. She was certain this was the ship involved in the trafficking. What they must do now was find the vessel that transferred them ashore and this end of the operation would crack wide open. Unfortunately, the carriage of AIS equipment was only mandated for ships over 300 gross tonnes engaged in international voyages. It was quite feasible that the two vessels travelled side by side, undetected. She would have to try a fresh approach to this problem. In the meantime, she had a name to pass on to the boss.

~§~

Xing Da was being most co-operative with the wealthy Arab gentleman; almost, but not quite the perfect host. Yes of course he could supply any number of girls, and absolutely, they would all be virgins.

He was lying of course. As allegedly inscrutable as the Chinese were, it showed on Xing's face when he said all the girls would be virgins. Harry played along with the lie, nodding his head in agreement.

The price asked was extortionate, as was only to be expected. After all, Mr Khalid was a wealthy gentleman and could afford to pay. Mr Khalid was also an Arab and excelled in the art of barter.

Xing explained he needed to confer with his business partner and stepped out to make a quick phone call.

117

Harry felt the first tingle of a warning. Nothing he could put his finger on yet, but why would the man go out of the room unless he suspected they spoke Cantonese and he had something to hide? On the other hand, maybe the man was just being cautious; whatever the reason, it didn't feel right and Harry listened to his instincts more than most.

While Xing and Harry negotiated, Emma remained busy working on her tablet, seemingly unconcerned with the discussion about young girls being shipped to the Middle East. Her presence seemed to unnerve Xing at first, which had been Harry's intention all along, but Xing realised she had no interest in these negotiations and appeared to be unfazed by the idea of girls being bought and sold in this way. Had he realised Emma was busy hacking into his computer through the WiFi, things may have been somewhat different.

Xing re-entered the room, smiling widely, the gaps in his teeth forming miniature cave entrances to the cavern within.

'My partner, he agree, but first you must see girl. You go with my men; they look after you. Take you see girl.'

'That is unnecessary, my friend. I have your word, and in my country, that is sufficient.'

Xing smiled.

'You in my country now. Please, go see girl.'

Two men entered through the same door from which Xing had recently re-emerged. Harry listened again to his internal watchdog. Although not large in stature, the men had a presence. Warriors recognised other warriors and these men knew how to handle themselves. This didn't smell right and if Xing's men were escorts for their safety, then he was a ballerina with the Bolshoi.

'We take my car?'

Xing shook his head.

'Not far. Two-minute walk.'

Although he still presented the air of someone calm and relaxed, the klaxon for action-stations sounded loudly within. This wasn't the place to take action, three to one was okay for Harry, especially as they didn't know Harry's background and training. To them he was an ageing Arab and nothing more.

The confined space and presence of Emma urged him to be cautious.

They followed the two men outside and along the street for a short distance before turning into a narrow and unusually quiet alleyway.

'Shortcut.'

I bet, Harry thought.

Harry stumbled and steadied himself on Emma's shoulder leaning towards her.

'This is wrong. Make sure you step back out of the way when it kicks off. If you can, get back to the car. Understand?'

Emma inclined her head and as she did so, the two men whirled round brandishing knives.

'Go, Emma.'

Harry found himself looking at the back of Emma's head as she rushed the nearest man; not quite the direction he was expecting her to take.

The spinning wheel kick took the knife out of the hand of the first assailant, the second kick went to the head dropping him like a stone, clearing the way for his colleague to take up the attack.

As Harry moved forward, the second man lunged towards Emma with the knife held low. This man knew his knifework and even in these circumstances, Harry admired a fellow professional at work. It mattered not. Harry heard the man's leg break as Emma's kick went in from the side, moving the knee joint in a direction it was never designed to go. He dropped the knife as he toppled sideways. Emma's rising foot made contact with the descending head; the resulting crack made Harry wince.

She stepped back and performed Bao Quan, the traditional martial art salute.

'Bloody hell, girl. Where did you learn that?'

Emma flicked back her hair.

'A pretty little blonde girl living in a rough part of town has to learn to look after herself.'

'Anything else I should know about you, my little flower?'

She smiled.

'Some things I like to keep secret.'

'Go on. What was it and what level are you? Those were not beginners' moves.'

'Shaolin Kung Fu, brown belt. My sensei believes I'm a black belt candidate now.'

Harry laughed.

'And there I was, about to do the gentlemanly thing and protect you. I'm more impressed by you every day, little flower. Impressed indeed, and I have to say a bit relieved too. These Arab robes are not the best thing to be wearing in a fight.'

He pulled out a polythene bag and a pair of nitrile gloves from his thobe. Holding a glove in his hand, he picked up one of the knives and dropped it in the bag. He smiled at Emma.

'Evidence. Now let's get out of here before someone sees us or they wake up' —

He looked at the two figures sprawled on the ground.

— 'although that might not be for a while. In the meantime, I think I need to reopen negotiations with Mr Xing.'

~§~

'Ah Mr Xing, how good of you to see us again.'

The pleasure seemed to be Harry's alone as that previously inscrutable face showed the first signs of fear.

'Something wrong, my friend? Were you not expecting us so soon, or indeed at all?'

Xing looked past Harry.

'Your men are not here, Mr Xing. My pretty, young assistant here, has caused them not an inconsiderable amount of pain I suspect. I believe they may not be here for some time. In my country, the host does not set thugs armed with knives upon the guests. Perhaps it is a different custom in your country, Mr Xing? Is it so?'

Xing shook his head.

'So please explain to me why you thought this necessary. I came here to do business. You were recommended to me by an associate in the UK. I took his word you were a man of honour. We need to put this right, do we not?'

Harry turned to Emma.

'I think you should go back to the hotel, my dear. I will call for a car when I am finished. Mr Xing and I are going to have a man to man talk.'

'But I —'

'My little flower, you have shown me what a tough cookie you are, but really, it is best if you are not here.'

Emma nodded and made for the door.

'Mr Khalid, please be careful.'

Harry nodded once in acknowledgment. She was one cool kid. Even in a time of stress she hadn't broken his cover, not that it would matter now. Xing would not be speaking to anyone, not now, and most definitely, not in the future. Not once Harry had finished explaining the error of his ways.

~§~

Dire Strait's *Money For Nothing* brought Helene out of her sleep. She reached for her mobile. This better be important at this time of the day, whatever time that was.

Her first attempt to speak resulted in a small croak. She cleared her throat and tried again. This time she managed to say her name.

'Did I wake you, Helene?'

'Hmm — Yes, sorry, give me a moment, James.'

She reached for the glass of water on the bedside table and took a sip.

'They must be working you too hard, whoever they are, I know — I know, you can't tell me, or you would have to kill me. You're asleep already and it's only just gone 8 p.m.'

Helene managed to focus one eye on her watch.

'Actually, James, it's five-past three in the morning.'

'No, it's — Where are you, Helene?'

'Hong Kong.'

'Bloody hell, why didn't you tell me you were going? I wouldn't have called at this time if I had known. I'll leave you to your beauty sleep, not that you need it, beauty that is —'

'James.'

'Yes?'

'Stop digging holes and tell me why you called.'

'It can wait, Helene.'

'James, tell me.'

'I got the tox reports back.'

'And?'

'Nothing. Not even alcohol.'

Helene took in the information. It didn't really make a difference whether the girls were drugged or not, other than they would be fully conscious when they were raped and murdered. She gathered her thoughts.

'Helene, did you hear me?'

'Yes, sorry, James, I was away with my thoughts. Go on.'

'I think I better hang up and let you get back to sleep.'

'I don't want you to go' — almost as an afterthought she added, — 'ever.'

'Sorry?'

She'd not intended to say it aloud, but there it was, out in the open.

This wasn't really the right time for this discussion, but as she already messed up the chance at the post-mortem, she didn't want to not have it either.

Helene shuffled up the bed and fluffed up the pillow behind her. Her heart raced and her mouth went dry. This was a make-or-break moment, and she was doing it over the telephone. What was she thinking?

'The other day at the PM, remember I said I wanted to tell you something?'

'Yes. You never got around to it.'

'No, well. I didn't think it was the ideal time to discuss it. James, I want you on my team.'

'I — are you offering me a job? Why couldn't you have told me then. After all I was — '

'James, shut up and listen. That's only part of the offer.'

'And the other part?'

'Me.'

'I don't quite — Oh.'

Helene could hear him breathing, fast shallow breaths.

'Are you okay?'

'I'm just a little bit taken aback, I — I didn't know you felt, I mean …'

'I'm sorry, perhaps I shouldn't have — '

'Oh God no. We need to talk when you get back.'

'Was that a no?'

'To the job, or you?'

'Either, both, I don't know.'

She closed her eyes again, hardly daring to listen to the response.

'We'll talk when you get back.'

'James, I'm not sure I can — '

'Helene, I love you. I've felt that way for a long time, but it was so wrong, and it would have been wrong to tell you. I was married and I didn't want you to get caught up in that, even if you were interested in me, which I wasn't sure about. That night, when we …, well when you never mentioned it again, I thought it was just a one-night thing and — '

'James, please stop rambling. I love you too.'

The line went quiet, and it was some seconds before James spoke again.

'I don't know what to — perhaps we — why didn't — we've done it now haven't we? When did you say you were coming back?'

'Good grief, James, are you going to be this incoherent from now on. We'll be here couple of days I suspect, no more.'

'Okay. I think we might have a lot to talk about. In the meantime, I'll give the job offer some thought. Now get some sleep. I'll see you when you come back.'

How the hell was she going to go back to sleep now? Her heart was singing, dancing, doing somersaults. Why had she wasted so much time before asking him? Some sort of detective she turned out to be. He'd felt that way all along. All that time wasted.

Suddenly, it was all too much. The tears welled up and she buried her head in the pillow, sobbing gently. She had never been so happy in her life.

~§~

She felt like shit. After the 3 a.m. phone call from James, sleep evaded her entirely. Now 6 a.m. she had to make a conference call with London. She was keen to find out what the other team had so far, if anything, and to catch up with Harry and Emma. She assumed they had little to report, or they would have called her last night while she was out to dinner with one of the HKPF senior officers and his wife.

The full team would not be on hand as it was now late in London, but it only needed one person to pass on the information.

A gentle tapping on the door alerted her to the presence of Harry and Emma.

'Just in time, Ruth is waiting for my call.'

Helene made the VOIP connection on her laptop.

'Hi Ruth. I've got you on speaker. Harry and Emma are here with me. What have you got?'

'Wow, boss. Sounds like you are in the same room. The wonders of the internet, eh? I've got some good news; I think I know the name of the ship they used to bring the victims to the UK.'

'Well spit it out girl.'

'Hamadryad.'

'You're going to have to spell that one.'

Helene wrote it down as Ruth spelled it out using the phonetic alphabet.

'Anything else?'

'Yes. I'm fairly sure I know where they landed. I got back onto Juliane, oh you don't know about Juliane, I'll tell you about her when you get back. Anyway, we took a look at the track of the ship again. I'm still working on the transfer vessel.'

'You're right about the ship, and we are definitely looking for a westerner for this.'

Helene looked at Harry and raised her eyebrows questioningly.

'I spoke with Xing Da last night. Not a nice chappie, tried to have Emma and myself killed. Most uncooperative at first, but he finally coughed up he'd sold some girls to a 'gweilo' by the name of Mr Don and confirmed the name of the ship. He has a cousin who works in logistics and is able to load containers onto the ships at the last minute, with the agreement of the captain of course. This was his first shipment, but his cousin told him he'd done it before for one of the triads.'

'Did you hear that, Ruth? We need to run through the possibles on the list see if any have the name Don, Donald, or anything that might sound remotely similar to a non-native English speaker. If you find a match, don't do anything just now other than put them under observation. I want the nuts of whoever is responsible in a vice and I want to be the one who squeezes them.'

'Okay, boss. Anything from your end?'

'I didn't think so but apparently there is. This is the first time I've seen Harry and Emma since yesterday afternoon. I'll catch up with you in the morning.'

Helene ended the call and turned to the other two.

'Okay, let's hear it.'

Harry recounted the story, with special emphasis on Emma's martial arts abilities.

'You never told me about that, Emma.'

'To be fair, it's not something I bring up in normal conversation.'

Helene conceded the point.

'So, when you went back to Xing, did you both go?'

She saw Emma glance at Harry and the almost imperceptible nod of Harry's head. These two were as thick as thieves. She wasn't sure if that was a good or bad thing for now.

'I came back to the hotel.'

Helene turned back to Harry, her head to one side.

'How much persuading?'

'Jeremiah 5:27.'

She closed her eyes for a moment. When she opened them, she could see the puzzled look on Emma's face. The bible reference meant nothing to Emma, but to Helene, it signified that Xing would not be taking another breath. Bible quotations formed part of Harry's MO. Although Emma remained unaware of it, she had been in the vicinity of Harry shortly before he dealt with a rapist in the Tower Hamlet's Cemetery Park a couple of years previously. As SIO on the case, Helene saw the transcript of Emma's phone call, reporting what she heard after she read about the murder in the newspaper.

Harry was a deeply religious, but flawed individual, however, Helene knew she could put his unique talents to good use which is why she recruited him to the Invidia team and didn't have him locked up for life.

'Jeez, Harry. I can't give you the same level of cover here you know?'

'I know, boss, but it was the only way. Anyway, one of his two henchmen did all the work. He left a knife covered in his prints.'

She could see Emma looking sideways at Harry. She was a bright kid, and it seemed the penny had just dropped. Strangely, she appeared unfazed. This girl was not your average geek at all. What a terrific find she had been for the team.

'Okay, we have something at last. I suggest we have breakfast in an hour, after which I'll make some calls about the ship. Then Emma and I, well Emma, with me watching will do some of that magic she does. The rest of the day is free. Tonight, we'll have dinner in the Ozone Bar, and tomorrow a sightseeing trip mixed with a little work. You've earned it.'

~§~

After breakfast, Helene returned to her room, dropped her phone on the bedside cabinet and sank onto the bed. She closed her eyes. Bad move, MacKay, she thought. She still had the phone calls to make before sleep.

On impulse she checked the bedside cabinet drawers. She would be surprised if one wasn't there. She pulled out the Gideon Bible and turned it over in her hands. She had yet to stay in a hotel and not find one in a drawer somewhere. She wasn't too familiar with this publication; never felt the need for it. The only thing she knew for certain was that there were two parts, the old and new testaments; that much she remembered from her enforced trips to Sunday school as a child. It took her a couple of minutes to find the passage; the book, chapter, and verse abbreviation, presumably carved somewhere on Xing's corpse by Harry.

Jeremiah 5:27. Like cages full of birds, their houses are full of deceit; they have become rich and powerful.

Another apt passage. She wondered how he managed to remember them all, she had never seen him reading the bible, nor did he mention his beliefs at all in his day to day conversations. Harry Fielding was most definitely a unique individual, and it seemed he wasn't the only one on the team.

~§~

'Okay, Harry. You have some explaining to do.'
'I don't know what you mean, my little flower.'
Emma stepped in front of him as they walked along the corridor from the lift. Helene had already returned to her room. She stopped, facing him with her hands on her hips.
'Don't you "little flower" me. Xing's men did nothing of the sort, and you know I know that, because you saw me beat the living shit out of them. So, if you want us to stay friends, you have a little — no — make that a lot of explaining to do.'
'Okay, okay, you're right, but not here. Come to my suite after dinner. What I need to tell you might take some time.'

CHAPTER FIFTEEN

In room 11314, "Miss Smith" settled down to work her magic. All the items she told Helene she would need had been delivered and set up; she was good to go. Helene sat by her side, watching her as she dipped in and out of various servers, seeking any information that would move the case forward.

When Emma worked, she imagined herself as mixture of Lara Croft and a Kung Fu master. The fearsome creatures, falling floors, and vicious, poison-tipped stakes ready to impale at the slightest mistake, were not real but the electronic equivalent. She ran, somersaulted and pirouetted her way through a virtual maze, seeking out the prize, before quietly departing with not a trace of her presence to be found.

This time, the task was far simpler than her recent foray into the hotel system. She searched for every bill of lading for Hamadryad over the past twelve months.

'Boss?'

Helene moved closer to the laptop.

'Have you found something?'

'I think so. Is it normal for ships to carry empty containers?'

'I'm not sure, probably. I suppose if there's no return load, they have to. Why?'

'Just a second.'

Emma's fingers moved deftly over the keys.

'Damn, I wish I had my monitor setup.'

As with many people who are regular computer users, Emma had a multiple screen set-up, both at the office and at home. Unlike most users, she also had several computers linked together. Sometimes, she needed a lot of processor power to achieve her results. Now she was having to make do with a laptop.

'Yes, see?'

'My darling, all I can see is a jumble of windows on a screen. What am I looking at?'

'Here. On the last three occasions Hamadryad sailed to the UK, it carried just one empty container.'

'Like I said, I'm sure they sometimes do.'

'Yes, but, as you said, they would be either returning the container, or maybe they are sending it empty to bring something back.'

'And?'

'These containers haven't moved anywhere else; they are still in the UK and they were all loaded at the last minute.'

'How do you know that?'

'Every container has a unique code. The first three letters signify the owner and the six numbers that follow are unique to that container. It's how the goods being shipped are tracked. What's more, these three belong to a company here in Hong Kong. So why would they ship just one empty container at a time and leave it there?'

'Where are they now?'

'Tilbury.'

Helene raised her eyebrows at her.

'Emma, did anyone ever tell you you're a genius?'

Emma smiled.

'Not very often. I'm more used to, "where are those damned figures, Johnson?" I like this better.'

'Send those serial numbers over to Ruth. If this is how they were transported, there will be evidence all over the inside.

She can get our crime techs over to Tilbury. You don't by any chance know where that ship is now, do you?'

'Yes. According to AIS, it's four days out of Hong Kong.'

'So, if I said you'd repaid your debt to society and you could go back to your old job, what would you say.'

'I'd say "don't push me, boss." I can wipe out your identity in the press of a key.'

'Sometimes you scare me — just a little — but enough. There is so much more to you than computer geek.'

'I know. That's why people like to have me around.'

Emma gave her one of her sweet little girl smiles and fluttered her eyelashes.

Helene giggled then grabbed her mobile to make a call. After a few minutes' discussion in Cantonese, she hung up.

Emma sat there shaking her head.

'You speak Chinese too?'

'Cantonese to be exact. That was my contact in HKPF. They are going to meet the ship when it gets here and arrest the captain. It would appear both he and the ship's owners have been on their radar for some time. Assuming we can find DNA evidence from the containers to match the victims, our captain is going to have a lot of explaining to do. Right, it's time sleeping beauty got out of bed and took his two assistants for dinner.'

~§~

Fresh from dinner together with Helene, Emma and Harry went back to his suite. She sank into the soft cushion of the rather sumptuous chair, gin and tonic in hand and looked inquisitively at Harry who dropped himself onto the matching sofa.

He inspected his fingers and avoided looking at her.

'I've, I — what I'm trying to say is, I'm not always the nice old man you know.'

He looked up.

Emma put on the face that only certain people can fully carry; the face that says, you are kidding me, right?

'What?'

She rolled her eyes.

'Remember what I do? I access things others don't want me to access. Who do you think got your locked records from the MOD?'

'That was you?'

Emma nodded.

'And there was me thinking the boss was a clever girl.'

'She is. She asked me to get the files, because the MOD didn't want to give them.'

Harry laughed.

'You know, I've spent a good portion of my life in the company of men, some pretty smart ones at that, but I'd back Ruth, you, and the boss against them any day. You three have given me a whole new outlook on the fairer sex.'

'Yeah? Good, but it doesn't stop there. After breakfast this morning, I accessed your Invidia files, but that's between you and me. I know what you did in that churchyard. Before you go any further, I understand, Harry.

'Perhaps it wasn't only my computer skills that got me here. I'm sure along the way somewhere, I may have had a discussion with Chris about how the world seems to favour those who do wrong. Injustice is a real problem for me, whether someone blames me for something I didn't do, or someone gets away with a crime, despite the evidence. I've never spoken to anyone else about it but Chris, and well, he seemed different.

'I couldn't do things the way you do, but neither does it bother me that things like that happen to some people. It should bother me, I know, but it doesn't.'

Once again Harry marvelled at this old head on such young shoulders.

'Does it still hurt Chris betrayed you when he got you caught hacking GCHQ?'

'No, yes, well, a little bit. He had no choice I suppose, and anyway, I would never have met you or come to Hong Kong otherwise.'

Harry studied her face then reached across to hold her hand.

'Don't ever lose sight of the fact those people I killed are human too. What they do is inhuman and indefensible, but at one time, they too were innocent children. They lost their way. I don't know if something happened to them or an evil grew from within, that isn't for me to judge but please, don't ever become callous or uncaring about death. It is final, and if we get it wrong, we can't apologise to someone once they are gone.'

'So, why do you do it if you feel that way?'

'I am different; a part of me is missing. I feel no remorse for what I do. If anything, I feel it's my duty. But deep down there must still be something, because I still have those thoughts, the ones I've just told you.'

Harry stopped studying her hand and looked up into her eyes.

'On the other hand, I do get pleasure from watching them die.'

He took a deep breath.

'You are the only person I have told this to. It's strange, but you're the only one I feel I can trust, one hundred per cent.'

She squeezed his hands.

'Thank you.'

Emma frowned as a thought occurred to her.

'Doesn't it contradict your beliefs?'

He shook his head.

'No. Not at all. It is God's will I am this way. I am a firm believer he puts us all on the path we must be on.'

Emma smiled at him. For some reason, she trusted him implicitly too. She would never understand the pleasure he derived from killing, nor his deep-seated religious beliefs, but she felt a bond between them, a kindred spirit in some way. Perhaps they are two lost souls travelling the same path for a while; she gained satisfaction in beating the system, Harry from protecting society in his own way. An unlikely pair to be friends, but that they are is without question.

CHAPTER FIFTEEN

~§~

The time difference, long flights and the pressure of the case were all taking their toll on Helene. She felt driven to solve this and bring these vermin to justice. She had seen some pretty rough cases in her time with the Met, but this one was getting under her skin, becoming personal. She should remain detached, all the experts, manuals and training sessions and psychologists said so, but she couldn't, not with so many young lives cut short for what appeared to be the personal gratification of a bunch of sick bastards - and she was fairly certain they were dealing with more than one individual, even though forensics had come up blank for any DNA evidence so far. Whoever was doing this knew about evidence and that in itself caused her worry, especially in light of the video tampering Brandon mentioned about the untraced vehicles. This could well involve a senior Met officer. She truly hoped not. The vast majority of the officers did a fine job, especially in the face of relentless budget cuts. Unfortunately, it only took a couple of rotten fish to spoil the entire catch. Of course, this may not be an officer at all but one of the many civilians employed by the force, only time would tell.

The journey back to the UK had once again been broken in Dubai and for sound reasons. On the way out to Hong Kong, Harry entered Dubai on his own passport and left for Hong Kong as Mr Khalid. He would need to reverse that so that Mr Khalid was back in his own country and Harry Fielding left Dubai after his 'vacation'. Immigration computers are simple souls and like to see one visitor in, same visitor out. Despite the attractions of downtown Dubai, none of them left the hotel that night grabbing an early night before the relatively early start in the morning.

Harry appeared to be deep in his own thoughts as all three of them passed through immigration, collected their bags, strolled through the green channel and exited into Heathrow T3 arrivals. Emma, on the other hand, chatted away like an excited six-year-old on her way back from Disneyland. Although tired and grumpy, Helene listened and responded with genuine interest. It was what made her such an excellent team leader.

It was clear to Helene that Emma relished the role she now played. This trip was the first time they had spent any time together and they bonded well. Helene had genuine affection for her, as clearly did Harry, who fussed over her like a father with his only daughter. She was smart, and according to Harry, more than able to take care of herself. Helene suspected she was so fond of her because she saw so much of herself in the young woman.

Despite Helene having what many would consider an idyllic upbringing, she'd not had an easy path, especially as she joined the Met when women were still considered ancillary, and racism was rife. The tenacity with which she stuck at the job was also the reason for her success. No case would get the better of her, and even though some would never be solved, it wasn't for the lack of trying; some cases just didn't present enough evidence. Underlings and bosses alike, found her to be compassionate, helpful and fair but also a tough opponent when crossed, something they learned not to do without a damned good reason.

They emerged through the sliding doors from the customs hall and passed into the arrivals area of the terminal with the inevitable gauntlet of the "meet and greet" crowd holding up a varied collection of name-boards. Some appeared to be professionally printed, others scrawled on a piece of paper, and a few, keeping up with the times, proudly glowing on electronic tablets. Already knowing where their car would be waiting, Helene took no notice until one sign, seemingly out of place, caught her eye. Bigger than the others and held high in the air, the sign displayed a single word, neatly formed in black marker pen on a Day-Glo orange background - 'YES!'.

Emma's chatter, and the hubbub of the terminal faded into the background as Helene's brain registered the face of the person holding the sign. She dropped her case and ran to throw her arms around James.

'Whoa, whoa. No one has ever shown such enthusiasm for me accepting a job before.'

Helene pulled her head back and looked him in the face.

'Just the job?'

'What do you think?'

Many different types of greeting can be seen in arrivals halls, anywhere in the world. Some shake hands, others embrace, or give a quick peck on the cheek. This was a full blown, hard on the lips, long, deep, and totally oblivious-to-the-world type of greeting that only lovers seem to understand.

An ageing, denim-clad rocker, holding a signboard declaring him to be a representative of Cryptic Music waiting for "Dead Heads Living", muttered, 'Find a room will ya?'

Harry grabbed Helene's bag and whispered to Emma.

'I think this may take a few minutes. Best we stand over by the wall and wait, my little flower.'

CHAPTER SIXTEEN

Ruth scoured the list of suspected traffickers. Their man had to be on here somewhere. In the end she had five "Dons".

She ran all five through immigration. Two had never left the country, one seemed to spend an amazing amount of time in Thailand, definitely worth looking at a bit closer and bingo, Donald Golding travelled to Hong Kong in December.

Ruth decided to use all five "Donalds" in setting up a VIPER session, along with others who bore a resemblance to each one of the suspects. If Kun picked out one of the suspects, it would be a significant step forward in the case. Fingers crossed.

VIPER was the modern way of creating an identity parade, but no longer requiring real people to turn up at a police station. Instead, they were paid to have their images added to a database that could pick out persons with similar features, and present to a witness, along with an image of the suspect; far more cost effective.

On Ruth's first visit to the hospital, she found Kun to be lucid, but still in considerable pain. Not surprising really, unless you were Wonder Woman, stopping a truck with your body is never a good plan.

As soon as Helene had news of Kun and her probable link to the killers, she had her moved to a private room; much better for Harry's men to keep an eye on her. Today it was Brian Martins, a.k.a. House, who stood guard, although standing was not an accurate description. To describe House as a big man, would be like saying tigers can be a touch unfriendly: 6ft 6in, in his stockinged feet, 16st 10lbs, and built like an American football player, except he had no need of the padding; one of those people naturally shaped that way. House didn't sit in a chair, he occupied it, much like an army occupies territory and it would probably require an army to have him vacate it. Light blond hair and bright blue eyes gave him a look of innocence, a gentle giant, a cuddly teddy bear of the human kind. On closer inspection, the eyes were alert, searching, and suggested a character comfortable in the knowledge little could come his way he couldn't handle.

To Ruth's surprise, House was outside the door, not in the room keeping Kun company as was the normal routine.

'Hi Ruth. She's awake but wanted a bit of alone time. Been through a lot, poor kid.'

'Do you think I should ...?'

Ruth nodded her head in the direction of the room.

'Give her a few minutes. She's having a tough time getting over Jing.'

Ruth nodded.

'She's an amazing kid. She has incredible recall of places and people. I think you'll get a lot more out of her now she's on the mend.'

'In what way?'

House leant forward.

'She was telling me earlier about when they'd just arrived from the boat and were taken to the warehouse. She could recall the graffiti on the walls. She never got a look at the VRN in the warehouse or she would remember them, but she did remember a partial plate from the final time they were transported. She's a remarkable young lady.'

'You have them written down?'

He gave her a look that made her apologise instantly.

'I know I'm not a copper, but I'm not dumb either.'

'Yes, I'm sorry. I'm sure once we all get to know each other a bit better, things will be easier.'

Ruth's mind was picking up speed. The police kept a database of tags, the names the graffiti artists painted. If she saw any one of those, then they would know what area to look for the warehouse. Who knows what clues that might offer? The partial index was a major bonus. That would narrow down the enormous list of white vans they were having to work through. Oh, she said the last van was blue, she would have to check that with her. Now she had something to work with, her list of questions for Kun just got bigger.

~§~

'This one. This is the man who took us to the old building where the angry man was.'

'You are sure about that?'

Kun nodded.

'This is really important, Kun. How sure?'

'I'm certain it is him.'

'Okay. Do you recognise any of the others?'

She shook her head.

'Only him. He is the one.'

Ruth smiled.

'Thank you. You have been really helpful. House, err — Brian, tells me you remembered some of the writing in the warehouse.'

Ruth held up the list House had given her.

'Yes. I remembered. I gave him everything I could.'

'And this number?'

Ruth indicated the partial index.

'I couldn't see it all. One of the men was in the way and it was dark, but these, I am sure. Will you catch him, this man?'

'Was this van white too?'

'No, it was blue, like these.'

She pointed to the bed curtains.

Ruth patted her hand.

CHAPTER SIXTEEN

'We'll get them, all of them, Kun. I promise.'

Such promises are difficult for police officers to make. It's unfair to make a promise you may not be able to keep, but on this occasion, Ruth had the confidence that if anyone could do this, it would be Invidia.

~§~

Kun reflected on her journey so far. She knew she'd led a privileged life while her parents were alive. She had no knowledge then of how seedy it could be and the realities some people faced on a daily basis. She'd been sheltered from the world. But that all changed once her uncle took her in. She had been used, abused and treated no better than equipment for hire; sold on by the hour, returned in worse condition than borrowed and no one cared, as long as she made money. Then as suddenly as it had all started, it was over.

She had no idea what the future held for her now, a sixteen-year-old girl in a foreign land, no friends or family, but whatever lay ahead, she was certain it would not be lying on her back for the amusement of some short-term thrill seeker, incapable of getting his kicks any other way.

Her experiences should have made Kun hate all men, but she didn't. She accepted not all men were bad. These men guarding her in the hospital, and she was under no illusions about the fact they were guards, she could see a steeliness about them, yet they only showed her understanding and tenderness; treated her with respect; treated her as a fellow human.

She wondered at a world where people could be sold, not just for the sex trade, but for all sorts of reasons. From her schooling she knew about the slavery, but she had genuinely believed society had moved on from humans being treated as "goods and chattels". She knew nothing of the working girls, the triads and the sex industry. Why would she? She was thirteen years old when her parents died; still a child, innocent of the world and its evil. The day her uncle handed her over to the Triad, he killed her childhood; ripped the innocence from her with a brutality that defied belief. She had done nothing to deserve that, none of them had; no one ever deserved such a life. Bào ying would be in his life and she hoped the retribution he suffered would be an appropriate one.

Now, she was without a home or money, but she had a calmness like never before; she had purpose. She could feel it burning in her soul; a beacon guiding her. Quite how she would fulfil that purpose she had not yet determined, but she would work tirelessly to free those in situations like hers, and to ensure this barbaric trade of men, women, and children was stamped out forever.

Her daytime guard today was Harry. He was older than the rest, different. Even at her tender age, she could tell his eyes had seen things they shouldn't. He too had a calmness. Perhaps this is what happened when you travelled to hell and returned; nothing could hurt you anymore. She noticed the doctors and nurses seemed wary of him, but she didn't fully understand why. He was funny and could talk about places she knew. She guessed he'd been a soldier at some time as he seemed well travelled but didn't seem to be a "businessman" type. She'd seen plenty of those at her house, when her father invited them for dinner. Harry was most definitely not one of those.

She liked all her guards, but if she had to choose one, it would be Harry. They all made her feel safe, but he made her feel the safest.

She picked up the reporter's notebook from her bedside cabinet. The crest and words emblazoned on the front proclaimed it to be the property of the Metropolitan Police. Little snippets of information still popped into Kun's head, so Sergeant Ruth left the notebook for her to write them down. This time she remembered the name of one of the men who held them captive; Tony. He'd yelled at the person who used it, not to call him by name.

~§~

This time it was Ruth who took the lead in the briefing room.

'Okay. Can we have the lights down please?'

Ruth used the remote to put the first of several slides on the screen.

'A number of developments have taken place in the past few days. Firstly, we have established where the victims were held in their final days. Thanks to Nicky, we were able to locate the' — she glanced at her notes — 'pillbox and the lab have confirmed by fibre and DNA analysis the victims were present inside, despite an attempt to cover up by spraying bleach everywhere. We also have several boot prints and on a wider sweep of the area, we picked up tyre tracks. These match the ones found at the scene on Wanstead Flats, all that remains is to find the owners of the boots and the vehicle. We believe this to be the blue van that Kun reported as the final transfer vehicle. However, a bit of good news on that front too. It appears the perpetrators got a bit sloppy. Perhaps they didn't expect the girls to live long enough to talk, whatever the reason, on the trip to the bunker they were loaded into the van from the back. Kun managed to obtain a partial index, six-one-sierra-mike. Of course, it's possible it was on cloned plates and obviously without a full index, or confirmed make of vehicle, it's going to be a process of elimination; good old-fashioned police slog, but at least it was a blue van and not white and we know the year of registration. That takes some of the pressure off.'

Ruth took a sip of water.

'Thanks to the "away" team, we also have a name to work with, Mr Don. Not the smoking gun we would like, but we do have a positive identification from Kun; this man.'

She changed the slide to show a thin faced, pasty looking man.

'Guilty.'

'What makes you say that?'

'His eyes are too close together.'

Helene joined in.

'If only it was that easy, Fitz, if only.'

Ruth continued.

'Donald William Golding is a small-time crook, occupying a reasonable amount of space on the PNC hard drives, but he appears to have moved into the human trafficking game, no doubt lured by the promise of big profits. UK Border Force confirmed he left the country in January, bound for Hong Kong. It would appear Mr Golding isn't the brightest of villains, travelling directly from Heathrow and on his own passport.

'An apparently empty container was shipped to Tilbury onboard the Hamadryad, a mixed cargo vessel. She docked at Tilbury two weeks before our victims were discovered. She has done this on all three occasions before the discovery of murdered young Asians. On each of these visits, the ship carried just one empty container. Deck space is valuable so moving an empty container is an expensive process. Moving three on successive trips seems to be more than a little bit extravagant, especially when they are then left sitting at Tilbury, or rather, were. They are now in our possession and have yielded a significant amount of forensic evidence tying them to some of the victims. Hamadryad is currently in the hands of the Hong Kong Police Force and the captain, a Russian national, is in custody. Word has it, he's not being too co-operative at the moment.

'This ship sailed for the UK four days after Golding returned. Now here's the interesting bit, Golding must be doing quite well for himself somehow, because he owns a ten-and-a-half metre fishing boat capable of around thirty-five knots. He's been boarded by Customs on a couple of occasions, but nothing found. The night before Hamadryad docked at Tilbury, Golding's boat, "The Drifter", left for an overnight fishing trip in the Thames Estuary, and returned the next morning. We may well be barking up the wrong tree here, but with all the other evidence, I think we have our trafficker. He's under twenty-four-hour surveillance, but so far is behaving. He has a company that rents out slums to the desperate and we are trying to obtain a full list of properties, but it isn't easy as it appears, because many aren't registered.'

'Why don't you just bring him in for questioning?'

'We are fairly sure he's not the killer. He may be a scrote, a supplier, but he's not shown any violent tendencies in the

past, Smoke. From what Kun says, we believe he's just the importer and we want the end users as well. He may just go 'no comment' on us and really, what we have is circumstantial'
—

A quiet voice interrupted.
'He'll cough for us.'
A ripple of laughter ran around the table.
'Yes, Twinkle Toes, I'm sure he would, but it makes a terrible mess. Besides, we want him to lead us to Mr Big — I don't believe I just said that. Did I really say, Mr Big, and did I really just call you Twinkle Toes?'
Laughter followed once again.
'Just how Golding came to be in the trafficking business, we aren't sure. But — and this is the puzzler — he wasn't out of the country on the previous two occasions when the Hamadryad came to the UK, and the bodies started turning up.'
'Could it be coincidence?'
'Yes, it could, Nicky, but you have a nose for this sort of thing, what do you think?'
'I'm no copper, but from what you have told us, I think he's as guilty as sin on this one. In my experience, someone with his pedigree would not trust others to do the buying for him. He probably doesn't even trust himself. So, if he's not been to Hong Kong before, then this is a new venture for him, but I agree with Smoke, he needs to answer some questions.'
'We have a saying in Arabic, shway, shway. Little by little or slowly, slowly. I think caution is the key here.'
'Thank you, Harry. Yes, slowly, slowly. Nicking Golding for trafficking is secondary to finding out who the killers are. That has to be our number one priority. If we pull Golding, they'll switch to someone else and we will have lost a good chance of getting to them. We may still have to do that and lean on him a little, but for the time being we just keep obs on him.
'This is why Emma is going to spend time on the Dark Net, whatever that is, to see if we can lure Golding into attempting to sell us something he shouldn't be doing. As I said, at the

moment, what we have is circumstantial, and if we can get something a bit more concrete, we have more leverage. She will also look for any possible buyers in the hope we can draw out the perpetrators.'

Helene watched with increasing admiration for Ruth. She handled this well, not being distracted by the input from others. A thorough briefing.

'Just tell us what angle you want him to lean at, and me and the lads will put him there.'

'Jeez, Twinkle, you guys are beginning to scare me.'

'Only beginning?' He turned to the others. 'We better go and do some work on our menacing skills, lads.'

'I have to say, you scare the crap out of me.'

'Aww, thanks, Nicky. Positive feedback is always welcomed.'

Nicky chuckled.

Ruth held up her hands.

'Right, back to business. Another piece of information from Kun was several graffiti tags from the warehouse. It would appear the young lady has a remarkable memory for detail. I've not had chance to run them through the database yet.'

She read out a list of four tags, Kun had been able to recall.

'Ruth?'

'Yes, boss?'

'I think I've seen one of those.'

She spelled out a name phonetically.

'Is that how she spells, Morvi?'

Ruth consulted the list.

'Yes, you know it?'

'I've seen it around Tower Hamlets. I remember because it looked artistic, not the usual hastily scrawled territory marker. This person has artistic skills. I'll follow up, Ruth. Good work.'

Ruth continued with the briefing.

'Any questions?'

'You said it was unlikely Golding was responsible for all the trafficking. What are we doing about the others?'

CHAPTER SIXTEEN

'Fair question, Harry, and the short answer is, nothing. Not for the time being anyway. We are going after this event while it's fresh and we have some solid leads. If, in the course of our investigations we pick up something that may lead us to the earlier traffic, we will follow up, but for now, the perpetrators remain our number one priority.

'Anything else? No? Well in that case, as the boss would say, go catch me some killers.'

~§~

To the general public, the Dark Web is something mysterious and associated with many activities that are criminal, distasteful, or both. To Emma, it is nothing more than another place to ply her trade. As a 'white hat', her computer hacking skills are not used for nefarious purposes - not yet, anyway. In fact, she rarely uses them for any purposes other than being nosey, and as a challenge; much like a mountaineer tackling a difficult route to a summit, just because it is there, Emma attempted to penetrate some of the most protected servers in the world. She would search for something specific this time and was unsure of her feelings. She would join groups whose activities, at best, would be described as abhorrent. Another foreseeable problem was that occasionally, a clever group admin would detect a member hiding their true gender; something as simple as a single word or phrase often gave them away. Emma could not risk the possibility of that happening and for that reason Chris a.k.a. Jack Sparrow, joined her.

Emma discovered during her briefing that the commonly held view suggesting men committed the majority of sexual offences, was somewhat simplistic. Many factors came into play such as reporting rates, and classification of offences. On the other hand, serial killers are predominantly male; statistically, the chances of these murders being carried out by a woman or women, remained extremely low. In this case, the boss suspected a group of men, possibly brought together for the purposes of sexual gratification by killing. Helene certainly believed it was ritualistic from the similarity of cause of death in the victims; three stabbed, the remaining five strangled. The five strangulations occurred almost at the same time, according to the post-mortem results. Either they had an extremely fast serial killer on their hands, or the more likely scenario, these deaths were the result of a sick ritual. The only way to find out was to catch those responsible.

The Dark Web is only a small part of the Deep Web, which in turn is part of what the public understands to be the internet. The Deep Web is not indexed by search engines and remains hidden to the public, unless you know where to look and how to access it; much of it made up by business intranets, web archives, user databases, password-protected websites, the list goes on. Emma saw this as her playground, her means of relaxation, her place of fun. The Dark Web, on the other hand, often contains user-groups, bulletin boards and illegal marketplaces. She sometimes went there out of curiosity, a nosey around; today, she would enter quietly, search for something specific and prepare her traps.

All around the world, small government departments emulated her activities for various purposes; cracking sex rackets, human trafficking gangs, paedophile rings, drug smugglers and finding stolen goods, to name but a few. The first two were her targets, and as the boss first suspected, it seemed likely they were two separate groups.

Emma and Chris worked well together when not co-located, as when she hacked into GCHQ, but when in the same room, that was another matter. She loved to have music playing as she wandered through the labyrinth of VPNs, firewalls and servers. Music changed her mood and for this kind of work, she must be alert; rock made her feel alive. Chris preferred silence but he knew when he was in the presence of a master, or in this case mistress, he must let them have their way.

It wasn't long before she found the first item of interest. A group advertising 'The Ultimate Sexual Experience'. Now that warranted a little more investigation. Emma didn't want to go in through the front door and make her presence known, so she snooped around the server a little looking for an unprotected port which she found straightaway. That in itself suggested whoever ran this site was an amateur; it shouldn't be that easy. Having said that, it was surprising how many IT managers left their companies open to attack by forgetting to change default passwords or close any unused ports. It wasn't rocket science really. You wouldn't leave a sign in your house window announcing the door wasn't locked, yet effectively, that is what they do.

Just as she suspected, the site was nothing more than a porn site, and not a very good one at that, not that she was a connoisseur of course, but she had certainly come across them before. This one was probably run by a spotty teenager who would run a mile in the presence of a real woman.

Whoa! Now this one showed promise. An understated advertisement for gentlemen of means to join an exclusive club exercising the ultimate control. All applicants would undergo rigorous and extensive vetting. Once again, she ignored the link and looked for a way into the server where the site was hosted.

The protection here was far better, in fact, whoever set this up was very good, but still no match for Emma's talents and it was only a matter of minutes before she was treading carefully through the site directories. Much of the site was subscriber only meaning it was password protected to the users, but by coming into the backend, she was able to peruse at will.

'Holy shit, Chris. Have you seen this? They are referring to so-called snuff movies allegedly made last century. They are offering people the chance to take part in their own movie. Are they seriously suggesting they are going to film people being murdered?'

Chris had been shadowing her at his own computer, marvelling at the way she sidestepped the security and waltzed in as if it was her own place.

'They can't be serious, can they?'

'Sick fucking bastards.'

Chris had grown used to Emma's use of some of the baser words in the English language and always felt somewhat uncomfortable but on this occasion, he had to agree with her Anglo-Saxon summation.

'I think the boss is going to want to see this.'

'The boss is going to want to see what?'

Emma jumped.

'Jeez, boss. Don't do that. When did you come in?'

'About ten seconds ago. You two were glued to your screens, not that it would make that much difference.'

Helene waved her hand in the direction of the speaker from where Green Day's *Last Ride In* emanated. She bent down to look at the information on Emma's monitor.

'Can you find out who runs the site?'

'I already know who the admin is, but wouldn't we be better trying to join?'

'See what you can find out first. I don't want to show our hand so soon in the game. Let's see if we can get some solid evidence. Well done, Emma.'

~§~

Once Helene had gone, Emma posted on a number of bulletin boards. This formed the second part of the operation; bait for the traffickers. Her advertisement was designed to be subtle, but draw out those who were either already trafficking, or willing to become involved in some way.

"Wealthy client seeks importation of live goods from the east for private enterprise. Must be top quality, tender and unspoiled. Seconds will not be tolerated. Ongoing requirement. Discretion required and assured. Principals only."

The first secret to the Dark Web was temptation, the second was getting your message across without being obvious. This was also a place where law enforcement hunted, exactly as she was doing. Bait had to be tasty, but not so tasty as to be obvious and scare away the prey. Softly, softly, catchee bad guy.

The format of the advertisement had been discussed at length between Helene, Chris and herself. She and Chris had experience in the web, but Helene knew law enforcement. One advantage they had was not being too concerned about entrapment. Working on what Helene described as the 'fringes of the law', gave them considerably more latitude than the mainstream investigations. This investigation was covert and would always remain so.

'Well, that's that, Jack.'

Emma was still unused to addressing him as Chris, sometimes slipping back to using his hacker's identity. He on the other hand, began to use her real name as soon as she was brought into Invidia. Perhaps he didn't like flowers.

'I thought I was good, but I've never seen anyone with skills remotely as good as yours. It's almost like you are inside the web, following a map.'

Emma looked surprised.

'I think you may be right about that. I do see it as a collection of pathways, doors, and traps. Perhaps that's the real secret of hacking. Visualise yourself inside the network. Fancy a coffee?'

Never one to turn down spending time with this amazing woman, Chris readily accepted.

~§~

He sat up with a start, his breathing fast and heavy. Rivulets of sweat ran from his forehead, some finding a path around his face, others preferring to drip from the end of his nose.

The nightmare ends at the same place each time when the knife pierces his heart. She's only young but has such strength as she stabs him in the chest, over, and over, and over again.

This couldn't be happening, not to him, a respected businessman, a pillar of the community. His wife lay asleep beside him, oblivious to her husband's distress. He had been faithful his entire life; his recent infidelity, a means to an end. It was meant to be an initiation, a way to allow him to rub shoulders with influential people; the social contact far more important to him than anything else the club offered.

What he got was beyond his comprehension; he killed another human being. Sure, technically they made him do it, controlled his hands while he wore a blindfold, but it had been his actions, nonetheless. Now he knew the meaning of 'ultimate control over life': not his life, that of another.

Those words whispered to him at the Masquerade Ball, those fleeting moments where he felt he would finally be one of the movers and shakers of the country; his business moving from the 'also rans' to the 'podium finishers', had him hooked. A short sentence that promised he would move in circles he only dreamt of; access to the inaccessible. Only, they didn't mean that at all.

He should have known it wouldn't be that easy, nothing ever is. A simple initiation then you'll be in. That's all it would need. Yeah, right. That's why he was waking up every night in a cold sweat. He must tell someone, get it off his chest. They say confession is good for the soul, whoever they are, but confessing to a murder would mean his life would be over too.

He looked at his wife, sleeping peacefully. What had he done? He risked everything in his life; wife, children, business, freedom, all to get an edge, an advantage over the others, move in different circles. Why? He was more than content with what he had right now. What drove him to risk it all for membership to an elite club?

He could not see a way out of this, no way at all.

CHAPTER SEVENTEEN

The National Graffiti Database first saw the light of day in the early years of the twenty-first century. Keeping a register of tags formed just part of the strategy to clamp down on graffiti. Although graffiti appears to be one of society's more harmless pastimes, it is often unsightly, takes place in dangerous places and costs the UK a staggering £1 billion a year to remove.

Working her way through the database, Helene soon found what she wanted. The artist was known, had been fined for "dubs" on the London Underground and hadn't been caught reoffending since. She hoped he still lived at the last address on file or she would have even more work to do.

~§~

In one of those strange coincidences that seem to crop up throughout life, Helene found herself in the same apartment block as a perpetrator from her last case with the Met. He had been both perpetrator and a victim, but try as she might, she found no sympathy for the toe-rag. He and his accomplice beat several homeless men, resulting in the death of one. A death that triggered a series of bloody reprisals on the ne'erdo-wells of the parish including him and his accomplice. Technically, the reprisals remained on the books as unsolved crimes, but the cases were unlikely to be reopened. Helene and her superiors were fully aware of the identity of the culprit and as long as he played ball there would be no further investigations.

To her surprise, the door opened to reveal a neatly dressed young man. Helene knew him to be in his mid-twenties. She showed him her warrant card.

'I'm DCI MacKay. I'd like to talk to you about some graffiti. Mind if I come in?'

The man rolled his eyes.

'I don't do that no more. Left it behind when I got nicked.'

'I'm aware of that, but I need to talk to you. You are not in any trouble, but I think you may be able to help us with a murder enquiry.'

The young man turned pale.

'I didn't murder no one. I used to dub, that was all. I ain't done no violence. Not never.'

Helene struggled to unravel all the double negatives, but she got the gist of it; he didn't do it.

She smiled sweetly.

'I didn't say you did. I said you may be able to help.'

He studied Helene as if weighing up whether to talk or not, then motioned her to go inside. As she stepped over the threshold, he popped his head out of the door, took a quick look round before closing the door behind her.

Helene raised her eyebrows questioningly.

'Worried about something?'

'Yeah, I'm a bit shook, but it ain't that. Just checking. This ain't a safe neighbourhood for us.'

'Us?'

'Yeah Bruvvas and Sistas, Girl. A lot of those "get back to where you came from" lot around here.'

He gestured towards a large leather sofa.

'Here, pop a seat.'

Helene thought she maybe was a little old to be addressed as 'girl', but then it comes with the territory when you are black. Sometimes it was complimentary, sometimes not. This time she took it to mean he was cool with her.

'Keith. It's okay to call you Keith?'

'It's my name, innit.'

'Okay, Keith. You aren't in any trouble, and I promise you won't be, but I need some honest answers about your graffiti.'

Helene held up her hand before he managed to voice his protestation of innocence.

'I need to know if you tagged any warehouses.'

'Yeah, a few.'

'Inside?'

'Nah. I never broke in anywhere to do it. Not unless you count getting on the railway as breaking in.'

'You sure about that?'

'Yeah, I'm positi— oh, wait. There was one. Didn't break in though, it was already open, even the gate at the front.'

'Where was this?'

The young man looked reluctant to answer.

'I'm not interested in the graffiti or who did it, but I need to find a location. It could be really important.'

The man searched her eyes, presumably weighing up if she was telling the truth or not.

'Down by the river. Did it while I was waiting for my court case. Last act of defiance, I suppose. Then I grew up a bit din't I? Got a proper job. Left all that behind.'

'Can you remember where it was, exactly?'

'I'll take you there, if you want, but I can't be seen leaving with you, you being the po-po an' all, no offence.'

'Po-po?'

'Yeah, Five-O — cops. I'll meet you on the corner by Denni's.'

Helene cocked her head again and the young man took the hint.

'The corner of Swaton and Rounton.'

~§~

On the way to the warehouse, Helene warmed to Keith. He had been a bit of a rebel without a cause but getting fined for graffiti had been a sharp lesson to him. Others he ran with hadn't been so lucky, some spent time in prison, and a couple got killed on the tracks. Getting caught made him re-evaluate his life. He was intelligent, and when it came to art, he had a talent. He soon discovered his sort of talent was much sought after by graphic design companies and he managed to land himself a decent job.

Helene believed him when he said his graffiti days were over.

The warehouse turned out to be close to the East India Basin on the Thames and remained one of the few places not turned into apartments, offices or demolished to make way for another Starbucks. As soon as she saw it, Helene was sure this was the place. Kun said she thought they were close to the river. Even though she couldn't give an accurate time for the trip in the van, this would fit into the timeframe suggested.

Helene told Keith not to touch anything and to make sure he followed her exactly. If any evidence remained here after so long, she didn't want either of them putting their feet in it.

They made their way inside the warehouse, keeping to the walls and Keith showed her where he sprayed his tag. Kun had been right. Helene checked off some of the other names on the list she'd copied into her phone, and they were all there. This was the place.

Back at the car, she called Ruth to send the crime techs team, pronto. If evidence remained, they couldn't waste any time.

~§~

These places used to be called scrapyards, but some PR guru felt this was perhaps a little bit of a misnomer, they weren't only for scrap after all. So, in an attempt to present a better public image, they underwent a metamorphosis to become car breakers. Clearly, someone, somewhere, didn't think that was upmarket enough either and so the latest terminology in use was vehicle dismantler.

It didn't matter what they were called on the outside, the ones encountered by PC Thomas all contained piles of broken vehicles, mounds of manky engines, gearboxes and axles and parts that would not be out of place on alien spacecraft. Everywhere, miniature lakes surfaced with shifting rainbows of petrol, oil and heaven knows what; probably containing species as yet unknown to man. And the smell, they all had the same smell of old; old cars, old oil and decay. Admittedly, she'd heard there were some, some of the more modern ones, which had floors you could almost dine from, everything neat and orderly.

Swallow's most definitely did not fall into the latter category. If a league existed for the dirtiest, most disorganised yard in the land, Swallow's name would be engraved on the cup every year since nineteen-fifty-four, when his father scrapped his first car. Tidy did not exist in the Swallow vocabulary. Strangely enough, he always knew the whereabouts of each car and whether a particular part was available.

Ron Swallow entered the business after leaving school at the age of fifteen, and not a moment too soon as far as he was concerned. School wasn't for the likes of him. He would never use trigonometry or need to know the life cycle of a frog. Ron was mechanically minded, a wizard with his hands. Why did he need all that book learning when he could learn all he would ever need from his father?

'Look, Ron, you know the rules.'

'You can't just barge your way in here like that. You have to give me notice. Those are the rules.'

Ron had a wheedling way of talking to people in a position of authority; subservient, yet with a defiance that was hard to place. A conversation with Ron always made Thomas want to wash her hands.

She shook her head. The Scrap Metal Dealers Act 2013 (SMDA) was supposed to make it harder for stolen scrap metal to be sold on. The idea was to introduce traceability by stopping cash payments and put everything through a bank. In practice, plenty of dealers like Ron existed, ones who would find a way to circumvent the regulations, which was precisely why PC Thomas was here.

'The gate is open, that hardly classes as barging in, and para 16 subsection 2b of the Act states, and I quote, "entry to the site is reasonably required for the purpose of ascertaining whether the provisions of this Act are being complied with or investigating offences under it and, in either case, the giving of notice would defeat that purpose." I would say that giving you notice falls into that category, wouldn't you agree, Ron? So, why don't you show me around, show me the records and show me some co-operation, before I show you the inside of a cell.'

Ron Swallow's core business was breaking vehicles, but he was long suspected of parting stolen vehicles as well as fencing stolen metals, although nothing had ever stuck to him. The local nick liked to rattle his cage now and again, as a reminder they were keeping an eye on him. Today was PC Thomas's lucky day to do the shaking.

'It's harassment, that's what it is.'

'You don't know the meaning of the word.'

As they stepped out of the upstairs office, Thomas's eye was caught by a vehicle in the yard near the crusher, seemingly out of place; her back had been towards it on the way up to the office. Swallow normally dealt with older or accident damaged vehicles. This one looked to be neither. Something about it looked wrong.

'Let's start with this van, Ron.'

'I thought you were here about scrap metal.'

'I am, but now I want to talk about this van, so talk, or get nicked for obstructing a police officer in the course of their duty.'

Swallow grumbled all the way to the van, but PC Thomas had more pressing thoughts on her mind. This may well be a stolen vehicle and if so, they would finally have something to lay on Swallow.

She examined the vehicle without touching it. She'd been on the force long enough to know better than to contaminate any potential evidence.

'So, what's the story, Ron?'

'There's no story. Some geyser dropped it off, twenty minutes, half an hour ago, something like that. Said it had to be crushed. I told him it was worth more to me broken for spares. He gave me five grand in cash to crush it. I was still going to part it out though. Five grand plus parts, how could I not, eh?'

'Did it not strike you as a little peculiar that someone wants to crush a perfectly good van?'

Swallow looked a little sheepish.

'Cash is cash, innit.'

Thomas called for a PNC check and was surprised to find the vehicle taxed, insured, ten months left on the MOT, and not reported stolen. Now why would someone have a vehicle crushed unless they were trying to hide something? It made no sense. Something decidedly dodgy was going on here.

'Ron, you are not to touch that van until I say so. Am I clear?'

'But —'

'Am I clear?'

Ron rolled his eyes.

'Yes, you made yourself clear.'

Thomas called it in.

CHAPTER EIGHTEEN

Emma adored her new workspace. She couldn't conceive how she'd managed at the bank. Whatever possessed her to go into the world of finance, must at some point have been exorcised. She lived, breathed and dreamed computers, and so she should. She was at the very pinnacle of her game.

She looked up from her book; the ping from her computer drawing her attention to the screen. Although the boss hadn't actually authorised it, and it was probably against all the rules, Emma had inserted a piece of code into the Police National Computer operating system. Now she had an alert on her screen every time someone used the search terms she had set on the PNC computer.

With so little to go on with the index number for the van, there had been one false alarm. Quite a few six-one-sierra-mikes existed in the system, but the one sitting on her screen right now may well be the proverbial needle in the haystack they'd been looking for.

The phone rang only once before being picked up.

'Boss, I think I might have a lead on one of the vehicles. Someone just did a PNC check for a blue Ford Transit, lima-zulu-six-one-sierra-mike-sierra. I can give you the details and the search reference if you want?'

~§~

Helene hung up and immediately dialled another number. The PNC check had only just happened. There was a good chance if they moved quickly enough, they may catch that much needed break. They had Golding as a backstop, but she doubted he knew little more than they did when it came to the murders. It just wasn't his style. Nevertheless, they still had the twenty-four-hour surveillance on him.

Helene used her newfound authority to find out the origin of the PNC request, then arranged to meet the officer concerned near the registered keeper's address. On the way over, it occurred to her that perhaps she should ask Emma how she knew about the check, then decided it was perhaps better not to know. Some things are just meant to be.

~§~

The message puzzled PC Thomas. On her way to the registered keeper's address, she had been told to stop short and await instructions from a DCI MacKay. She didn't know this DCI and had no idea why they would be interested in the case. Something illegal was behind the disposal of the van, of that she was sure. Maybe it had been used in a robbery, if so, why use the original plates and not cloned ones? The plates matched the VIN, so unless the van was a ringer, the keeper was going to have a lot of explaining to do.

Thomas parked in a street adjacent to the address of the keeper, as per instructions. Now all she had to do was wait for this DCI to turn up.

A well-dressed woman tapped on the passenger window and she lowered it.

'Can I help you, madam?'

'I hope so, PC Thomas?'

'DCI MacKay?'

'Surprised?'

'No, yes — I was expecting — '

'A white, middle-aged man in a raincoat? I know I get that a lot.'

The DCI got into the car and briefed her on the interest her team had in the van. Thomas had the feeling she was only getting the tip of the information iceberg, just enough to allow her to fulfil her duties, which was fine. There are times when knowledge is only a burden.

'I have no idea who we are dealing with, but for now I just want a chat with him about the van. You go around the back, just in case he doesn't want to talk.'

Fortunately, this was one of the easier houses to get behind; no clambering over garden fences this time. On this estate, the houses were built in rows. The back of one row faced the back of the next. A high wall ran along the entire length of each row separating the gardens from the path which ran between the two sets of houses; a modern variation of the houses built for the mill workers, the difference being, these had gardens, not a flagged area and no outside privy. Thomas checked twice to make sure she was at the correct gate. It wouldn't be the first time a constable stood outside the wrong house only to watch a suspect leg it from further along the street.

A few moments later, the back door clattered as someone flung it open. Thomas positioned herself to the side of the gate with her back against the wall. The gate suffered a similar fate as the door, and Thomas stuck her leg out as the suspect ran out of the garden onto the path. His escape turned into a short flight as his legs disappeared from under him and he came to rest face down on the hard tarmacadam walk. Before he could gather his wits, Thomas had him cuffed.

'Going somewhere?'

The man struggled but with PC Thomas's knee in his back and the rigid cuffs on his wrists, he wasn't going anywhere.

'Well done.'

Thomas turned to see the DCI leaning casually against the gatepost.

'Thanks, ma'am.'

The DCI explained to Thomas that the man would be taken by her team for interview; the van already recovered from the scrapyard by her crime tech team. Thomas wasn't sure, but she had the impression this was a counter-terrorism operation, whatever it was it certainly beat doing a scrapyard check.

'That was good police work on your part, with the van. I'll make sure your inspector gets to hear about it.'

Thomas had heard it all before and she must have shown it on her face.

'I know, I know, but I really do support my officers, or ones I work with. That is something you can count on.'

'What's he wanted for, ma'am?'

'We believe he's involved in a major ringing racket, commercial vehicles.'

'Swallow involved too?'

'We have no evidence to suggest so.'

'I find that hard to believe, ma'am. We've been after him for years. That's why I was there, doing an SMDA check.'

'I'll bear that in mind, but for now, this is the chappie we want to talk to.'

'If he's ringing them, why did he want this one crushed?'

'That's what we intend to find out.'

Thomas, now more than ever, believed this to be a counter-terrorism operation and the story about ringing was a smokescreen.

The DCI squatted down beside the man on the ground.

'I'm DCI Helene MacKay and it's my good fortune to tell you that you are under arrest on suspicion of converting criminal property. You do not have to say anything, but it may harm your defence if you do not mention when questioned something which you later rely on in court. Anything you do say may be given in evidence. Do you understand why you've been arrested?'

'What the fuck are you on about? I haven't done any converting or whatever it is. Is that what this is about because if it is, I'll have your job, bitch.'

The DCI looked back to Thomas who applied a little more pressure with her knee to the man's back and winked.

~§~

Thomas watched as a police van took the man away. There was something odd about this whole set-up. She'd been in the force long enough to know most of the local guys, and these certainly weren't local. Then there was the DCI. She hadn't recognised the name at first, but now she realised who it was, and she knew her by reputation, although rumour had it, MacKay moved on from the Met. So, what was she doing getting involved in a ringing racket? And if Swallow wasn't involved, what was the van doing in his yard?

Something didn't add up and when she got the chance, she would do a bit of digging, but first things first, time for a cuppa.

CHAPTER NINETEEN

An electric door squealed and ground its way open to allow the police van to enter the building via the ramp into an underground garage. A second electric door, clearly an aural twin of the first, opened to allow entry into the custody delivery area. The duty sergeant listened to the arresting officer, in this case Helene, entering the details of the arrest on a computer. Formalities completed, a constable escorted the man to a cell to await interview.

A further two hours passed before he was escorted from the cell, past the custody desk, along a corridor, then up a flight of stairs to the interview room. Although the offices had windows, through which a nearby red-brick building could be seen, the interview rooms were windowless. As with most police stations in London, the sound of nearby traffic served as a constant reminder of a city that never sleeps.

Had anyone questioned him about the length of the journey in the van, he may have thought it to be longer than usual, but no one had asked and he hadn't remarked on it. He would be surprised to learn they were not in Central London, but a former Manor House in Hampstead Heath; the traffic noise came from speakers, and the uniformed staff members were Invidia office staff.

This part of the Invidia headquarters was purpose built to look like other police stations in London. Should a case go to court, nothing must point to the fact the interview had taken place somewhere other than a regular police station and the written records would show that to be the case.

Helene watched on a CCTV monitor as Ruth interviewed the suspect who they had now established as being Alan Anthony Bridgedale, a former bouncer with a reputation for being a little rough when ejecting unwanted clientele. Three years previously, Bridgedale had been lucky not to get a custodial sentence after head-butting a drunk trying to get back into the club where he worked, but he did lose his SIA Door Supervisor Licence and his employment.

Ever since then he'd drifted from job to job, often providing his services as a 'man with van', which begged the question as to why he would want it crushed; a question the crime techs were working hard to answer, even as the interview was taking place.

Contrary to what is portrayed in many popular TV series, the senior officer rarely carries out an interview with the subject. Nothing so glamorous as that; the majority of their duties lay with the paperwork, but who would want to watch a TV series that solely consisted of the detective sitting behind a desk shuffling papers? Helene was thankful that ninety percent of the paperwork that previously bogged her down was no longer necessary in her present role, giving her the opportunity to watch Ruth who she already knew to have an excellent track record as an interviewer.

Gone were the days of trying to wring a confession out of the suspect. Interviews were now directed at getting to the truth, probing the answers of the suspect, comparing them with known facts about the case. At least that would be how it would go if the suspect answered the questions, but the right to remain silent is enshrined in UK law, even with the rider that it "may harm your defence", introduced by PACE.

'So, is it Alan or Anthony?'

'Tony, if you must.'

Ruth gently and subtly probed what Bridgedale knew about the vehicle ringing enterprise and he in turn denied all knowledge, which was fine by Helene. Ruth was merely stalling for time while the crime techs did their thing. Surprisingly, Bridgedale hadn't yet asked for a lawyer. Whether that was because he felt he didn't need one, because he really did know nothing about the stolen vehicles, or for some other reason, Helene didn't know, but if he did ask for one, a genuine lawyer stood by ready to step in. At the moment they were playing this one by the book, almost.

A gentle knock at the door attracted Helene's attention.

'Result, boss. DNA found in the van matches the profiles of three of the murder victims. We are still processing the others. We also have fibres that match those found at the pillbox and the tyres are a match in pattern for both the pillbox and Wanstead.'

Helene loved this team. In a matter of a couple of hours they had achieved what might have taken days or even weeks in her old job. Now they could hit Bridgedale hard.

Helene pressed the transmit button on the headset cable so she could speak to Ruth who was wearing a tiny insert in her right ear.

'Show him the photos of the girls. We have a DNA match for three of them. Fibres match with the pillbox and tyre tracks from the pillbox and Wanstead.'

Ruth showed no sign of having heard other than putting her hand on the manila folder in front of her.

'Tony, why don't we go over it one more time?'

'I've told ya. I know jack shit about nicking vans or any other dodgy motors.'

'Does anyone else ever drive your van?'

'No.'

'Never?'

'I said no, didn't I?'

'Why were you having it crushed, Tony?'

Bridgedale stared at her but didn't answer.

'Would it be because of these?'

CHAPTER NINETEEN

Ruth opened the folder and laid out the mortuary photographs of the dead girls on the table in front of him.

'You see, we have DNA evidence these girls were in your van, and that your van was at two different crime scenes. Eight bodies Tony, one on life support and you've just told me you never let anyone else drive your van. That puts you in the same place as the murder victims, so as of now, you are the number one suspect in their murder.'

This was the first time he showed any sign of anxiety.

'Yes, Tony. One of them is still alive. So, where's that going to leave you?'

Ruth kept the news of Kun to herself. That was the ace up her sleeve.

'I still don't know what you are talking about, I didn't murder anyone.'

'Maybe you didn't actually do it, Tony, I don't know.'

Ruth stopped talking, letting the silence tear at Bridgedale's mind. Fear would be starting to release the maggots of insecurity, eating away at his rotting soul.

She never took her eyes off him while Bridgedale examined every last detail of his grubby pork sausage fingers.

'Do you know about joint enterprise law and secondary liability?'

Ruth watched as his eyes looked everywhere except at her.

'I'll take that as a no then. We can tie your van to the victims, we can also tie the van to where they were found as well as where we suspect they were held. You said yourself that no one else drives your van. That means you were a party to the murders and the disposal of the bodies. As such, you can be charged with the offence, even if you did not actually commit that offence.'

'That's bullshit.'

'If you say so. Now would you like to explain how their DNA came to be in your van?'

'I'm saying fuck all, until I get a lawyer.'

~§~

Once Bridgedale had returned to his cell, Helene and Ruth reviewed a rerun of the CCTV in the observation room. Often, details would emerge that for a variety of reasons may have been missed during the interview itself. This time, there was nothing; Ruth was a damned fine investigative interviewer and she'd picked up on every one of Bridgedale's answers.

The one thing that stood out from the whole interview was the change in his demeanour when confronted with the evidence. His initial attitude had been one of annoyance, tinged with indifference; arrested for something of which he knew nothing. Once he realised the real purpose, he used aggression in an attempt to hide his fear and had clearly been rattled.

It was likely that Bridgedale was a relatively small fish in a big pond and Invidia wanted the sharks, the ones at the top of the food chain. Sure, he'd asked for a lawyer and because he hadn't asked for anyone in particular, one would be appointed.

Invidia employed two lawyers, ones who were not averse to passing on information they may glean in the course of the discussions with their client, if they deemed it necessary to steer the case in the right direction. On the other hand, they would still work in court on a client's behalf, when and if the case came to trial in the British courts.

Had he asked for his own lawyer, he would have found himself being transferred to a local police station before his brief arrived. No one in the legal system outside Invidia would be aware of the location of this building. He would then be processed through the courts in the normal way. Should the case be dropped, or there be a miscarriage of justice, Invidia would intervene and Bridgedale would find himself in detention anyway, facing a private trial.

He was going down, of that there was no doubt. Just how deep, for how long and in what way, now entirely in his hands. Once they had information on others involved, the case would go to a specially convened court. Of course, the records would show he attended a regular court, complete with the court transcripts; Invidia's reach, extensive. Not quite how the criminal justice system usually worked, but the raison d'être for Invidia.

~§~

'Whoever set this up knows their stuff. They are using several VPNs and each one traces back to a different location: public places with free WiFi mostly coffee shops. The admin on the website goes to an anonymous email service and the username appears to be a random group of letters. I tried to follow the anonymous email, but it is forwarded through four more anonymous services and is forwarded again to a throwaway email. That one changes weekly. This person is wary, clever, and going to a great deal of effort to remain anonymous. Unless we can catch them actually logged into the site it is going to be very difficult to prove anything.'

Helene thought about her options. Despite having far better resources than she had in the MIT, she still couldn't hope to catch them in flagrante; what place didn't have WiFi these days?

'Do they have a preference for which coffee shops?'

'Pretty even between Starbucks and Costa, but several others too.'

'Okay, let's put the locations on a map and see where we go from there.'

Helene and Emma logged each location where the website had been accessed and the time of day.

Humans like to think they can be random, but in truth, they conform to patterns far more often than they think. It soon became apparent from the pins on the Google map, this person was not being as random as they probably thought they were, and two distinct clusters appeared, each with their own timescales. Cluster one centred around Liverpool Street Station. These locations were visited around lunchtime or in the early afternoon on weekdays. The second cluster appeared to centre around Camden town, in the evenings and at weekends.

'That, my young Emma, is what we call a clue. There is a theory that the perpetrators of crimes, particularly violent ones, tend to distribute their crimes in a circle around their area. It doesn't always hold true and is subject to variation for many reasons, but in this case, we do seem to have the classic circle. Check the dates and you will see that the second connection in either area was made on the opposite side of the circle from the first. Of course, these two circles are dependent on coffee shops with WiFi, so are not perfect. Tell me, what is the first thing you think when you look at the website and its membership requirements?'

'Disgusting, sick, perverted, bastards.'

'I asked for that. Who do you think is behind this and who are their clients, besides what you've just stated?'

'The clientele have to be wealthy and if they are going to set up an operation like this, so must the people behind it.'

Helene gave Emma a sideways look.

'You are a damned quick thinker, my girl.'

She pointed to the map. 'I'm hazarding a guess you know this area reasonably well?'

'I should do, I worked there. Whoever runs the site works in finance and lives in Camden.'

A huge smile spread across Helene's face.

'You know that's what I like about this team, Emma, we've been able to recruit people like you, quick, bright and focussed. I'm loving it.'

'You and me both, boss. I can't imagine doing anything else now. It's amazing what can happen when you break the law. I almost wet myself when they took me to the MI6 offices. I really thought I was going to prison. You better not let the rest of the world know jobs like this are an alternative to being locked up. You'll have a crime wave on your hands.'

As she studied the map, Helene decided on the next course of action. She motioned to Emma to stay where she was as she picked up the phone.

'Ruth, I am going to send you a list of cafes along with dates and times. I want you to get someone over to them and see if we can get CCTV footage. Emma has managed to trace them from inside their own website,' she listened for a moment, 'I know. I think she's some sort of witch too.' She winked at Emma then continued, 'If we can find someone common to these locations then we may just have found our perps.'

After hanging up she spoke to Emma.

'I think now is the time to see about membership. Will you be okay with this or would you like Chris to take over? Trying to join a so-called snuff club was never meant to be in your job description. Not that you ever had one in the first place.'

Emma held Helene's gaze.

'People like this make me sick to the stomach. This isn't about feminine equality, it's about human decency. I might have led something of a sheltered life up to now and can't possibly imagine the things you've had to deal with, but one thing's for certain, I'm going to help catch these people and see them rot in hell.'

~§~

Back in her office, Helene found James waiting for her. It didn't matter how many times a day she saw him, her heart fluttered.

He gave her a kiss. Not the full-of-passion type she longed for, they were at work after all, but an appropriate-for-the-circumstances-with-a-promise-of-more-later type. She would take what she could for now.

'Just came to see how you are?'

'I'm fine, James. For now, anyway. How's the move?'

The decision had been made that James would move in with Helene and let his rented flat go. His ex-wife already had possession of the house. He was spending all his time with Helene, he may as well move in.

'Yeah, that's what I wanted to talk to you about.'

She felt a moment of panic.

'What?'

'I just don't want you to get mad when we go home.'

She opened her mouth to speak and then closed it again.

'It's just that, it's a bit of a mess just now, boxes everywhere.'

'James.'

'Yes?'

'You said "home". You never said that before.'

She kissed him hard on the mouth. To hell with what the others thought.

~§~

Emma stared at the screen. She liked the office in darkness when she was working, so Chris had abandoned his desk and taken his laptop to work in another office, somewhere a bit brighter. Even though she admired Chris and his abilities, she preferred to work alone, she always had. There was one field in which he outshone her, the male perspective, and that would be why she would call him back to her, right now. Her little fishing expedition had paid off; someone had answered the advert.

The responder came straight to the point and suggested he could provide 'fresh goods' sourced from the Far East, and at a reasonable price. Well, that succinctly dealt with the requirements of the ad placed on the various bulletin boards.

Emma noted the pseudonym given in the reply and smiled. Just as she'd suspected Chris to be a fan of Pirates of the Caribbean with his hacker handle of Jack Sparrow, something that subsequently proved to be true, she now believed a certain person of interest had played right into their hands.

Not so clever, Mr Amicoauri, she thought as she started to write her response. You couldn't think of anything better? Who said learning Latin was a waste of time?

Emma did not want to get this wrong. Although it was not unknown for women to be involved in trafficking, the team felt it best that the person negotiating appeared to be male. She began to formulate her response.

~§~

Chris came into the room as Emma typed away. He watched her fingers moving deftly over the keys. She rarely made a mistake, yet she must be typing around one-hundred words a minute; a phenomenal rate for someone who was not a professional typist.

Before she hit 'send', she asked him to cast a male eye over it and he could see nothing that would suggest the sender's gender to the recipient, one way or another.

For once, he didn't feel to be playing second fiddle to Emma. She was the best, of that there was no doubt, but sometimes being acknowledged as someone who wasn't half bad at things himself certainly didn't go amiss. In fact, he wasn't so far behind Emma as some may imagine. After all, he had devised the code that proved to be her undoing and brought her here.

Was he jealous? Yes, just a little. On the other hand, he knew what a formidable team they made. Besides, who could be mad at Emma. She was the brightest thing ever to grace his life.

'Well?'

'If that doesn't hook him, nothing will.'

Amicoauri. Thank you for your quick response. You may well be the person we have been seeking for some months now. Despite many promises to deliver our requirements, we have been let down on most occasions. Should you prove to have the wherewithal to satisfy our needs this time, then I believe we may have a long and prosperous future ahead of us. Our requirements are ongoing, and we have substantial funds for the correct goods.

In order to facilitate an expeditious conclusion to our negotiations, I suggest we meet, at a place of your choosing, in the very near future.

CHAPTER TWENTY

'Boss?'

DC Jason Burns held out a piece of paper as Helene entered the incident room. After the interview with Bridgedale, she'd briefed Michael Strong on their progress so far. Now she was returning to what she considered to be her war office, located in the incident room. From here she could keep an eye on things and be available if something cropped up requiring her input, which invariably it did.

Although this was her working office, she had another, larger office, elsewhere in the building, the one she called 'the bullshit room.' It was here she would meet the grown-ups with a vested interest in the Invidia Syndicate; the room for politics, not the day-to-day running of an investigation.

'Have you seen this? Some background info on trafficking. I would like say it makes for interesting reading, but interesting isn't a word I would choose in this case.'

Helene took the proffered paper and sat at the desk alongside Jason while she scanned through the document. She reached the end and closed her eyes. It didn't require an over-active imagination to understand the significance of the information on that sheet of paper. A maelstrom of emotions played inside her; anger, sorrow, incredulity and sheer frustration, all intertwining and in the fight for the lead role. A solitary tear rolled down her right cheek. Her eyes opened, wet and bleary.

She took several deep breaths; the words, when they came, delivered with more growl than voice.

'Two — fucking — dollars? That's how little a life can be worth? How dare these people walk on this planet?' She shook her head. 'I cannot get my head around this. How can these, these — I have no words for them that fit. How can they sleep at night? And the girls we are investigating? Little comfort to them is it, that they were worth more?'

She handed the sheet back to Jason.

'I want everyone in the boardroom for briefing in one hour, everyone involved with this case, if they are in the building or in town, I want them here. Mozambique? Two fucking dollars. We are going to nail these sons of bitches and when we do, you better not let me near them because I will not be responsible for my actions.'

Jason watched his boss quietly close her office door. He'd never seen it in action before, but there could be no doubt that what he had just witnessed could be described as 'incandescent with rage'. Clearly, the information he'd found triggered something primal in her, as it had in him although to a lesser degree.

They always say, remain detached from the case, focus on the facts and leave the emotions behind. Once in a while, one would come along that got under your skin, touched a nerve, bit deep into your soul. This was the one getting under the boss's skin, but if a grave full of young women, or discovering that young African girls can fetch as little as two dollars, didn't affect you in some way, then perhaps you were not a member of the human race.

She had an excellent reputation, he wouldn't have taken the job otherwise, but he wondered if this was getting a bit too personal for her. Could Helene bring it under control, focus and do the job? He believed so, but right now she needed to take a couple of paces back and calm down.

Only time would tell how she would handle it, in the meantime, the team needed to be assembled. Jason picked up the phone and started to make the calls.

~§~

Such were the numbers for this meeting, the briefing room had been abandoned in favour of the training room where a greater number of seats were available; every one of them occupied plus some brought in from adjacent rooms. Not since Invidia's inception had such a large meeting been convened, but Helene wanted every person working on this case to hear about what she had read in the file from Jason.

She waited until everyone had found a place to sit.

'An hour ago, Jason' — she indicated the man seated on her right as not every member of the group knew each other yet — 'brought to my attention some figures on human trafficking. Make no mistake, the victims in the case we are dealing with were trafficked. We know where they originated, and we believe we have one of those involved in custody. Now I'm going show you those figures before we go any further.'

Helene turned to the SMART board and touched the screen. She let everyone have time to read through the entire document before continuing.

'Murder is abhorrent at the best of times, but when the victims have been sold to be used as seen fit, and are nothing more than a commodity to be traded in the market place, then it reaches new depths for me, and I suspect, for all of you too, especially when you see how little value is placed on some of these lives.

'I know you are all working hard on this case and your efforts are appreciated, but I also wanted you to know the kind of world in which we are working. This world is why Invidia was conceived in the first place, because in law enforcement there are times when our hands are tied, but the sort of scum who perpetrate these acts have no such restrictions.

'There will be some of you for whom it would appear I am letting this become personal. You are right, it is personal, because this could happen to any one of us, male or female. Make no mistake, trafficking is not something that happens only in poorer countries, you have seen the figures, it happens everywhere, including right here in this country.

'Each time we put one of these bastards behind bars, someone, somewhere, will not disappear, will not be taken from their families and friends, will not suffer for the rest of their lives, however long that may be.

'If any one of you have an idea, come across a piece of evidence, have a theory, anything at all that you might think could help the case, no matter how trivial, bring it to me or one of the investigation team. It doesn't matter what it is, we want to hear it and we will listen to you. Thank you all for coming here at such short notice. I would like to see the investigation team in the briefing room in five minutes. Thank you.'

Helene left, but not before noticing there were a few tears in the room. She was grateful she'd managed to hold back her own.

~§~

'Okay, where are we up to on the web, Emma?'

'I was just about to come and see you when we got the call from Jason. We've had a response to the ad for girls and it seems that the person is keen to do a trade. We've requested a meeting. I sent that about forty minutes ago.'

'Do you think it's a genuine response?'

'Not only do I think it's genuine, I think I know who it is.'

Helene raised her eyebrows and canted her head. Chris whipped his head round and stared at Emma in astonishment.

'You know I like to sometimes browse the internet, just out of curiosity.'

Helene nodded.

'Well, one of the things I like to look at is the origin of words and names. One particular name cropped up recently, so I looked it up. The response to the ad was signed "Amicoauri", but it is actually made up of two words, amico and auri, which is Latin for "friend of gold". Two days ago, the origin of the name I looked up was Golding. Apparently, it comes from the Anglo Saxon for son of Goldwin — Goldwin means, friend of gold.'

Helene shook her head slowly.

'I think I've missed something here Emma. You were in banking, right?'

Emma nodded.

'What the hell were you wasting your time there for? You, my little Orchid, are an absolute gem. That is detective work worthy of Sherlock Holmes himself.'

She turned to Smoke and Gypsy.

'Are you ready to meet if this comes off?'

'Yes, we've been ready since Howard. Same set up and IDs. The real Mr and Mrs Smith are still enjoying our hospitality in the Lancashire Pennines, I believe.'

'Good. Harry, you and the boys good to go?'

'Raring, I would say.'

'Okay. Let's hope our Mr Golding swallows the rest of the bait and sets up a meet.'

'That's not all, boss.'

Helene raised an eyebrow.

'Jack Sparrow has been working on an algorithm to determine where our snuff club member might log in next.'

Helene looked at Chris with a frown.

'I know I said humans were not that random, but are they really that predictable?'

'In this case, I think he is. He definitely has a favourite coffee shop in Camden, and Saturday afternoon is his favourite time, particularly when the weather is good.'

'When the weather is good? You've put the weather data into your algorithm.'

Before Chris could answer, Emma jumped in again.

'Yeah, Jack likes mathematical modelling. Me, I'm more of a "let's sneak in the back door and rummage around" kind of girl.'

'So, what do you have in mind?'

Chris answered.

'Boss, we figured that' — he glanced at Emma — 'we'd like to go over to Camden and see if we can spot him.'

'I'm not sure that's a good idea, you aren't trained officers, and, in any case, you have no idea what this guy looks like.'

'I can't imagine there will be too many there with a laptop and besides, we can take a picture on his camera.'

'You can take a picture on his camera?'

'Yes, on the laptop. He logged into the site at lunchtime from the City and Emma uploaded some code. We now control his webcam. Once we know who he is we can keep an eye on him.'

'I thought the light came on when the camera comes on.'

'Boss, we really need to sit down together sometime and get you into this century. I disabled the light. It's not difficult. Not only can we take a picture on his camera, we can get a screenshot to show what he's looking at. We get him and we might just be able to get the others involved.'

Helene looked at the rest of the team.

Jason held up his hands in a gesture of acceptance.

'I can go with them if you think we have enough on these guys already. Pull him in and see where we go from there.'

'We have no evidence at all that they've carried out the murders, but with what they are posting and the fact they are taking money, we certainly have enough for conspiracy to commit and encouraging. Those two things alone will put them away. Be absolutely sure. I don't want you pulling in some kid on Skype to his granny in Australia. Ruth, you go with them too.'

She looked at the assembled group. They all looked how she felt, dog-tired. They were all putting in long hours to bring this case to a conclusion. The work was paying off. The owner of the blue van, Bridgedale, realising he had little hope of getting off scot-free had cut a deal for a reduced sentence.

While he couldn't offer any information on the end users, he did give them the location of the house where the girls were taken; a property undergoing extensive reservation, isolated but relatively accessible. Unfortunately, the property had recently been gutted by fire, thought to have been started by a halogen lamp left on by the builders and placed too close to some kitchen cabinets. Helene suspected that was not a coincidence. The property owners were on an extended world cruise; the team were still trying to contact them.

Bridgedale had no idea of who had supplied the girls. He'd been told where to park and when. Another van had pulled up alongside, transferred the girls through the side door and driven off. He didn't remember the make and certainly didn't take a note of the registration. Yes, it was white.

At the moment, the investigation seemed to be stalled in the middle with no means of connecting the dots at either end. Perhaps the proposed operation this afternoon would shed further light on the case. In the meantime, they just had to work methodically and consistently.

'Emma, see if you can set up a meeting with this supplier then?'

'I already did on the off chance you would ask. 6 p.m., Captain Kidd, Wapping High Street.'

Before Helene could say a word, Smoke answered.

'I know it, we'll be there.'

~§~

Hazelton settled down with his Americano, screw what Anthony said. He liked his coffee strong and black and it would stay that way. The cafe was busy today; his favourite table occupied by what he guessed to be a mid-thirties couple. He'd grab a table here and wait until they'd gone so he could sit at what he now considered his own personal table. Even though he knew that there was no such thing, it irked him that someone else was sitting at it.

Things were going well with the snuff club. There were any number of clients wanting to invest. When Hendricks first proposed the idea, he thought he'd lost his mind, but he could now see Hendricks was something of a visionary with this idea.

After setting up his VPNs and relays, he logged into the site to check for messages. As when he had been startled by Hendricks in this very spot in the early days, Hazelton found the outside world disappearing as he focused on the task in hand.

Five more messages to read; the first from a web SEO company telling him they could rank the site number one on Google. Holy shit, how stupid did they get? Clearly this was a site which was not one to be indexed by Google, or any other search engine if it came to that, and it certainly didn't want to be number one. What did they think they would use as keywords, murder, death, and we did it?

The second email came from a General offering a share in the $6.3 million dollars he'd found in an abandoned bank. How did these people find the site? They clearly had the intelligence of a toilet brush.

The third email, well, that was more like it. Someone wanted to buy in. He fired off the standard response with the buy-in price. If they were serious, they would be back, if not, oh well, shit happens.

The final two emails were from recently joined members wanting to know when they could expect some action. Soon gentlemen, soon. As with all good things, you must wait.

Emails answered or deleted as necessary, he looked and noticed the couple were about to leave his table. He reached to close the screen on his laptop and saw a pop-up appear.

"Smile you are on Candid Camera."

'What the fuck?'

He became aware of someone approaching; it was the couple who now stood right in front of him.

The man smiled and held up a badge.

'Hello. I'm DC Burns and this is DS Cannon and those two over there are right now taking an image of your hard drive so don't try to do anything silly. I'm arresting you on suspicion of conspiracy to commit murder and encouragement — '

Hazelton jumped to his feet and then collapsed as his knees gave way.

~§~

He landed heavily on the bench and Ruth grabbed hold of him before he toppled onto the floor.

She looked up at Burns.

'Clearly they've been teaching some new arrest techniques since I went to training school. You're going to have to show me that one or are you one of those Jedi the boss was on about? I could have done with something like that on a few arrests, I can tell you.'

Jason laughed.

'You have much to learn, my young Padawan.'

'Jason, I haven't got a bloody clue what you are talking about. Now give me a hand to sit this lump back up and wait for him to come round.'

~§~

Once inside the Starbucks, Hendricks spotted Casey Hazelton out on the terrace, sitting at a different table from usual. That wouldn't please him. Never mind, perhaps another ridiculously strong black coffee would appease him. Hendricks ordered the drinks and watched as the barista took his time over each order. Why did it take so long? He was making a drink for goodness sake, not building Rome. It took less time to get a haircut than buy a coffee.

Finally, his own order was called out, "Andrex". Oh, for goodness sake, it wasn't a difficult name. Why did these people have so much trouble getting it right? Perhaps he should write his name on the cup himself, but then they would probably mangle the pronunciation anyway, so what was the point?

He grabbed the drinks with a glare at the barista who had already moved on to the next order in the caffeine production line. He made his way towards the terrace, managing to stop the door from closing with his foot as it swung shut behind a departing customer. He glanced through the window and froze.

He'd looked out in time to see Hazelton collapse onto the table in front of a man and woman who were clearly holding up some sort of identification. The woman reached out to Hazelton to save him from rolling onto the floor.

To Hendricks, this all happened in slow motion. He had time to look at each of them in turn as if they were participants in a still life tableau.

He removed his foot from the door and stepped cautiously backwards trying to merge into the crowd. He placed Hazelton's Americano on an empty table and made his way to the main entrance; the green tea would go with him and help calm him so he could work out his next move.

~§~

'As I was saying, Mr Gold — '

'Please, call me Don.'

'— as I was saying, Don, our operation is for high end clients. The girls have to be the best available. Our clients will not settle for second best. They have a liking for Asian girls in particular, young ones.'

Unlike Charlie Palmer, Golding did not have a penchant for meeting in locations suitable for Hollywood gangster movies, often opting for a local pub in which to conduct his business. On this occasion, the Captain Kidd public house on the High Street in Wapping had been favoured. Golding varied his meeting places, but Captain Kidd was one of his favourites, especially in good weather. An outside terrace overlooking the Thames kept the conversations more private and there was something satisfying about conducting illicit business overlooking the pontoon belonging to the Thames River Police.

'You mentioned in your response, the possibility of an ongoing arrangement — Daniel, was it?'

'Yes.'

'Well, Daniel, maybe I can help you in your little enterprise, and maybe I can't. How do I know you are who you say you are? I don't know you from Adam. For all I know, you could be the filth.'

'I could and that is for you to decide. You might have gathered from my accent, I'm not from around here, but ask around Manchester. Someone there will vouch for me.'

Golding studied the man opposite for several seconds, before taking a swig of his Old Brewery Bitter.

'I don't know anyone from Manchester, Daniel, and if you give me a name of someone there who could vouch for you, I'll have the same problem, I don't know them from Adam either. So that leaves me still not knowing anyone from Manchester.'

Golding kept a close watch on the man opposite and was startled when he rose to his feet abruptly and downed the last of his gin and tonic.

'You do now. Sorry to have wasted your time, but while we are on the subject, how do I know you aren't the law?'

The man reached into his jacket and pulled out a business card.

'If you change your mind, give me a call, but don't leave it too long. My clients want action now, not in a few weeks.'

The well-dressed man turned and left, stopping on the way out to collect an equally well-dressed brunette from a nearby table. Several of the customers turned their heads to watch as she passed by.

Golding held the card for several seconds after the couple had gone from sight, before reading it.

Daniel Smith

Nothing else, other than a phone number.

This intrigued Golding. Never before had anyone walked out from a meeting with him so soon; that usually came when a price couldn't be agreed. The man clearly valued discretion which made Golding think he would be someone with whom he could do business. If only he knew something about him.

He tapped the card on the table, took another drink from his glass. On the other hand, this could be a fortuitous event.

CHAPTER TWENTY

He made a decision. As much as it irked him to do so after the warehouse incident, he would give Palmer a call, he had contacts in Manchester. Perhaps he could shed some light on this Daniel Smith.

~§~

'That was short and sweet, hon.'

Gypsy linked arms with Smoke as they passed through the seemingly old bar. Captain Kidd occupied a former warehouse and gave the appearance of an establishment much older than its thirty or forty years. Amazing what some beams and a wooden floor can do for ambience.

As they passed through the small courtyard entrance, Smoke responded.

'He questioned my legitimacy, suggested it could be a sting. I switched it around and left him. He's got my card; he'll be in touch.'

Gypsy looked sideways at her companion.

'How can you be so sure?'

'He can smell the money, honey. He's cautious, but he's hooked.'

'I wish I had your confidence. What if he doesn't call?'

Smoke shrugged.

'Then we have to tell the boss we gave it our best shot.'

CHAPTER TWENTY-ONE

As when Bridgedale was interviewed, Helene observed on the monitor. This time they weren't dealing with someone who had no fear of the law, this guy was clearly scared. He fidgeted nervously at the desk while a PC stood watch over him, waiting for Ruth to enter the room.

He was not the only one waiting with eager anticipation. This man set up a website offering the chance to take another's life for the payment of what was quite a princely sum. Perhaps this interview would allow them to round up all those involved in the deaths of the young victims. Although Helene had been surprised in the past, she couldn't see this quivering wreck as a killer. He didn't seem the type, more schoolboy than scum. Still, he had been caught red-handed logged into the site and answering emails.

Ruth entered the room and Hazelton visibly jumped.

Helene watched as Ruth logged into the secure digital network and informed Hazelton that the interview was being recorded digitally, both on audio and video.

He quickly scanned the room and for the first time, spotted the camera discreetly tucked away in a corner of the ceiling.

She then reminded him he was still under caution and he had a right to a solicitor being present.

'I don't need a solicitor, we did it.'

'Did what Casey? You don't mind being called Casey, do you?'

He shook his head.

'We set up the site.'

Ruth slid the screenshot across the table, clearly showing the website back end and Hazelton's image taken by the webcam.

'This site.'

'Yes.'

'Who's we?'

Hazelton looked up sharply.

'You haven't arrested Anthony?'

'Who is Anthony?'

Hazelton slapped his palm on his forehead.

'Anthony Hendricks. I knew this would happen. I knew it from the start he would wriggle away. He does it to people all the time.'

Ruth stayed quiet and let him ramble on.

'I told him this would get us into trouble, but it's not us is it? It's me, just me. He's buggered off and left me to carry the can. He wasn't home when you got there, was he? I never should have trusted him. This was all his idea. I just went along with it because I thought we could have a bit of fun.'

He stopped talking and looked up at Ruth again.

'So, this was your idea of fun was it?'

She showed him pictures from the mass grave.

Hazelton paled.

'I don't know anything about those.'

'Really? These are the young girls your "clients" murdered.'

'Murdered? What are you talking about? We haven't done anything apart from set up a website. Sure, Anthony rented a property, but as for murder, we haven't done a thing. We took money from clients but that's it. You can't pin murder on us because we didn't do that.'

'You were going to though, weren't you?'

'You can't prove what we were going to do, and I don't for one moment think Anthony meant to go through with it.'

'You don't? So why did he rent a house to use?'

'Well, that is just Anthony isn't it? Impulsive.'

'So, you are asking me to believe you set all this up for a bit of fun, you didn't kill anyone, and you never intended to?'

'We didn't kill anyone. No one did. You can take my DNA, whatever you need. I don't know anything about any murder.'

Sure of his ground now, Hazelton stopped being the angst-ridden person at the start of the interview and started to get cocky. Helene had seen it many times before. Whatever was thrown at him, he was sure either they couldn't prove it, or money could make it go away. Why did some people believe laws only concerned others?

'What about the "ultimate control" you mentioned?'

'That? That was just a bit of bull we put on there as a teaser.'

Ruth kept his gaze.

'And you expect me to believe that?'

'Quite frankly, I don't care what you believe we were going to do. We didn't do anything, and you can't prove the rest.'

Ruth closed the folder and leant back in her chair.

'It's a pity you didn't look into that before you started all this.'

'What do you mean?'

'A list of everyone you've taken money from.'

'That's not possible, my files are encrypted.'

'Yes, I believe Emma mentioned that.'

'Who the hell is Emma?'

Ruth smiled.

'She's the one who kept tabs on every move from inside your site. She's the one who noted times, dates and locations of every coffee shop from where you logged on. She's the one who uploaded a file from your own site to take that picture with your computer's camera, and she's the one who knows every little thing you have done.'

'You're bluffing.'

Ruth opened the folder again and pulled out a list of names. She handed it to Hazelton.

'How did —? I mean — that's not possible.'

'Here's another bit of bad news for you. Conspiracy to commit murder doesn't require a murder to be committed. The act of conspiracy is the offence in itself. The same applies to assisting or encouraging an offence to be committed. It looks like your Anthony has dropped you right in it. Maybe you would like to tell me about him.'

Hazelton appeared to make a decision.

'I need to see your SIO.'

'Sorry?'

'Your SIO — Senior Investigating Officer.'

'Yes, I know what an SIO is. The question is what do you know about them and why do you want to talk to her?'

'Because it would appear that eighteen months of work is about to go down the pan. Let me introduce myself properly. I'm Casey Hazelton attached to the National Crime Agency.'

~§~

Helene swore as Hazelton announced his identity. She would of course check out his credentials, but she had no reason to doubt he was telling the truth and they had just arrested an undercover operative of the NCA; the department responsible for investigation of crimes requiring specialists in a variety of disciplines. Effectively, they worked for the same boss, albeit with somewhat different remits.

Helene directed Ruth to stop the interview and return Hazelton to the cell until she could unravel this monumental cock-up. Not only would it appear they were back to square one in their own investigation, but they had screwed up an NCA operation into the bargain.

What Helene couldn't fathom at the moment was why someone of Hazelton's financial standing would be working for the NCA.

She picked up the phone and dialled. This was one conversation she didn't want to have.

~§~

Helene motioned Hazelton to take a seat in her office.

'Drink?'

'Black coffee please.'

Helene spoke into the intercom to order two black coffees.

'A fellow psychopath.'

Helene frowned.

'Apparently, black coffee drinkers are psychopaths.'

'Ah, that does explain a lot.'

They waited in uncomfortable silence until the coffees arrived then both spoke at the same time.

Hazelton laughed nervously.

'After you.'

Helene smiled and spoke again.

'I'm sorry about your case but I don't quite understand what you were doing with this website.'

Hazelton rubbed his chin with one hand.

'Where to start? Okay. I've known Hendricks for a few years. We started our financial careers at the same bank. While I was there, I discovered some irregularities. Nothing to do with Hendricks but one of the senior partners. It was well hidden, and I wasn't sure at first if I was making a mistake, but I decided someone needed to look at it and decide what could be done.'

Hazelton noticed Helene was frowning again.

'Sorry, I need to explain this to justify how we got here.'

She motioned for him to continue.

'I couldn't approach any of the partners, so I decided to report it to the what was then the National Crime Squad. After passing on the information, the partner was arrested and found guilty of embezzlement. I was offered a position with the squad which I turned down, but I did agree to help them with future cases wherever possible. Officially, I'm now a consultant and they are now the NCA.'

'I did wonder why someone with your wealth was tied up in a case like this.'

'Yeah, well, the truth is the NCA have been after Hendricks for some time. I have to confess, at one time I really liked the guy, said what he thought and damn the consequences. Then I realised that he actually didn't care about anyone but himself, and when I left the bank to start out on my own, we kind of drifted apart. Finance isn't a big world, and we did cross paths frequently, but we never had the same relationship we'd had at the bank.'

'You said the NCA have been looking at Hendricks?'

'Yes. They've long suspected him of insider dealing and tax evasion but have never been able to work out how he was doing it and how he was getting the money out without being noticed. HMRC looked into his finances on more than one occasion and he seemed squeaky clean but somehow, he's managing to get money through the system without paying tax.

'Then out of the blue he called me about this so-called snuff club. He needed my internet expertise and apparently, I'm the only one he could trust. He knows I'm something of a control freak which is how he thinks he sold it to me, the ultimate control.'

'Ah, yes.'

Hazelton nodded.

'Yes, not a pleasant thought at all especially as he believes I'm capable of doing that sort of thing. Anyway, I turned him down flat but then I realised that's how he does it. He sets up these organisations, uses fictitious clients to invest in them and moves the money into shell companies that on the surface are not linked to him in any way. I believe his plan with the snuff club was that at some point we would be blackmailed by one of the fictitious investors and coerced into handing over the money. Only it would be Hendricks doing the blackmailing. Any real clients we had, and I need to point them out to you because we have several, wouldn't say a dicky bird. Why would they? They're committing conspiracy to murder, as your sergeant so clearly pointed out. Anyway, the money vanishes from our account and Hendricks once again gets his money tax free. The blackmailer vanishes from the face of the earth because he never existed in the first place taking the laundered money and that of several others into the bargain.'

'Are you sure he wasn't serious about killing?'

'I'm not at all sure. He's a bit of an oddball, money can buy anything as far as he's concerned, and he bores easily so it is possible this was for real, the rest is just a theory.'

'And what about you?'

'What about me?'

'Do you think money can buy anything?'

'Yes, but that doesn't mean I think it should, which is why I took this job in the first place. I do have some morals you know.'

Helene sipped at her coffee and wagged her forefinger while she swallowed.

'There is something that's been bugging me. I read the arrest report and when my officers spoke to you, you collapsed.'

Hazelton nodded and smiled.

'Hendricks was there. When that message flashed up on the screen I glanced around, as you would when someone says smile, you are being filmed. I saw Hendricks in the open doorway, about to come out onto the terrace. I could have shown my credentials there and then, but that would have given the game away to Hendricks, so I did what he probably thought I would do if ever I was arrested, I fainted. I was still hopeful we could salvage the case.'

'You may still be able to. He doesn't know why you were arrested, does he?'

'I presume not.'

'You could say it was in relation to a trade you made, and it turned out to be a malicious complaint.'

'Possibly, but I don't think he'll go near the snuff club, or me for a while. Having said that, there is a significant amount of money invested.'

'How did you know which investors were real and which were Hendricks?'

'Like I said, he's not that tech savvy. Even when I explained to him the importance of using different places, he didn't. All the fake investors had different email addresses but came from just two IPs. The chances of that are so slim, it had to be him.'

'You and Emma should have a talk.'

'I'd love to. I want to know how she got past the encryption.'

'I'll set it up. In the meantime, we'll take you back to Camden. I'm afraid it will be in the back of the van again. The location of this place is only known to those who work here.'

This time it was Hazelton's turn to frown.

'Who exactly are you?'

'We have the same bosses, and that's all I can tell you.'

~§~

'See, I told you he was hooked. He's come good. Apparently, there's a shipment of girls coming in from Hong Kong next week. He wants to meet to discuss terms.'

Gypsy stuck her tongue out at her partner. As a married couple they made a formidable undercover team for Her Majesty's Revenue and Customs Investigative Branch, still their official employers, and on secondment to the Invidia team, but everyone knew the secondment was permanent, unless the team disbanded, or they were forced to leave for some operational reasons. Gypsy hoped not. She liked her new boss. The old one wasn't too bad, but this one had something special about her. She was approachable, efficient, talented and pretty good looking too. Even though Gypsy wasn't that way inclined, she could still appreciate the beauty in another woman, and this one had plenty.

Gypsy frowned.

'Either he has another way of bringing them here, or he's telling porkies, hon. The ship is in the hands of the Hong Kong Police, remember.'

'Oh, you know what these guys are like, we saw it all the time in our last job. They like to brag about what they have when really, they are only telling us what they might be able to get. He wants to meet at a different venue this time, The Prospect of Whitby.'

'Where's that?'

'It's just behind the Shadwell Basin. The only thing is' —

Smoke paused and compressed his lips.

— 'he wants me to come alone this time.'

'Honey, I don't think' —

Smoke kissed her on the lips to stop her from talking.

'It's fine. It's a public house. I'll be in view all the time. It went fine with Howard didn't it? This could be the break we've been waiting for, Kat.'

Gypsy had returned to being a natural red head, which shimmered in the light as she shook her head.

'I didn't feel the same about Howard. This guy's a sleaze ball and I don't trust him one bit. I don't think you should go alone.'

'You worry too much. It'll be fine.'

Smoke mulled it over for a moment.

'Look, if it makes you feel any better, take the bike. There'll be somewhere to park and keep an eye on the entrance. If it all kicks off, I can always jump on the back.'

'Do you think it will?'

'No, but there's no harm in having contingency plans is there?'

They had done scores of these operations before, but she had a bad feeling about this one. There was nothing she could put a finger on; that in the stomach feeling, the just out of reach thought, the sixth sense of danger all investigators seem to develop. She couldn't understand why Dan wasn't feeling it too. Maybe he was too close to the job to notice and too eager to please the boss on their first case. She would take the bike and at the first sign of trouble they would be out of there, investigation or not.

~§~

Smoke could see Gypsy leaning against the wall along the road, cigarette in hand; her Harley Davidson parked at the kerb. Every inch the biker chick. To the casual observer that's exactly what she was, a biker chick who'd stopped for a smoke.

Cigarettes can be a useful tool. Asking for a light can be a great way to talk to someone who would otherwise be suspicious of an approach, and they can be used as an excuse to loiter somewhere, as Gypsy was doing now. The less than casual observer would notice she never inhaled; Gypsy didn't smoke.

Smoke ignored her. You never knew who might be watching, and as the instructions were clear, 'come alone', you could bet your bottom dollar someone would be keeping an eye on him; wherever they were, they were not being obvious and he couldn't be either so he refrained from anything more than a casual glance of the surroundings.

Unlike its counterpart along the road, The Prospect of Whitby was an old establishment, dating back to 1520. Previously a notorious den of smugglers, thieves and pirates, these days it occasionally entertained more respectable celebrities, although Smoke felt Golding to be firmly established in the former group.

He made his way to the terrace overlooking the Thames, where Golding was waiting at a table. On the way in but without making it obvious, Smoke scanned the other tables for any sign of Golding's minders but no one obvious jumped out at him, although there were one or two people at the bar who had their back to the room. Maybe he had come alone after all.

'I took the liberty of getting you a drink, G and T wasn't it?'

Smoke nodded then shook hands with Golding.

'So, I understand you might have something for me?'

Golding wagged his finger.

'Tut tut, Daniel. Don't be so eager to rush into business. Take a moment to relax, savour the atmosphere, enjoy a few moments to reflect by the river.'

Smoke looked out across the Thames. It must have been close to high tide; the river lapped against the pilings supporting the terrace, tripping up and down the steps leading to the inn. Smoke wondered what it was like in the old days; probably far more intense and cut-throat than it was now. He took another sip of his drink.

The two men remained silent, staring across the water.

'You're right Mr — Don. This is just what the doctor ordered.'

The two chatted about world affairs for some time as they drank. Golding insisted on going to the bar for a second round, even though he'd bought the first. Smoke saw him speak briefly to a man seated there, a broad backed man he had noted earlier; still facing the bar and not quite visible in the mirror behind the inevitable array of spirit bottles and mixers adorning the shelves. The conversation seemed casual and nothing more so he didn't give it a second thought.

They were well into their second, before Golding broached the subject of the meeting.

'Well, Daniel. I've done a lot of asking around and no one in London seems to know you. So, I asked a business associate to check you out in Manchester. You were right you are known there, but no one has heard from you for a while.'

Smoke smiled and raised his glass to Golding.

'I'm impressed, Don. I like a person who doesn't take things at face value. Of course they haven't seen me. I haven't been in Manchester for some weeks now. I'm here.'

'Why's that, Daniel? You were quite a somebody up there. Why would you give that up? What brings you down here? Surely the competition here is far more intense?'

'Let's say, I was getting a little heat, and thought I'd do a bit of business down here for a while. Let things cool off a bit. I like that you are asking these questions. It gives me a — a — feeling' — Smoke shook his head. He felt sleepy — 'a feeling of ...'

He became aware of someone else at the table. A well-built, round faced man, balding, wearing glasses. He pulled the face into focus.

'Hello Daniel, or should I say, Smoke. You're doing well for yourself I must say. The last time I saw you, now, let me see, that would be that time I was arrested for possession with intent, wasn't it? But of course, you were arrested too. You must have had as good a lawyer as me, son, to be on the streets so soon.'

Smoke struggled to recall the name; he struggled to recall anything. Bastards must have drugged him. Palmer, that was it, Charlie Palmer.

The last thing he remembered was being bundled out of the pub, along an alleyway to some steps, then into a RIB moored alongside the pub wall. He heard someone say, 'yes, he's fine. Just had one over the odds, that's all.'

~§~

'I need to speak to a detective.'

The civilian desk clerk looked up from the report on the desk and reached for her notepad.

'If I could just take a few details, sir, then I can pass on your — '

'I won't talk to anyone but a detective.'

'I'll take this, Sally.' The speaker turned to the man at the counter. 'Detective Chief Superintendent Brandon. How can I help?'

The man's shoulders slumped. The reality of it all flooding into him.

'I — I killed someone.'

Brandon put his hand on the man's shoulder.

'You do not have to say anything. But it may harm your defence if you do not mention when questioned something which you later rely on in court. Anything you do say may be given in evidence. Do you understand?'

The man dropped his head then nodded.

'You are not under arrest at this time and you have the right to legal representation at any time if you so wish. As you are not under arrest you are free to leave at any time, but I must warn that given the nature of what you have just said, doing so may lead to your arrest. With that in mind, do you wish to continue?'

The man mumbled a yes.

'Would you like to wait for legal representation?'

The man looked at Brandon.

'It won't make any difference. I did it.'

Brandon nodded.

'Sally, we need an interview room and you better find me a trained interviewer. Once you've done that, please make a record of what was said here.'

Sally buzzed them through. 'Take room one. I'll call upstairs and see who is free.'

Detective Superintendent Brandon led the man through the door and into the bowels of Bethnal Green Police Station.

CHAPTER TWENTY-TWO

'Not my problem, Donald, my son. You got yourself into this now it's up to you to get yourself out of it.'

The man Palmer knew only as Smoke, lay unconscious in the basement of the shabby house where the girls had been kept before Golding sold them on. Golding still remained unaware that Palmer and the buyer were in it together. Had he known, it's doubtful he would be quite as comfortable having Palmer in the property.

'I'm no killer, Charlie. I do a lot of things, but I've never taken a life.'

Palmer almost wanted to scream in his face that's exactly what he had done when he sold the girls, but he wasn't about to let Golding know he had any involvement in their fate. Technically, he hadn't, he was far too clever for that. Palmer had distanced himself nicely, while still making a tidy profit, and if the rozzers ever came sniffing around, he had what the politicians called plausible deniability. Ironic really, given that at least one politician was in it up to their neck and likely there were more.

Now, a golden opportunity presented itself for him to get rid of a proverbial thorn from his past while keeping his hands clean at the same time. Although he had no evidence, he knew Smoke must somehow be involved in law enforcement, which department, he had no idea and quite frankly he didn't care. His suspicions came from the fact that since the arrest he'd not heard a whisper about any court case involving Smoke. Okay, his real name was unknown but that didn't matter. Anyone being tried for selling heroin with a street value of a quarter of a million pounds was bound to be in the news, and there had been nothing. Unless of course he'd made a deal but Palmer didn't think so. This whole thing smelled like a sting operation and this man was the law.

As for his own part in the drugs case, his lawyer had cast sufficient doubt on the circumstances of the arrest to cause the CPS to drop the charges. Good man - and that is exactly why Charlie paid him so handsomely.

The fact this man was now dressed smartly, walking the streets and as far away from being a Hells Angel as was possible, only served to confirm his suspicions. Golding was going to have to step up and get rid of him, one way or another, or he would get rid of them both.

'Listen. I don't care how you do it, or where, but you don't have a choice. He can identify us, Donald.'

'Can't one of your — '

'Oh, I see. You want me to be involved so that when it all goes pear-shaped, you walk away smelling of roses and I'm the one left to carry the can. Not going to happen, Donald. Sort it quickly or nasty things are going to happen. Now if you don't mind, I'm going to get the fuck out of here and leave you to it.'

Golding stared at the door after Palmer slammed it shut behind him. He was a lot of things, but cold-blooded killer wasn't one of them. He needed time to think, to find a way out of this mess.

Buying the girls had been Palmer's idea in the first place. Then he didn't want them, and Golding had to take a lot less for them than he'd planned from another buyer. Then along comes this guy, answer to all his prayers, wanting to buy Asian girls and he turns out to be the law. At least, that's what Palmer was suggesting.

He needed to sleep on this and clear his head. Whoever he was, he'd be secure enough in the basement. What could he do down there? The door was locked, and his feet and hands were zip-tied. No way was he going anywhere.

Golding slipped quietly out of the door. If the worse came to the worst, he would leave the guy where he was. He could deny all knowledge, force the door to make it look like someone else had taken him there. Maybe that was the answer.

~§~

Helene listened as Gypsy spoke, her voice on the verge of breaking down, but not quite there yet. She must appear calm for Gypsy's sake. She had to keep this grounded to avoid Gypsy becoming hysterical. She was calm, relatively speaking. Helene had always been able to maintain a cool head, be analytical and think things through when it all went wrong. Rising to this rank as quickly as she did would never have happened if she had been one who was open to panic.

'So, the last time you saw him was when he entered the pub?'

'Yes. I waited outside for an hour, and when he didn't come out, I went in to see if I could find him. He wasn't there.'

Helene's mind swung into gear.

'Did you see Golding go in?'

'No, he must have already been inside, but I didn't see him come out either.'

'Any other exits?'

'There's an alleyway to the side, but that comes out on the same street and I don't know if there is access to it from inside.'

'Could you have missed them coming out?'

'No. I had my eyes on the entrance the whole time.'

'What's the address?'

'Prospect of Whitby, Wapping Wall. I only know the street name because I was looking at the sign for an hour. It's on the banks of the — shit — shit.'

'What?'

'I did lose sight of the entrance for a few seconds when the bus went past. That alleyway to the side, I can see along it now. It leads to the river.'

'Stay there. I'm going to round up Harry and the boys, just in case. We'll be over as soon as we can. In the meantime, don't move, don't call him, but let me know if he calls you.'

She placed her first call.

'Emma, I want you to get a location for Smoke's cell phone. Urgent. Don't call it, just locate it. I can't explain.'

She hung up and dialled Harry. Damn. This was not good.

~§~

Helene remained deep in thought as Ruth weaved her way through the evening traffic. Even with the blues and twos, progress remained heavy going. People did their best to move out of the way, but it wasn't always that easy on a crowded street. Helene had to admit to herself, she always enjoyed blue light runs. Something immensely satisfying to the rebel inside occurred when driving the wrong side of a keep left sign, cautiously passing through a red light, or seeing the flash of a speed camera, knowing that as long as the task justified breaking the rules, there would be no repercussions. A potential life or death situation certainly met those criteria. Now she had to be content to watch someone else getting that satisfaction.

She hoped Gypsy was mistaken, that Smoke had gone with Golding to another location, but Gypsy was a seasoned undercover officer herself, most definitely not the panicking type. Undercover operations can go south very quickly, and Helene hoped this was a false alarm.

Helene's phone rang, breaking her train of thought, and she grabbed it from the centre console. Cup holders were rarely used for the purpose they were intended; phone holder and a receptacle for loose change being their primary role in many vehicles.

'Yes, Emma?'

Helene listened briefly.

'Shit! Okay — Thanks, Emma.'

Ruth glanced at her boss questioningly.

'You need to keep this to yourself when we reach Gypsy. Smoke's phone ceased transmitting to the cell towers just over an hour ago. As far as Emma can tell, they were on the river at the time, upstream from the Prospect. It was sudden with no shutdown message to network, so it wasn't switched off.'

'Fuck! — if you'll pardon the expression, boss.'

'My thoughts exactly. Jason alerted the River Police to look out for Golding's boat, that's if he's stupid enough to use his own boat. Mobile phones do not jump into rivers on their own; this is no false alarm.'

Her phone rang again.

Helene listened with a frown.

'Okay. Thanks.'

She turned to Ruth.

'That was the obs team. Golding's car is where he left it, still at the Prospect. So, if his car is still parked there, he must have other transport unless he intends to stay on the river, but where? Anyway, I can't see him doing that. He must have sussed Smoke is undercover. He can't be that dumb to keep him on his own boat, surely?'

'He was dumb enough to use his own passport.'

'He probably didn't see any reason not to. As far as he was aware, no one would be tracing his movements. I don't think he ever thought these girls would end up dead. His sole interest was bringing them in, selling them on. Had it not been for the mass grave, it's doubtful we would have even investigated where they came from in this way. Jeez my head hurts.'

'I'm not surprised.'

Another call interrupted them.

Helene looked at her watch.

'Okay. Thanks.' She took a deep breath. 'That was Jason. He got someone to check, apparently Golding's boat is still at the marina. Which leaves us without a single way to trace where Smoke is, assuming he hasn't really been dumped in the river along with his phone. How much longer?'

'About another fifteen minutes.'

Ruth took another keep left sign on the wrong side and several pedestrians turned to watch the car go by. Ruth hit the brakes as a young woman stepped off the kerb, headphones on and totally focused on her mobile phone; completely oblivious to the unmarked police car now standing two feet away with flashing blue lights in the grill and two-tone siren still announcing its request for right of way. The woman visibly jumped as she finally noted the presence of the car and stepped back smartly onto the pavement.

Ruth said a few choice words under her breath.

'They should be banned for pedestrians too, never mind just drivers.'

She set off again but not before giving the woman a look which told her exactly what she thought of her.

She picked up again on the conversation.

'Okay, assuming they did leave by boat and he's not using his own, then whose boat is he using?'

Helene let out a deep sigh. This was not good at all.

~§~

Ruth turned off the blues and siren as they passed Shadwell Basin and slowed to a more appropriate speed for the road. Even though events suggested Smoke's cover had been blown, it may not have been, and keeping a low profile until they were absolutely sure was the best thing to do.

'Take the next right into Glamis Street and your destination will be on the right.'

Ruth did as the satnav ordered; never having worked in this district she'd entered the address before they left Invidia HQ.

'Whatever did we do before satnav, boss?'

'We learned to read maps and didn't find forty-ton trucks stuck down alleyways, that's what we did.'

Ruth eased up as she crossed over the now defunct lift bridge. Since the 1980s, Shadwell Basin had been isolated from the Thames by a concrete barrier. The bridge remained permanently lowered, a frozen tribute to the once busy docks.

At the far end, Gypsy paced up and down near the bike, close to the wall of one of the numerous apartment blocks that gave the East End docklands a new lease of life. From here, Gypsy could observe The Prospect of Whitby without being too obvious.

She jumped in the back of the car, her motorcycle leathers squeaking on the leather seats.

'Neither of them are in there. I don't know what to do.'

Her voice quavered, on the edge of hysteria but she was just about keeping things together.

'Gypsy, you know this city has more CCTV cameras than any other in the world. Once we have a lead, we'll find him.'

Helene's instinct was to keep the news of the cell phone from Gypsy. She was having enough trouble coping, without that piece of information.

'I knew he shouldn't have gone alone. I had a feeling this was all wrong. We've never done that before, and never been asked. Even when we met Howard, we had a man on the inside. It just did not feel right. Dan thought I was being paranoid. He should listen to me more.'

'We're doing everything we can. Golding's car is still here so we don't know for sure how they are travelling. Wherever he is, it won't be long before we catch up with him.'

Gypsy buried her head in her hands, sobbing quietly.

Ruth glanced at Helene. There was little either of them could say at this moment.

Helene's phone broke the silence.

She listened then hung up. Ruth looked at her questioningly and she shook her head.

'Nothing so far.'

She turned to address Gypsy.

'We are going to take you back to HQ. You can use one of the overnight rooms. There's nothing you can do here. We've got officers covering Golding's car, home address and the boatyard. Harry and some of the lads are also in the area, so if anything turns up, we'll be the first to know. If nothing else, Golding has to come back for his car sooner or later and we'll nab him then.'

'That might be too late.'

'It won't. Golding's no angel, but I don't think he's got it in him to be violent. Besides, we don't know if Smoke has been taken against his will or gone with him voluntarily. He is undercover, after all.'

Even as Helene was saying it, she couldn't think of any reason why he would throw his cell phone in the river, but some things are best left unsaid.

'Why would he do that?'

'I don't know.'

'He would have found a way of letting me know.'

Ruth started the engine and Gypsy put her hand on Helene's shoulder.

'What about the bike?'

'Gypsy! Smoke is missing and you are worried about your bike?'

Gypsy let out a stifled laugh through the tears.

'I suppose once a biker chick, always a biker chick.'

Helene shook her head.

'That's something I've never understood. When I was in uniform, we'd attend an RTC, there would be some slightly mangled, leather-clad guy lying on the ground, and almost always the first words would be, "how's my bike?" What is it with you lot? We'll get a van to collect it in the morning.'

'Boss, I don't want to appear ungrateful, but I'm not leaving it there overnight, so if we can arrange that now?'

Helene shook her head and picked up her phone once again.

~§~

Gypsy remained adamant that she wasn't going anywhere until the van collected the bike. Helene, equally adamant they had to get back to headquarters and Gypsy would be accompanying them. There would be no second option.

The unstoppable force of Helene and the immovable object of Gypsy settled on a compromise that one of the two members of the obs team would keep an eye on the bike, but Gypsy still insisted they wouldn't be moving until he arrived.

The compromise did not fill Helene with glee. Should Golding come back for his car, there would not be time to pick up the obs team member guarding the bike and the obs car would have to go single crew. On the other hand, Gypsy had made it abundantly clear she was going nowhere unless the bike was safe. Helene did not doubt she meant every word. Strong team members were a blessing, but at times like this they could be an absolute pain in the arse and Helene was blessed with a full house of such team members. Still, she wouldn't want things any other way. The female members were particularly strong, almost as if Brandon had compensated for effectively railroading Helene into joining the team by his previous chauvinistic treatment of her. That man had so much to answer for.

Now back at headquarters, Gypsy was equally adamant she would not be going to bed, at least not just yet. As she rightly pointed out, sleep would not be coming anytime soon unless delivered in tablet form.

Although now getting quite late, almost all the investigation team were in the briefing room. After twenty minutes of discussion it was clear that they had nothing. Smoke and Golding's whereabouts were still unknown, as was their direction of travel. A second obs team, despatched to Golding's home address as soon as Gypsy reported Smoke to be missing, confirmed he still hadn't returned, and as far as they could tell the house remained unoccupied. A similar report ensued from the officer now watching over Golding's fishing boat at Gallions Point Marina.

They concluded that calling for an air asset would be non-productive with no solid lead to work with. The Thames River

Police were maintaining a patrol but with Golding's boat under guard, they weren't sure what they were looking for either. Golding had gone to ground somewhere, and Helene hoped Smoke was with him.

CHAPTER TWENTY-THREE

Why did this happen every time he got involved with Palmer? Things would run smoothly, he'd make a bit of money here, do a bit of business there, some legit, like the fishing trips, and some not so much, smuggling booze and fags from France for instance. Palmer then suggests people-trading would be far more profitable and like the mug that he is, he falls for it, hook, line and sinker. He should have just walked away, but no. He has to give it a try because the promise of big money is too much to resist. What was the old adage? If it looks too good to be true, then it is too good to be true.

And now? Now, he had some cop or whatever, tied up in the basement of one of his rentals and not a clue what to do with him. Thank goodness the house was in the name of a holding company; it would take time to trace it back to him. Although, with the way things were going, no doubt they would have made that link by now.

So, what to do next? He couldn't go home, because if this Daniel Smith was the law, they would be at his house, and for the same reason the boat was out of the question. His car remained parked near the pub and would stay there indefinitely, because no doubt that was under observation too.

Things couldn't get that much worse really, unless his minder, Leon, turned out to be a snitch.

As luck would have it, Leon had a spare room, a stroke of good fortune. His missus didn't seem too keen on the idea of putting him up for a couple of nights, but at least it would tide him over until he could decide what to do with the copper, or whatever he was.

He didn't like sleeping in strange beds, not unless they came with some fringe benefits and they were few and far between these days. Come to think of it, they almost always were. Ladies seemed to ignore him pretty much. He never understood that but those were the cards he'd been dealt.

At least the RIB they used had been nicked from the boatyard; that made one less thing to worry about. There was no way that could be traced to him. Besides, Leon and his mate did the nicking; he had no involvement whatsoever.

He had to give Palmer credit for that. Figuring out that the meeting would be at high tide and then using the RIB to escape along the river was a stroke of genius, or so he thought at the time but in hindsight that plan left him with bigger headache; they were clearly onto him and he had no viable transport. It seemed a good idea to sneak out of the pub with this Daniel fella, avoid any colleagues of his but before all this happened, he could have denied any wrongdoing, perhaps say he'd been having a laugh answering the advert. Now? Now he was facing charge of kidnap at the very least.

He would lie low for as long as he could then slip out of the country somehow. He couldn't use his own boat, that was for sure. Maybe Leon could nick another and ferry him across the channel.

He had a thought, one which instantly raised his level of angst. Supposing this Daniel wasn't law, but belonged to one of the gangs? Daniel might have set up Palmer for the drugs, get him out of the way so a rival gang could move in on his turf. But then how did he get away from the cops? He was arrested too, according to Palmer. No, he must be a copper or even HM Customs. That was the only reasonable explanation and one which didn't help him one iota. Kidnapping a member of Her Majesty's law enforcement community was not a good plan under any circumstances. Then again, Palmer got off, so maybe this Daniel wasn't law after all but had a good brief too, and that meant he was a gang member and senior one at that.

His mind whirled, going around in circles with the what-ifs and the maybes; trying to think of a solution now was just impossible. He needed to sleep on it, but sleep wouldn't come because his mind reeled: a right Catch 22 situation. Perhaps another shot of whisky would help. Leon wouldn't mind, would he? Didn't matter if he did, that's what he got paid for, looking after his boss.

~§~

With Smoke missing, none of the team members went home, most only managing to grab snatches of sleep during the night. With only two bedrooms available and Gypsy occupying one of those, people slept at their desks or on the floor. The news so far was there was no news.

Jason hung up the phone and changed that in an instant.

'That was the Marine Unit, boss. They had a call this morning from someone reporting a boat at — ' he looked at his notebook — 'Pier Head. Apparently one of the residents made a 101 call last night to report a bit of an altercation; assessed as R grade by the operator, as the alleged perpetrators left the area before the reporter made the call.

'He rang again an hour or so ago, to say the boat was still on the shore and in danger of drifting away on the tide. Apparently, the original call log makes no mention of a boat, he's adamant he told the operator that the three men arrived on an inflatable. This time they advised him to call the Marine Unit as they are literally a stone's throw away and the incident involves a boat. They checked the area and found a RIB beached at Pier Head. They called the registered owner and as far as he was concerned, it should still be at Gallions Point Marina.'

Helene and Jason spoke in unison.

'Where Golding keeps his boat.'

'Jason, get over there and get a statement from this guy, see if he can give a description of the three men.'

'I don't need to, boss, the Marine Unit did that already. He says he saw two men assisting a third who appeared to be worse the wear for drink. According to the descriptions, that could be Smoke and one of the others is a match for Golding. But the beauty is, they drove away in a van and he got an index number.'

Jason checked his notebook.

'Belongs to a Leon Mills, bit of a rogue and known to do the odd job for Golding. He matches the description of the third man. I've got his last known.'

'Brilliant. Where is this Pier Head?'

'Off Wapping High Street, not far from the pub, just over half a mile.'

Jason put Google maps on the screen and added the aerial view overlay.

'This is the Prospect here' —

He shone the laser pointer on the screen indicating a road near one corner of Shadwell Basin and then moved it a few centimetres to the left.

— 'and this — yes, here. This is Pier Head.'

He adjusted the pointer once more but only by a couple of centimetres.

'And this, here, is the River Police mooring.'

'Right under their bloody noses. Still, they weren't to know. Emma check whether the van pinged any ANPR cameras and see if you can spot anything on the traffic cams. We need to know where they went. I don't have time to ask permission to access the databases, so I'll ask forgiveness later, just get into the system and see what you can find.'

'What time frame?'

'Oh yeah, Jason?'

He consulted his notebook once more.

'The call was logged at 21.35.'

'On it, boss.'

Emma dashed out of the room, preferring to use her own computers rather than the ones in the ops room.

'Ideas anyone?'

The evidence still remained circumstantial, albeit growing stronger by the hour, to the point of being on the verge of overwhelming. Golding's disappearance appeared to confirm their suspicions of his involvement in the human trafficking element.

To move forward they would need to hear what Mills had to say for himself and if Emma could track the van on CCTV.

At least Emma had a rough time period to work with and wouldn't need to trawl through hours of footage.

'Right, let's get to it. Jason, Ruth, you two bring in Mills.'

~§~

The route from Invidia Headquarters to Wapping was becoming familiar to Ruth, although this time they would be going to an address in Mile End, one of Wapping's near neighbours.

Ruth had already developed a liking for working with Jason; technically she was his immediate superior, but the nature of the unit made for more informal arrangements; everyone on first name terms, except the boss.

Ruth had never worked with a Northerner before and found the straight-speaking, say-it-as-it-bloody-is approach, quite refreshing. She could see how some people might find that to be a little too honest, but they were here to do a job not stand for parliament.

Of course, she now worked with not just one, but two Northerners, although she didn't spend as much time with Harry as he was on the 'special ops' side of things. She hoped the whole of the team would adopt their approach; everyone knew where they stood.

Now there was a bit of an odd fish, Harry. He had a quiet way about him, slow, steady, but Ruth recognised the look in his eyes; a man who had seen things, done things, and feared little. All Harry's team all had that look, but Harry especially.

'What made you decide to join Invidia, Jason? I take it you were recruited like the rest of us?'

'Aye. My ACC called me in one day. I thought I was in for a bollocking about something, but Brandon was there. I've never seen an ACC be deferential to a Chief Super before, and then up he gets and leaves us to it. I suspect you had a similar deal and much the same questions. I told him I was sick o' knocking my pan in, only for it to be thrown away by the CPS. Sick o' toe rags gettin' off scot-free. Sound familiar?'

'Not quite the words I used, but I get the gist.'

'I don't suppose you would, with you speaking like the Queen.'

'I'll take that as a compliment.'

Jason laughed.

'You are "job" aren't you? You take what you can, when you can, compliment intended or not. Not like some of the buggers down here.'

'What do you mean?'

'Some of you Southerners.'

'Having trouble fitting in?'

'Nah, not really.'

He turned towards her.

'The one thing I don't get is, when you speak to someone on the tube, or the bus, or in the street, they look at you like you've escaped from a loony bin or something. Do none of you talk to each other down here?'

It was Ruth's turn to laugh.

'Not if we can avoid it. Head down in the paper or a book, although these days it's mobiles that take our attention.'

'Well, I suppose that's cos we're a friendlier bunch up north. We'd talk hind leg off a donkey given half a chance, we would.'

Ruth eased the car into Brokesely Street.

'Do you see what I see?'

Jason sang it out Christmas carol style.

'Don't give up the day job, mate. Yes, I see it. Looks like the intel was right.'

Parked further along the street was a white van bearing the same index number identified as the one belonging to Mills.

Ruth drove past, then parked up. She called the boss.

'The van's here so I'm guessing he's here too — yeah, should be fine.'

She hung up and turned to Jason.

'There's no way out the back?'

'Not as far as I could see on Google Earth. It's a complete block with the gardens back-to-back, no path between them. There's a ginnel at the far end but it's gated and belongs to the houses at that end.'

'There's a what?'

'Ginnel, snicket. What are you looking at me like that for?'

'What the hell is a ginnel and a snicket?'

'It's a — ginnel, you know, passageway.'

'Why the hell didn't you say so?'

'I did. It's not my fault you don't understand English down here.'

'I'm not sure it is! And you got this info from Google Earth?'

'And Street. Cracking tool for sussing locations beforehand.'

'What did we do before good old Google Earth? No, don't answer that. I asked the boss the same about satnav and got a lecture about the old days.'

'Really? She can't be a day over thirty-five.'

Ruth looked sideways at him.

'You angling after a promotion already?'

Jason jumped out of the car.

'Come on. Let's get this done.'

A harassed-looking woman holding a toddler answered the door on the second knock.

'Yeah?'

'Is your husband home?'

'Wot's it gotta do wiv you?'

They both showed their warrant cards - the Invidia version.

'DS Ruth Cannon and DC Burns. We'd like to have a few words with him.'

The woman looked up and down the street before turning back into the house and yelling.

'Lee. Get yer arse down here. It's the filf — again.'

A short while later, a stocky man appeared at the door, dressed in pyjama bottoms and a string vest. His hair looked as though it hadn't been combed since his twelfth birthday, the bags under his eyes, dark and puffy.

'What?'

'Leon Mills?'

'Yeah, what of it?'

Jason got hold of one wrist as he arrested Mills. As Jason suspected, Mills attempted to slam the door shut, but found himself on the floor with one arm behind his back and Ruth bringing the other wrist around to finish the job by putting on the rigid cuffs.

'Now that wasn't very nice was it?'

Mills spat on the pavement.

'Now, now, Lee, less of that.'

The commotion had drawn the woman back to the door and she was now spraying out a string of words that would make a trooper blush.

Whilst the torrent of abuse continued, Ruth and Jason got Mills on his feet.

Ruth called for the van to come for a pickup. Fairly sure they would be making an arrest, the van had followed them to the address and parked around the corner, waiting for such a call.

They bundled Mills into the back. Jason was about to give the driver the signal to leave when movement caught his eye.

Jason waited for a gap in the invective still pouring from the doorway.

'Is there anyone else in the house apart from you and the child?'

'I've got three more kids; not that it's got nuffink to do wiv you.'

'No other adults?'

'No, and I wouldn't tell you if there were.'

'That's what I thought.'

'Ruth, upstairs. Top floor!'

Jason pushed past the woman and into the house.

They clattered up the stairs to the top floor, front bedroom, accompanied by yells of 'Get the fuck outta my house, you got no right. Where's yer warrant? I know my rights.'

Jason flung open the door to the top floor bedroom. Thrown back bedclothes and a depression still visible in the mattress showed this bed was no exception to all the other beds that recently played host to a human body.

'You're seeing things mate. There's no one here.'

The duvet hung off the side of the bed nearest the door, masking the space beneath. As Ruth spoke, she gestured underneath. This was not one of the better games of hide-and-seek either of the two detectives had played in their careers.

She lifted the duvet and bent forward to look underneath. A pair of eyes, as Fitz noted during the earlier briefing, most definitely too close together, peered back at her from between a discarded Buzz Lightyear and an old sock.

'Hello Donald. Fancy seeing you here. We're having a bit of a party down at the nick. Why don't you come and join us? Leon has his ticket already. Free entry, but as always, there is a catch. You might not be leaving anytime soon.'

Jason cautioned and cuffed Golding as Ruth called the boss again.

'You'll never believe who we found hiding under a bed — yep, got it in one. We need another transport ASAP.'

Minutes later, the van containing Mills, drove away. Golding would need to wait for a second set of wheels to collect him. They didn't want him and Mills working out a story on the way back and they couldn't transport Golding themselves, or they would give away their location and the fact it wasn't a normal nick. Besides, they were going to give the house a good going over, in case Golding and Mills had Smoke tied up somewhere inside.

~§~

Helene ended the call and allowed herself a little smile. They now had two suspects for the price of one. What a bonus. Unfortunately, until they got one of them to admit to the abduction, it didn't help them to locate Smoke. If neither prisoner was willing to talk, then perhaps she would let a couple of Harry's boys have a chat with them, persuade them the error of their ways. She did say at the first briefing that she wouldn't allow forced confessions, but a confession wasn't needed; the location of Smoke would do just fine.

She called the Transport section, arranged for a recovery vehicle to collect Mills' van and for a second transport van to be mobilised, advising them this was a significant response call; they could use lights and sirens as they saw fit. She wanted Golding back here as soon as possible. Even so, it would be at least another hour before they returned.

Helene hoped against hope that Golding hadn't done something stupid and out of character. She had never lost an officer under her command over the years, she certainly didn't want this to be the first. She wondered what tipped off Golding that Smoke was a law enforcement officer, indeed, if that was the reason behind his disappearance. It could be something else entirely. Only time and Golding would tell.

Helene returned to her war office to take a step back and look at the problem from a new perspective, to see if they missed anything.

She had been in the office for only a couple of minutes when Emma entered.

'I've got something.'

She brought up a map on Helene's SMART board.

'Okay. Although the traffic cams are ANPR equipped, not all of them catch sight of the vehicle plates in every direction, so we had to do this another way. Fortunately, Jack — I mean Chris — has been working on a little program that helps us spot the same vehicle in the footage, even without a registration, so we don't spend hours trawling through it. Once we feed the parameters in, it alerts us to all similar vehicles within a set time period.'

Helene listened impatiently waiting for Emma to get to the point.

Emma drew breath.

'Anyway, we first picked up the van here, camera 225 on the A1203, but it didn't appear on camera 505 at all. There's about six hundred metres between those cameras. A couple of minutes later a similar vehicle appeared up here.'

Emma pointed to the junction of Cannon Street and Commercial Road.

'This was one of the ones that didn't get the plate because of this car following close behind. You can see they turn left to head west along Commercial Road, then shortly after, the van and the car signal right. They don't take the first street, and the second has bollards blocking the entrance, so they must have turned into this one, Settles Street. Now this is where things become interesting. The van didn't show up when expected on any of the other cameras. We thought either he took a route to avoid them, or he parked up somewhere. Forty-five minutes later he turns up on this camera on Whitechapel Road, here, so it must have parked. From there he goes to his home address.

'Unfortunately, there are no traffic cams in the area where they spent those forty-five minutes, but I did find some CCTV cameras belonging to Tower Hamlets Council and I took the liberty of having a look on their servers. One is very conveniently placed at the end of Settles Street, and even more conveniently it was pointing in the right direction, otherwise we would never have seen this.'

Emma brought up a couple of still images on Helene's screen clearly showing two men carrying a third into a house.

'That's fantastic, Emma.'

'It doesn't stop there.' She showed Helene a clip of a fourth man entering the house.

'So, he had two accomplices?'

'I don't think he's an accomplice, but he must be involved, because Chris spotted this in the footage.'

Emma showed a sequence of video clips showing the same car behind the van in every clip.

'I am reliably informed by Chris, this is a Bentley Mulsanne, a black one.'

'Fuck!'

CHAPTER TWENTY-THREE

'Exactly, boss. Fuck. I think we have "angry man" as Kun would call him.'

'We need to run the index through PNC.'

'I already did. Charles William Palmer. I did an ANPR on his plate, and he tripped this one.'

She showed Helene the image from the camera at the junction of Whitechapel Road and Plumbers Row.

'We ran out of cameras but from the direction he was travelling, I suspect he was going home.'

'You don't have access to PN — oh, of course you do.'

Emma smiled sweetly.

'The government really needs to spend some money on security, you know, and that's how I knew Mills had gone to his home address, you forgot to give that to me in the briefing. So, I took the liberty of checking that too.'

'So, all we need to do is work out which one of these houses is the one where they took Smoke.'

'There are two in the street showing as unoccupied, according to the council tax records. This one I think is the where he'll be; the other is much farther along the street.'

Helene grabbed her phone, called Ruth and apprised her of the situation.

Phone call over, she turned to Emma with a look of puzzlement on her face.

'This piece of software, is this something you dreamed up?'

'Chris, actually. I told you I'm more of a rummage around sort of girl. My software work is to get me in somewhere, that's all. Chris is the thinker. He read a paper on it earlier this year. Thought he would give it a go himself. He's really rather good, but don't tell him I told you.'

'You guys are making me feel old. Half the time I haven't got a clue what you are talking about, so I just nod and smile sweetly.'

'But you do that so well, boss.'

~§~

Ruth watched as the van containing Golding drove away.

'Yes, he's just on his way.'

As she listened, she tapped Jason on the shoulder and indicated he should get in the car. Ruth jumped in the driving seat and started the engine while still listening to Helene. She hung up and held up a finger to stop Jason speaking while she entered the address into the satnav. The time to destination said thirteen minutes, Ruth intended to do it in less.

She put on the blue lights, did a quick three-point-turn, then hit the siren as they reached the main road.

'I thought we were going to search the house?'

'The boss thinks Emma's found where Smoke might be.'

'How the hell? — No, don't tell me. I sometimes think that young lady is capable of casting spells. The less I know about her, the better.'

Ruth laughed.

'Yes, she does seem to have that ability. She tracked' —

She stopped speaking while she negotiated a set of red traffic lights; her total concentration needed for the driving.

— 'yeah, she tracked the van. Spotted a big gap in the timeline and used local CCTV to find where he went.'

'Council CCTV?'

'Yeah.'

'I though those servers were secure?'

'So did the council.'

~§~

Smoke couldn't work out which was worse, the pounding head, the lack of memory or the fact his arms seemed to be glued behind his back. He felt groggy. It was a long time since he'd been on a bender like that, only he couldn't remember being on a bender. He couldn't remember much at all about last night. Except — no, it was too difficult to try to recall anything.

Wherever, he was, it needed a good clean, the place smelled old and damp. He wanted to look around, figure out where he was, but his eyes refused to give him anything more than a blurry image of what appeared to be a wooden staircase.

He didn't have a wooden staircase so what was it doing in his flat and why was Gypsy not there?

He tried to call out, but his voice merely croaked, so he tried to move once again. His legs seemed to be stuck together and would only move in unison; his arms were a different prospect; they didn't seem to want to move at all. None of this made sense.

He had no idea where he could be or why he felt so uncomfortable, and for the moment, the answer would continue to elude him. He drifted back into the relatively cosy darkness.

~§~

As Ruth and Jason pulled up at the address, a Trojan unit, otherwise known to the public as an ARV or Armed Response Vehicle, approached from the opposite end of the street. Easily identifiable by the two yellow discs shown in the windscreen, rear window and one either side in the rear quarter-lights, the vehicle carried a number of firearms for the officers' use, but these were not of interest to them today. The ARVs also carried a "big red key" the colloquial name for an enforcer, the sixteen-kilogram battering ram utilised to open doors when either the occupant wasn't present or was and refused to open the door. Other units also carried them, but this Trojan was the closest and had responded to the call.

One swing of the enforcer and the door flew open. Clearly the owner of the property didn't spend a great deal of money on securing the house but that was to their benefit if this was indeed the location where Smoke was being held. The armed officers entered first and began to search the rooms, calling out Daniel's name rather than his nickname. The property was obviously unoccupied and in a state of what an estate agent may call 'requiring some modernisation'. The ground floor comprised of three rooms and took only moments to clear. A search of the upper two floors also revealed nothing, which left only one place to look, the basement. The door proved to be in the hall, underneath the staircase. This time they didn't need the enforcer as the key was still in the lock.

One of the SCO19 officers led the way with his Glock 17 drawn, the others followed. The officer paused at the bottom of the stairs, scanned the single room then holstered his weapon.

'Over here.'

He led the way to Smoke, still lying where he'd been dumped the night before. Smoke stared at them wide-eyed.

'Smoke?'

Ruth was the first to speak to him.

'You okay?'

'I — I don't know. What happened?'

'We were rather hoping you could tell us that.'

'I don't remember, Kat and I went for a drink, I think. I'm not sure.'

He looked at Ruth with fear in his eyes as he realised Gypsy was not there.

'Kat, where is Kat?'

'She's fine. She's at headquarters, worried sick about you. You've been missing overnight.'

'Why?'

'We were hoping you could tell us that too. We'll take you back and have the doc check you over.'

'You're sure Kat's okay?'

'Yes, she's fine.'

Ruth motioned to Jason to call the boss and give her and Gypsy the good news.

~§~

Helene knocked gently on the door to the bedroom. Gypsy didn't reply, so she checked the handle and found the door to be unlocked. She quietly slipped in and found Gypsy fast asleep on top of the bed, still fully clothed. Not surprising, the poor girl was shattered. Helene felt tempted to leave her there, heaven knows she needed the rest, but she was certain Gypsy would want to hear the news right away. Helene moved to the bed, sat beside her and began softly stroking her hair.

'Gypsy.'

She gave her a gentle shake.

'Gypsy. I have some news.'

She opened her eyes and sat up with a start.

'What? What's happened?'

Her eyes were wide open now, searching Helene's face for a hint of the nature of the news she brought.

Helene smiled.

'They found him, he's fine. They are on the way here now. We'll have the doc give him the once over, but he's okay, if a little groggy. He can't remember much, so the chances are he was drugged. We'll know that for sure after a few tests.'

Gypsy threw her arms around Helene.

'Thank you! Thank you! When can I see him?'

'Hey, we are family; never forget that. You can see him as soon as he gets here.'

She held Gypsy as the tears started.

'I thought I'd lost him. I don't know what I would do without him.'

She held Gypsy close until the sobbing subsided then left her to compose herself before the others got back.

As Helene closed the door behind her, she wiped away her own tears.

CHAPTER TWENTY-FOUR

While Gypsy freshened up, Helene returned to the ops room and gathered everyone together.

'Okay. Many of you will already have heard this but for those of you who haven't, the news is good. Smoke has been found. He seems to be okay and he's on his way back here' —

A loud cheer went up, and Helene held her hands up for silence.

— 'and so is Don Golding, arrested by Ruth and Jason along with a known associate, Leon Mills. I want everyone in the briefing room in thirty minutes. We still have no one fully in the frame for the murders. Now we have Smoke back in the fold, we can get back to concentrating on that. I know it's been a rough night for us all, but I feel we are close to finding the culprits.'

~§~

Helene stood at the front of the room; this would be her brief.

'So, what do we have so far?'

She brought up the points on the SMART board and continued. 'We have Bridgedale, the owner of the van left at the scrap yard. He's insisting his only involvement is in the detention of the girls and disposal of the bodies. He lawyered up once he heard the forensic evidence we have against him, but on the understanding there will be a reduction in sentence, he has been telling us what he knows, which is scant little. The deal was on the proviso of no further evidence coming to light to indicate he was present when the murders took place; we already have sufficient evidence to charge him with joint enterprise. I think he's as guilty as sin, in which case all deals will be off the table. He thinks he has us convinced but he's in for a shock.

'We have positive DNA evidence of the presence of the victims inside his van and evidence linking the vehicle to both scenes. We don't have the footwear, but we do have matching prints at the pillbox and the burial site. We also have him on video saying that only he drives the van, which puts him in the frame for the joint enterprise. We are analysing his phone records to try to establish a link to others, but that takes time.'

Helene saw a movement out of the corner of her eye.

'Yes, Chris? And you don't need to put up your hand, I'm not your teacher.'

Chris looked a little sheepish as he scanned the room while a couple of the team sniggered.

'Erm, it's not going to take that long at all, actually. I have some results if I could ...'

He nodded toward the front of the room.

'Go ahead.'

He took up position beside the SMART board.

'We analysed call data from Bridgedale's phone. One number appeared over the three-night period we believe coincides with the disappearance of three of the victims from the pillbox. The following evening, Bridgedale made a call to that same number, which we, err — that is Emma and me, believe may have been when they discovered Kun missing. This number called Bridgedale again the day after the team found the pillbox. Coincidence? Doubtful, but this is pure conjecture at the moment. For the purposes of this exercise, we labelled this number M1, to avoid getting confused.'

'M1?'

'Yes. Mystery 1.'

The briefing was interrupted by the arrival of Ruth and Jason, to the accompaniment of a round of applause.

Chris waited for the room to settle down.

'What did we miss, Chris?'

'And that concludes what we do next.'

Laughter erupted around the room.

Helene sat fascinated by the contrast between the capable Chris giving the briefing and the meek and mild geek everyone took him for. He was on home territory and showing the confidence of someone who had a complete mastery of their subject, even to the point of being able to deliver a briefing to a bunch of experienced law enforcement officers.

He gave a little smile and waited once again for things to settle down.

He addressed the newly arrived pair.

'I'll tell you the bits you missed once I finish. So, where were we? Oh yes. We looked at the record of M1 and came in for a bit of a surprise. The number was only in use for two weeks, and only ever used to call three numbers, one being Bridgedale's, the others we designated M2 and M3. It also received calls from only two numbers, Bridgedale's, and M3. Our interest initially lay in M2. On the three occasions M1 called M2, M2 then called three other numbers immediately afterwards. Bet you can't guess what numbers come next. I could go on with this but I'm sure you are all familiar with a cascade calling system and you are falling asleep now. What I'm trying to say is we are now up to M33, all from that one number. The interesting thing is that we found several more numbers prior to M1 that delivered the same pattern. We believe these all belonged to the one person and he, or she of course, was changing SIM cards on a regular basis.'

'Do we know who these numbers belong to?'

'Some are pay-as-you-go, but quite a few are on contract' — he glanced at Helene — 'I would like to discuss that in private with you, boss.'

Helene's eyebrows shot up.

'Okaaaay. Right — Was this another piece of your magic software that managed to work all this out?'

'I'm afraid I can't take credit for this, but I do wish I had written it, Bill Gates made quite a tidy sum from this program. All done in an Excel spreadsheet.'

'Seriously?'

'Seriously.'

'Anything else?'

Chris shook his head and returned to his seat.

Emma leaned over and whispered in his ear, 'Well done, hot-shot.'

Another little smile flickered across his face.

'Golding and Mills processed, Ruth?'

'Yep, and Golding is squealing for a brief.'

'Then a brief he shall have, eventually. Let him stew. Smoke?'

'With the doc and Gypsy.'

'Good. Right, back to the "where are we?" Golding, who, as you've just heard, is now in custody, is our prime suspect in the trafficking of the victims and as such, may be able to lead us up the chain. We shall see. We also had in custody, Casey Hazelton, one of the two owners of a so-called snuff club website. He's not a happy-chappy because he wasn't who he appeared to be, and we have possibly destroyed an eighteen-month operation by the NCA. I'm not going to go into too much detail, but that operation was against Anthony Hendricks, the other "owner" of the snuff club website. As much as I would like to have words with this Hendricks myself, it would appear this site was possibly no more than a money laundering exercise. There is no evidence of any involvement in the murders and although I feel sorry for trampling on Casey's operation, our priority is catching the perpetrators.

'At the moment, that is where we are. The next step is to interview those still in custody, process the van belonging to Mills, debrief Smoke, and try to establish a link between Golding and Bridgedale. If we can do that then I think we can move forward. Anybody any questions?

'No? Okay, let's get to it. Chris, my office in five minutes, please.'

~§~

'Shut the door please, Chris. Take a seat.'

Chris knew Helene recognised the importance of what he had to tell her. Her open-door policy was literally that, the door was always slightly ajar although everyone still knocked. For it to be completely closed was a rare event. What he was about to show her must be kept under wraps for the time being. The fewer people in the know, the better.

'What couldn't you tell me about the numbers in the briefing?'

Chris handed her a printed list without saying a word.

Helene scanned through names on the list, her eyebrows getting higher and her eyes growing ever wider.

'Shit, Chris. Who else knows about this?'

'Just me and Emma, and now you.'

A knock on the door interrupted them.

Chief Superintendent Brandon peered through the glass and Helene beckoned him in. Chris got up to leave.

'No, Chris, I want you to stay for a minute, I think the Chief Super will want to see this.'

Chris nodded his agreement.

She handed Brandon the paper Chris had given to her moments earlier.

Brandon read through the list and looked questioningly at Helene.

'Numbers retrieved by Chris from a mobile number linked to Bridgedale, and matched to contract phone records. We think these people are involved somehow. Makes for scary reading doesn't it? All we have to do now is prove it.'

Brandon turned to Chris.

'How did you manage to obtain these numbers?'

Chris explained how they had put all the numbers from each phone record into a column along with the time of the call then used the "duplicate values" function in the "conditional formatting" menu to find the matches.

'I didn't understand a word of that so I'm going to take your word, Chris, but well done. Well done indeed. Who else has seen this?'

Chris reiterated what he had told Helene, adding Brandon himself to the select group.

'Good. Let's keep a lid on this for now. Would you mind giving DCI MacKay and myself a few moments please?'

~§~

Brandon waited for Chris to close the door.

'He's one switched on lad, that one.'

He looked at Helene and grimaced.

'I can confirm the involvement of some of those.'

'Holy fuck.'

'Indeed Helene, as you so eloquently said, Holy fuck just about covers it. Quite apart from a few household names as you've seen, there are many lesser known but nonetheless pretty influential people on that list. This is a political hotcake because we have no idea who else is involved.'

'If you've only just seen this list, how can you confirm some of these people are involved, sir?'

'Colin, please. You've earned that right, and I understand first names is your policy here.'

'Not that the buggers listen, they still call me boss.'

Brandon laughed then continued.

'Yesterday afternoon, a man walked into Bethnal Green and asked to talk to a detective. I just happened to be passing the front desk and offered my assistance. He wanted to confess to a murder.'

Brandon described the interview in detail.

'So, what you are saying is there is an "elite" club for want of a better word, that uses the murder of young girls as an initiation rite?'

'Appears so.'

'And have we evidence he is linked to this case, sir — Colin?'

Brandon pointed out a name on the list.

'That's him.'

'We only have his word though. We would be hard pushed to prove this without any form of physical evidence. They can just deny knowing him and say nothing ever happened.'

Brandon pursed his lips and nodded.

'Agreed, but as the final part of the initiation, they take a photograph of the initiate holding the knife, which they retain as an insurance. Only that person's DNA will be on the knife because the rest wear surgical gloves, and of course the photograph itself will support the physical evidence. They do seem to be forensic savvy.'

'Isn't everybody these days? We need to find that evidence.'

Brandon nodded.

'We do.'

'It could be anywhere.'

'It's going to be kept easily accessible. My guess is that one of the group's organisers will be in possession' — he pointed the sheet of names — 'M1 or M2 would be my guess.'

'As M1 is still unidentified to us, M2 seems a sensible place to start. Keep things discreet, Helene. These are high-powered people.'

'What if we can't find the physical evidence? The threat of exposure may be enough to convince any would-be informant to stay quiet and then the evidence is disposed of.'

'That scenario makes for a huge problem for us. We can't talk to anyone outside Invidia; who do we trust? Any one of these unknown numbers could be the very person we are talking to. But my feeling is that the evidence is still there.'

'Do you think it likely anyone associated with Invidia is involved?'

'No, I don't, otherwise I doubt they would allow this investigation to continue, but for now we'll keep our cards close. We'll bring this guy in and search his house. If we turn up anything, we can take it from there.'

'He will lawyer up straight away, and it will undoubtedly be his own brief. He's not going to settle for some Saturday night, legal aid solicitor.'

'I know, that's why I've arranged for him to be arrested under section 41.'

'Shit, sir — Colin. Terrorism laws? We have no evidence this is terrorist related.' She smiled. 'Oh — yes, less evidence required and longer holding. We can round up the others if we get the physical evidence, and it's all kept hush-hush.'

'Exactly. They are going to clam up tighter than a duck's arse in water. So, if we already have the evidence, we don't even need to interview. They will be begging us to talk to them. I just hope I'm right about where this evidence is stored, but I'm of the opinion that M1 or M2 will either have it at home or know its whereabouts.'

'Who is making the arrest?'

'SO15 will bring him in then Invidia will take over under the guise of NCA. It's your op.'

'By the way, who did the interview?'

'You're thinking of leaks to someone on the list, one of the unknown numbers?'

'Well, I'm thinking you didn't do the interview yourself.'

'No, my days of rattling people's cages has long gone. Apparently, I'm a dinosaur when it comes to interviews. No, a DS at Bethnal did the deed. I had a word with her afterwards. She's sound. A possible candidate for here too, but not yet.'

Brandon leant back in his chair.

'So, where does this leave us with Casey Hazelton?'

'I feel sorry for him, Colin, I really do but murder trumps fraud. However, he has given us a few names of people who were willing to invest in this snuff club. We will definitely follow up on that once we have this one solved. Casey also suggested Hendricks may have been willing to go through with what he proposed. Apparently, he has some unusual tastes when it comes to the fairer sex, violence being one of them. He would definitely be worth talking to if we can track him down.'

Brandon shrugged.

'You know how it goes Helene; some you win ...'

She studied him for a moment.

'I wish you'd been like this with me when you came to the Met. Things would have been so different. Instead, I finished up in therapy, did things I'm not proud of, left a job I loved.'

'What about this job?'

'I think it's going to be fine, but self-doubt is something that's been hanging over me for many months. It scares me. I don't have that cosy feeling I had in the Met. I feel more isolated somehow, more exposed.'

Brandon lowered his head, closed his eyes and massaged the bridge of his nose before answering.

'If it's any consolation, and I don't suppose it is, my treatment of you has caused me many a sleepless night, both then and since.'

'Would you do it again if you thought it necessary?'

Brandon sighed deeply.

'You know as well as I, there are some aspects to this job that we don't like, yet we have no choice but to do them anyway —'

'That's what I thought and that does not make me feel good. How do I know you haven't or currently doing that to someone else to drive them to the team? It does not make for a good working environment — sir.'

Helene chose not to call him by his first name this time.

'— Jeez, Helene, I wish more of my officers had a fire in them like you, but I hadn't quite finished speaking when you set fire to my arse. What I was about to say was that this was not one of those tasks. I would not do it again under any circumstances. It was wrong. It hurt you deeply and in the long term, may well have ruined my best officer. Michael and I have spoken at length about the matter and although he is happy with the final outcome, he agrees it was wrong, but you have to remember Michael is Whitehall. He's basically an undercover politician, and we all know how they are so adept in making the end justify the means. But, and you have my word on this, if he ever tries anything like that again he will have me to deal with and although you might not know it now,

I once had your fire. It might not be as visible or as strong, but rest assured it still burns well.

'I'm not one of the graduate career coppers who have no idea what it's like at the sharp end. Like you, I came up through the ranks and had to prove my worth at every step of the way' —

He held up his hands.

— 'and before you say anything, I know you had it twice as hard if not worse. The Met wasn't, and to a degree still isn't, a place where men and women or blacks and whites necessarily get the same opportunities. But if you want my honest opinion, that is precisely what made you the officer you are now. It's wrong. I know it, you know it, and they know it and yet we all know it still happens.'

Helene studied his face, searching for the slightest hint of insincerity.

'That's the longest speech I've ever heard you make, apart from in a press briefing.'

She cocked her head to one side.

'You know something — Colin? I think this arrangement might just work out after all.'

~§~

Ruth exchanged greetings with Brandon in the ops room and then knocked on the door to Helene's office.

'What now, boss?'

'Good question. We have to hope Golding gives us something, but I'm not holding my breath. Failing that, we will have Brocklehurst in custody by tomorrow.'

'Who?'

'Ah, you aren't supposed to know that. M2 on the phone list you haven't seen.'

'That name sounds familiar.'

'It should, you drive past one of his places on the way here every day.'

'Not — you mean the owner of Fit-Faster Tyres and Exhausts?'

Helene nodded her head and gave Ruth a knowing look.

'Holy fuck.'

'My words exactly when I found out, and he's not the only one on Chris's list that would make your hair curl. Okay, this isn't public knowledge, not even in the group, but I think you need to know as you are going to be conducting some of the interviews.'

Helene brought Ruth up to date with the events since the last briefing and Ruth agreed to the need for the secrecy.

'Some of these interviews will be done at other stations as no doubt many of those involved will use their own solicitors. We just have to hope we find that physical evidence. The arrest will be made under section 41 and we'll have a search warrant, so fingers crossed the search team comes up trumps.'

Ruth closed her eyes and shook her head.

'What gets me is the scale of it. Have all those people been involved in murders? Why haven't we heard about this before. You didn't have that many unexplained cases before, did you?'

Helene looked thoughtful.

'That's a very good point. Either there are a lot more bodies out there or only certain members have to go through this sick ceremony; maybe the ones they aren't entirely sure of. It doesn't bear thinking about if there is a victim for every member.'

~§~

The phone buzzed in his pocket, but he waited until he was alone before checking the message. None of the others knew of this phone and he intended for things to stay that way. This would be difficult to explain away.

Now in his car, he checked the message. A new phone number. He would receive a call that night unless he sent a warning message saying he would not be alone. He slid the phone back in his pocket, started the car and made for home.

CHAPTER TWENTY-FIVE

Smoke was still feeling the effects of whatever had happened to him. He had to take their word that he had likely been drugged because he had no recollection of anything after first meeting Golding. The events leading up to it were now clear, but the more he tried to remember the rest, the more his mind felt full of treacle. Tantalising glimpses of images slipped in and out but each time he tried to focus on one, it vanished.

Gypsy accompanied him to the debrief, totally against protocol but Helene agreed that under the circumstances, protocol could take a back seat.

The debrief would take place in one of the rest areas rather than an interview room; Smoke was a victim not a suspect. Helene would conduct the proceedings with Ruth alongside.

'Take me through what happened after you entered the pub.'

Smoke described the events as far as he could remember but still struggled to recall much after the second drink. Nothing would come except a jumble of blurred images and the feeling he had been on a boat. The next thing he remembered was being in the room where he was found, but he didn't remember it as a basement; only the confusion as to why he couldn't move. The knowledge he was in a basement came later when Ruth, Jason and the SCO19 officers found him.

'James sent the results back from your tests. Your urine sample came back positive for benzodiazepine, flunitrazepam to be exact.'

'Roofies? No wonder I can't remember a bloody thing!'

Smoke started to laugh. Gypsy looked at him anxiously.

'Sorry, Kat. It's just the irony of it. I'm hit with a date rape drug, from a guy who doesn't even fancy me.'

'It's not funny, Dan. You could be dead by now.'

'I know, I know, I'm sorry, but it does have a funny side.'

Gypsy glared at him as he chuckled away.

He stopped suddenly.

'There was someone else. It just flashed into my head, someone else came to the table and spoke to me.'

'Do you remember anything about them?'

' No, just that they were — wait — I — I think I knew him.'

Smoke buried his head into his hands as he tried to think.

'Sorry, it just won't come.'

'It's okay. We have Golding. We'll ask him who else was with him, because I'm sure once he knows how hard he's going down, he won't mind taking anyone else involved down with him.'

Helene got up to leave.

'Right, I'll leave you two to have a rest.'

Helene reached the door when Smoke blurted out a name.

'Palmer. Charlie Palmer.'

'Is that who came to the table?'

'Yes. He's the reason me and Kat are here. Our last case with HMRC.'

'Yes, I remember it from your file. You're sure it was him and you aren't mixing things up in your head.'

'I'm positive. He called me Smoke. It was him, I'm sure of it.'

'I couldn't tell you before because I wanted to see if you could recall it on your own. We have video footage from the traffic cams and CCTV of Palmer's Bentley following the van you were transported in. We also have footage of whoever was driving that car entering the house where you were held. The image isn't clear enough for an ID, but it looks like Palmer is involved in some way.'

'Oh, I do hope so. I want that bastard going down for a long time. Nasty piece of work he is.'

'Unfortunately, he's going to have to wait for a little while, because we are about to bring in a prime suspect for the murders and we hope to obtain physical evidence. I'll bring you up to speed when I get chance. Now, get some rest, both of you. That's an order.'

~§~

The bleary-eyed, unshaven and dishevelled looking man, clothed in Paisley pyjamas and a plain grey dressing gown, bore no resemblance to the captain of industry the public knew so well. Armed police officers presenting a search warrant upon entering a house at 3 a.m. tend to create that state in anyone present at the time.

Appearing in all the advertisements for his tyre and exhaust business, Brocklehurst quickly became a household name. Now he sat on a sofa watching SO15 officers search his house, the sergeant in charge of the team stood beside him.

'This is preposterous. I have nothing to do with terrorism at all.'

'We had a tip off that weapons are coming into the country hidden in shipments of exhaust parts. I've explained this already, Sir Desmond.'

'And I've told you it's nonsense.'

One of the SO15 search team entered the room.

'Sarge, there's a safe in the study.'

'Sir Desmond, you need to open that for us.'

'Poppycock. I need do no such thing. There is nothing of interest to you in there.'

The sergeant, beginning to lose his patience, asserted, 'There are two ways we can play this. Either you open it, or we open it for you. I suggest the former as we aren't too fussy about the condition of the safe afterwards — sir.'

Brocklehurst reluctantly accompanied them to the study and opened the safe, all the while muttering under his breath.

'See, nothing of interest to you.'

The officer smiled.

'Let us be the judge of that, sir.'

The contents of the safe were placed in an evidence bag and sealed.

The sergeant looked around him. His entire lifetime salary probably wouldn't pay for this house, yet the old fool wasn't content and wanted to make even more money through arms smuggling, or so the tip-off said. Maybe that's how he got rich and the tyre and exhaust business was a front. All the sergeant knew was they would be here for a while until the search finished. Brocklehurst would then be taken to Bethnal Green. Why Bethnal Green, the sergeant didn't know. It wasn't the closest station, nor the usual place a person suspected of being involved in terrorism would be taken, but things went on far above his pay grade and he was content to keep it that way.

An hour later, the search was in its final throes. All paperwork had been confiscated and placed in evidence bags to accompany them back to Bethnal Green Police Station, along with desktop and laptop computers.

As they boarded the minibus, one of the search team approached the sergeant.

'Sarge, have you got a minute. Something's bugging me and I want you to check it out with me.'

The officer led the sergeant to an outbuilding. To call it a garden shed would be an insult to any self-respecting garden shed. Some families lived in smaller houses, although garden shed was clearly its purpose.

'What is it?'

'Look inside and tell me what you see.'

'I see a lot of gardening equipment, not surprising given the size of the garden.'

'What about the size of the shed?'

'Enormous. What are you —? Oh, I see it now. It's not big enough inside compared to the outside.'

'Exactly, Sarge. I can't think of a reason to have a part sealed off, can you?'

'No. Not any legitimate ones. If it was something like a water tank, there would be easy access.'

He called on the radio for them to hold everyone in situ.

'No other doors?'

'No.'

'Okay, Let's take a closer look at this wall.'

The sergeant started at the left-hand side, tapping at the brickwork. It sounded solid enough but as he reached the right-hand side, the sound became hollow.

He turned to look at the officer.

'What have we here?'

They examined the wall more closely with their torches and spotted what appeared to be a hairline crack running through the mortar. Not easy to see as it ran between two bricks vertically before moving horizontally along the course, then moving vertically again.

The officer pushed hard against the wall and was rewarded with the entire section moving back slightly more than the thickness of one brick, but that was as far as it went. There appeared to be no means of moving it.

As he examined the bricks, he noticed another with cracks around it. He pushed and nothing happened, so he pressed just one end of the brick and it swivelled to form a handle.

They pushed sideways and the door slid open.

The back wall of the small room contained a rack of shelves. Neatly spaced on them were a number of boxes, each with a name and a date written on it; the dates went back almost four years.

The sergeant had no idea what was in the boxes, but he knew that whatever it was, the owner clearly did not want them found. He counted them; forty-seven in all.

'I think we're going to need more evidence bags.'

~§~

CHAPTER TWENTY-FIVE

Helene arrived in her office at 6 a.m. to find Brandon already waiting for her.

'Morning, sir — err Colin. You must have news to be in this early. Good I hope?'

Brandon grimaced.

'It's both, I'm afraid. We have the evidence.'

He went on to explain how the secret room had been found and the boxes with names and dates, each containing a photograph and a bloody knife.

'We have them, Helene.'

'And the bad news?'

'There are forty-seven of them. All containing evidence of a murder.'

Helene closed her eyes and shook her head. When she opened them, they were full of tears.

'Forty-seven young girls murdered for what, some sort of "boys' club" for the wealthy?'

Brandon shook his head.

'They aren't all girls, there are boys too.'

'For fuck's sake, what is wrong with this world that lives are worth so little?'

Helene stormed out of the office leaving Brandon at a loss what to do. He thought it best to wait and let her calm down. She returned a few minutes later with two steaming mugs, one of tea and the other black coffee.

'You once suggested I was only fit to make the tea, so there, get that down you. You may have noticed I'm somewhat grumpy until after my first coffee.'

'Can't say as I have.'

Helene looked at him and burst out laughing. 'Sorry.'

'It's understandable, especially as you do feel each case you work on. I would normally say that isn't necessarily a good thing, but clearly it works for you. Just don't ever take it out on yourself if you don't have the result you were hoping for. You are not Superwoman — although you aren't far off.'

Helene turned away and bit her lip. She would never become used to being praised; it made her well up inside.

Brandon continued. 'The really good news to this is that we have names, so those wise enough to use a pay-as-you-go are coming in too, once we've matched them to the phones. We will have to process them through several stations as we don't have the capacity here, and I suspect many of them will have their own solicitors anyway. Are you okay with that?'

'Frankly, I don't give a damn where they're processed, as long as they are, and they go down for what they have done. I'm betting though, our M1 isn't amongst those involved. So, when will the arrests be made?'

'They've started. We can't afford to let this drag on and word get out to those involved. It's using a lot of manpower I can tell you, but the AC Rowley himself signed off on the overtime.'

'You are still using section 41?'

'For the time being.'

Helene squinted her eyes.

'I'm not sure that's a wise thing but I will defer to your judgement on that. On another note, Golding told us that he only got involved at Palmer's bidding. I suspect Palmer had been running his own trafficking racket. Now you've told me how many cases there are, I can see why he might back off and have someone else take the risk.'

'You think he's involved in this group?'

Helene shrugged again.

'I can see it's the sort of thing he might be involved in. Come to think of it, he may be our M1. He fits the profile. He'll be getting a visit from us tonight; we've already got surveillance in place. He's going nowhere without us knowing.'

Brandon took a deep breath.

'Helene, where do we stand? I mean us personally.'

'Your tea's in the cup, not on your head.'

Brandon roared with laughter.

'I'll take that.'

~§~

The previous night's conversation had been somewhat one-sided; they talked, he listened. The other party wanted more but he could only give them what he had, which at the moment wasn't much.

Today was quiet, everyone seemed to be preoccupied with something, but no one was saying a word.

His pocket vibrated. This time it wasn't a message but a call. It must be urgent. He couldn't answer now.

'Just nipping out to the shop, anyone want anything?'

With replies all in the negative, he slipped out of the entrance and around the side of the building.

He called the number given to him previously.

'Why didn't you warn me?'

'About what?'

'The arrests?'

'I have no idea what you are talking about.'

The phone went dead. He glared at it for a few moments before making his way down the short drive to the car park. He'd grab a bar of chocolate from the paper shop to back up his story.

~§~

A pair of eyes watched thoughtfully as he went past.

Now why did he need to come out of the building to make a call?

CHAPTER TWENTY-SIX

The white Georgian house stood in almost four acres of land on the edge of Epping Forest. Oak, beech and silver birch ringed the immaculately kept lawn, as though the forest sought to absorb and protect its cultivated neighbour. A grey river of a gravel driveway cut a meandering path through the grass, before spilling into a wide parking area in front of a white portico, flanked either side by potted cedars; arboreal keepers of the gate. Enormous bay windows dominated the front of the house on both floors; divided horizontally by a rambling hydrangea, spanning the full width of the house.

An urgent buzzing attracted Charlie's attention. The outer perimeter alarm had not been activated, but someone had breached the inner perimeter. That someone either knew about the outer alarm and bypassed it, or they dropped from the sky. Charlie himself had installed the tremblers buried in the lawn. Only he knew of their existence, and they formed his inner perimeter system. Can't be too careful in this day and age; you don't know who might want to sneak into your house.

A quick glance at the monitor told him all he needed to know. The infrared cameras picked up four figures, clad all in black and carrying automatic weapons, moving with purpose across the lawn; two towards the back of the house, the remaining two, straight for the front door.

Whether the law, or a rival group wasn't relevant. Clearly these people were not on a social visit. The fact they had already reached the second perimeter gave him very little time, but still enough to do what he needed; not long enough to pack or grab anything. Not that it mattered anyway, he needed to take nothing from here. Fake documents lay in several places around the city, and clothes were hardly worth losing your freedom or life for; they could easily be replaced. Offshore banking ensured his money remained accessible from anywhere in the world.

No one could expect to run their lives the way Charlie ran his and be surprised when this day came; the knock at the door, the sound of smashing glass. That he would be forced to flee at some point and leave the UK forever didn't bother him in the slightest. It was almost a relief. A permanent loan, using the house as collateral, meant the loss of the £3.3m property was more of a loss to the bank than to him. By the time they found out, his account would be empty and a new one opened in another country.

The men approached the front door; time to move. He pulled on a pair of jeans and a t-shirt, before slipping into a pair of trainers. As he wriggled his feet into the footwear he reached under the shelf on the bedside cabinet and pressed a hidden button.

A home-made thermic lance, installed by Charlie, protected the contents of the safe from prying eyes; another precaution should this day arrive. The steel brake pipe, wire wool, a portable oxygen bottle and a small incendiary charge created the perfect way to destroy the contents of his safe concealed behind the Picasso copy in his study. Sure, he kept some cash there, but not enough to worry about. Pressing the button started a chain reaction inside the safe, setting off the incendiary and igniting the steel wool. Seconds later an electromechanical valve opened introducing the oxygen along the pipe making the wool burn hotter, sufficiently hot to ignite the steel pipe. Certain items he had deemed vital to destroy were arranged closest to the pipe. Even so, burning at a temperature in excess of 4000°C, he was confident that by the time they managed to open the safe, the contents would be ash. Amazing what can be learned by a quick search on the internet, and what a mockery it made of movies where the safecrackers used a thermic lance to cut open the safe; there would be nothing left to steal by the time they got in.

Charlie dashed into the library and pulled on one of the well-stocked bookcases. It rotated smoothly to reveal a door. He was through in seconds, pulling the bookcase closed behind him. They would find it, but not for some time. He descended the stone steps into the wine cellar, part of the original building from the early eighteen-hundreds. The more recent addition was the tunnel leading off the cellar in the direction of the nearby woods. Charlie built it himself, digging a deep trench across the lawn and gardens under the pretext of upgrading the drainage system. Large bore sewage pipes made an ideal escape route, if a little cramped. No one noticed when he continued the trench well beyond the borders of his property and into the trees. Why would they? His was the only property bordering the forest here, and the public rarely frequented this corner.

At the end of the tunnel, a small chamber stored a motorcycle jacket, trousers, helmet and gloves, which he donned before the short climb up a vertical ladder, finally emerging from a well-covered hatch in the forest floor. Even without the gibbous moon filtering through the trees, he would be able to find his way; he'd practiced often enough.

The sound of a helicopter reached him, rising and falling as it circled. Given the direction of the sound, he surmised his nearby neighbours, the Metropolitan Police Helicopter Unit at Lippitts Hill, had been tasked to assist whoever was undoubtedly now searching his house. He hoped the thermal camera stayed trained on the building and not the nearby forest.

He wasn't sure if realising the intruders were law officers was advantageous or not; at least his rivals couldn't put a watch on all the ports and airports.

After fifteen minutes of trampling through the undergrowth, Charlie reached his objective; a seemingly overgrown area between a beech and oak tree and close to the nearby lane. He reached into the bush and pulled, lifting netting away to reveal a Kawasaki Versys 650 motorcycle. It was a bit of a pain in the backside to keep it maintained and hidden from prying eyes, but in doing so ensured he would always have a means of escape. No one was going to put one over on Charlie Palmer. That pain was now paying dividends.

The engine didn't so much roar into life as purr, just as he wanted. No sense in sneaking away from your house only to advertise your escape with a noisy machine. Charlie gently opened the throttle and eased his way onto the nearby lane. Within minutes he was on the clockwise carriageway of the M25; his destination a mere twenty miles away. A gap in the trees to his right allowed him to glance in the direction of the house. He could make out the anti-collision beacon on the helicopter, clearly still circling the now empty building.

You would have to try harder to catch old Charlie Palmer he thought, as he settled into the ride.

~§~

The four men moved quietly and efficiently. Not a word spoken between them; hand gestures and nods of the head, the only form of communication. As each room in the large house proved empty, the team moved on to the next one, weapons at the ready position. Helene, Smoke and Gypsy remained in the hallway, their own weapons drawn, but Harry's men were experts at this sort of warfare, and that's what it was, warfare.

'Clear.'

The call came from upstairs. Now they knew for sure the house itself was empty.

Helene was at a loss to explain it. The observation teams were certain Palmer was still inside; they saw him enter and were equally certain he hadn't left. He had to be here somewhere.

'Boss, better take a look at this.'

Helene made a move towards the stairs.

'You better come in here quick, boss.'

This time the voice came from downstairs and carried some urgency. The room turned out to be an office of some sort. Helene supposed in a house of this grandeur it would be known as a study, and her attention was immediately drawn to a painting on one of the walls. White smoke curled lazily from behind the picture frame, growing denser by the second.

Fitz grabbed the edge of the frame and pulled on it; nothing happened. He tried again on the opposite side of the picture and the painting swung away from the wall revealing a small safe set into the wall.

Helene dropped her head for a moment then let out a sigh.

'Oh, bloody funny, Mister Palmer, bloody funny.'

Fitz gave her a quizzical look.

'Boss?'

'Oh, I doubt he would have known it would be a woman, but nevertheless.'

Helene gestured at the painting.

'The painting, it's a Picasso; Weeping Woman. Bloody ironic isn't it? I don't suppose we'll be getting very much out of there now. Keep an eye on it, Fitz, make sure it doesn't burn down the house. I'll go and see what Twinkle wants.'

The staircase wasn't grand, but it did have an elegance about it not found in the average semi. Helene found Lightfoot in one of the bedrooms off the landing.

'Thought you'd want to see this, boss; CCTV coverage of the lawn.'

'I thought that was triggered by the alarm?'

'It is. Seems there is a second alarm somewhere, see?'

Lightfoot pointed to the flashing caption in the bottom right corner of the screen.

'Bed's still warm too. He was here not too long ago. Either he's still here and hiding or there's another way out.'

'Neither Surveillance, nor the helicopter have seen any movement around the house other than us, so we better start searching the rooms thoroughly. Start with downstairs.'

Twenty minutes later they had their answer. Smoke spotted a mark on the carpet in front of one of the bookcases in the library. Many years of being a customs officer had taught him to look out for the little things; a freshly marked screw holding on a piece of trim in a car, or a carpet not fitting quite right in the saloon of a boat; anything showing a recent disturbance.

The tunnel wasn't readily visible in the wine cellar, but neither was it fully concealed. Helene checked the time.

'Assuming he left when we came in and went directly to the marina, he could be there by now, but he had to go through here which would have cost him some time and then he had to get some form of transport. We may be one step ahead of him, finally. Harry?' — Helene looked around.

— 'Where's Harry?'

It was the first time she'd noticed Harry was missing. No one recalled seeing him after the raid started. Helene returned to the library to get a signal on her phone. Her first call was to the team at St. Katherine's Docks where Palmer kept a private yacht, advising them of the escape; her second, to Harry; voicemail. A quick call to the team member left with the vehicles revealed Harry left shortly after the team penetrated the grounds; announcing he would go to the marina.

Helene stamped her foot: damn it. She needed him here and he was nowhere to be found. She would deal with this later. Right now, locating Palmer was the priority. He would not get away this time.

~§~

Ha! They can't put one over on old Charlie William Palmer. Oh no sir, he was too smart for that. Even that run in when they caught him with the four keys of heroin, they still didn't manage to pin it on him. He was sensible enough to surround himself with fall guys and smart lawyers; especially the lawyers.

Once again, he managed to slip through the net. They may have had him surrounded but they weren't expecting him to pop up in the woods, were they?

Nor did they expect him to have another cruiser moored in a different marina. While they were undoubtedly busy watching the one they knew about, he went to the other. As they said in the insurance advert, 'simples.'

The Sunseeker 90 gleamed under the marina lights. A private purchase by someone who had been paid a lot of money to keep quiet, ensured it would not be traced back to him. He was absolutely certain he would be home free once he left the marina, after all, boats came and went every day. They couldn't stop them all.

No, he was definitely home free. The riskiest part of this would be crossing the Bay of Biscay. With a cruising speed of 23 knots and a top speed of 26 knots he would be able to make the passage in three and a half days including three fuel stops and some sleep. That's all he needed and, as they didn't know about this boat, he didn't have to worry about them tracking him. North Africa beckoned, and with the money he had stashed in his offshore accounts he would be guaranteed a lifestyle fit for a king. Casablanca here I come.

Charlie keyed in the code for the gate to the pontoon. One of the reasons for choosing this marina was the exceptionally good security. No one in or out without the code, and only one place to obtain that, the marina office.

He relaxed. They couldn't reach him now. The boat was fully fuelled and provisioned, kept on a permanent readiness for such eventualities, taken out on a regular basis, always in the morning, so his departure tomorrow would not arouse any suspicion. The authorities had no reason to suspect this boat. On the few occasions the Customs Officers had checked it out after the regular trips to France they had found nothing, nor would they, nothing was ever smuggled on this boat, unlike several of the others he owned, with their underwater compartments. People, drugs, alcohol; it was all the same to him; commodities, that's all they were, commodities to be traded like fish fingers or coffee. That was the only thing he and that loser Golding had in common.

He stepped on board giving the marina a quick scan for lurkers. Of the few people who were around, no one paid him the slightest attention; no one lurking or pretending to be occupied.

He stepped aboard onto the aft deck and took another swift look around before unlocking the saloon doors. He let out a sigh of relief as he locked the door behind him. He was safe now.

The mood lighting was enough for him to navigate his way to the well-stocked, granite-topped bar on the port side of the vessel. He needed a drink after that close call at the house; a drink, followed by a good night's sleep and an early start. He dropped some ice in a tumbler and added a small measure of Glen Morangie. He didn't want to overdo it and have a hangover in the morning; a quick nightcap, no more.

The pain in his neck was as sudden as it was intense. The tumbler lived up to its name and fell to the floor as the darkness descended on him.

~§~

Charlie's eyelids fluttered as the oxygen, so vital to the brain's activity, was restored as the blood was allowed to flow once again, and consciousness returned.

'Welcome back, Mr Palmer, or may I call you Charlie? I think I should as we are going to become well acquainted with each other over the next few hours.'

The recumbent figure struggled against his bonds; a low growl emanated from behind the gaffer tape covering his mouth.

'Now, now, Charlie, it's no use struggling like that, those knots are not going to give way, you see, I was in the Navy, well, kind of; the one thing I do know how to do is tie knots. I've been dying to meet you for some time. Oh wait — no. I think that should be you will be dying from meeting me — or something like that. Oh, how remiss of me, we haven't been introduced. My name is Harry and I'm so pleased to finally make your acquaintance.'

Harry was rewarded with that first realisation of mortality entering Palmer's eyes. It still gave Harry a buzz to watch the thought of impending death enter someone's mind for the first time; almost as satisfying as watching the final vestiges of life vanish from the eyes as they died. Something to be savoured for as long as possible, much like a fine wine, or an exquisite meal; Harry, a true connoisseur.

The news announcer shuffled her papers and looked up at the camera as the titles of BBC News at One faded away to the local news studio.

'Good afternoon. I'm Alice Bhandhukravi.

'A well-known East End nightclub owner has been found dead in the water at Limehouse Marina. He had been wanted by the police in connection with an ongoing investigation. A statement released by the police earlier today says the body of Mr Charles William Palmer was spotted by a passer-by early this morning. It is thought he became entangled in a fender rope and fell overboard from his luxury yacht. A post-mortem will be carried out later today. At this stage of the investigation, the police are not looking for anyone else in connection with their enquiries.

'In other news, the fallout continues over the arrests of a number of high-profile businessmen. Police are still unwilling to release details of the arrests, but it is our understanding they were arrested under anti-terrorism legislation and have subsequently been charged with murder.

'Among those arrested are Sir Desmond Brocklehurst, owner and CEO of the Fit-Faster chain of exhaust and tyre centres. His lawyer released a statement saying that the allegations are without foundation and that Sir Desmond will be vindicated by the evidence presented in court.'

CHAPTER TWENTY-SEVEN

Helene reflected as she stood with Kun that were this in a TV drama, they would be holding umbrellas, watching the coffins being lowered into the sodden earth as the priest, vicar or celebrant said a few words. Mourners would be, well, mournful, and at least one lady dressed head to toe in black would dab her eyes with a white handkerchief as she sobbed gently.

Instead, the late afternoon sun shone intermittently through cumulus clouds providing a shimmering sunbeam backdrop to the solemn occasion in Highgate Cemetery. Normally restricted to a few burials a year, on learning of the circumstances of the deaths, the Trust were only too happy to provide a space for the victims.

Of the mourners, only one did not come from Invidia. Kun took the role of the sobbing lady as the coffin of her friend Jing and seven other members of their container-community took their places in the ground one by one; the final member of the group remained in a coma. Another mass grave, but this one with ceremony and dignity.

Although none were blood relatives, Kun wore light blue, a Chinese tradition for family members of the deceased; these were her sisters.

Helene put her arm around Kun to comfort her. She had gone from being part of a happy family to facing life alone in a strange land; the Home Office granted her permanent residency without question on the direction of someone in the Invidia hierarchy. That person had no recollection of making the request but allowed it to remain in force on the understanding a certain young lady stopped using her computer to do things in his name.

Michael Strong and Helene joined Kun in the car as they left the burial. They would go to a nearby public house and hold a small wake for the girls. But first they needed to talk.

'Do you know what you want to do?'

Still sobbing gently, Kun shook her head.

'I don't know, I have no money and I never finished my education. I only know how to do one thing now. I don't want to do that.'

Helene patted her on the shoulder.

'You don't need to. We have an offer for you. You don't have to take it, but I think when you hear what we have to say you might consider it.'

Kun looked at her through watery eyes. Helene glanced at Michael, sat facing them with his back to the driver. He nodded almost imperceptibly.

'You have been such a help to us, and we want to help you in return. You know you have an amazing ability for recall, don't you?'

Kun acknowledged.

'We are willing to put you through school then university, fund your degree. When you have finished, we'd like you to consider working for us. You don't have to, but we'd like you to think about it while you are studying.'

'I can't pay you back. I have no money.'

'It's a gift, Kun. You don't need to pay it back.'

'Why?'

'Because we think you deserve a break in life. It's not exactly been the best start for you has it?'

Unused to kindness over the past few years, and overwhelmed by the day's events, Kun could no longer rein in her emotions, prompting Helene to hold her even tighter.

~§~

Once Kun left the wake, the members of Invidia returned to headquarters, or the "factory" as it had come to be known by all members of the team; another sign of the influence that some of the police officers in the unit were having over the civilian and former military members of staff.

Helene called together everyone involved in the case to meet in the lecture theatre where she would bring them up to date with the proceedings.

The arrests totalled forty-seven from the physical evidence alone. Although Brocklehurst didn't have a box in his name, he was charged with conspiracy and encouragement to murder. The fact no box was found for Brocklehurst was no surprise really as these boxes held evidence against the members; more than likely another held the one for him, if one existed, but nothing came to light during the arrests.

The Borough Operation Command Units had taken over operations now and were responsible for processing all those arrested with the exception of Golding and Bridgedale who were still under the jurisdiction of Invidia.

The whereabouts of Hendricks remained unknown, but undoubtedly, he would turn up again and Hazelton would get his man.

'This was something of a baptism of fire for us all, but apart from a couple of hiccoughs' — Helene glanced at Smoke who grinned back at her — 'things went exceedingly well. You will be pleased to know that Bridgedale no longer has a deal; those involved in guarding the victims while they were in captivity are all under arrest and singing like the proverbial. As suspected, he was up to his neck in it.

CHAPTER TWENTY-SEVEN

'We did have one slip away from us, Charles Palmer. However, as you may have heard on the news, he met with an untimely end on his boat in what appears to be an unfortunate accident whilst he was making his escape. Unfortunate for him that is. As for me, well I won't be shedding any tears over him.' Helene avoided making eye contact with Harry.

'Having all departments, forensics, cyber, legal and of course, the foot soldiers under one roof made an enormous difference in the way we were able to progress the investigation. Being able to obtain same day results from the labs and from the PMs' — She couldn't help but look at James and smile, — 'is such a benefit to the whole process which, unless you have been operational in crime investigations before, you will perhaps not appreciate. You have shown the people responsible for this team that it is worth all the heartache and organisation that went into its formation.

'I want to thank them for letting us get on with it without any interference but most of all I want to thank each and every one of you for your immense efforts in what turned out to be the most horrendous of cases. Let's hope we can now have a short break before we are tasked with something new.'

A round of applause peppered with the cheers, rose in the lecture room.

Helene held up her hands to subdue the noise, but even so had to shout over the top of it to be heard.

'One final thing. When I was serving in the Met, at the end of a successful case we would allow ourselves a small celebratory drink in a local watering hole. For those of you still unfamiliar with police terminology, piss up tonight at 7 p.m. in The Prospect of Whitby' —

A massive cheer went up and Helene had to shout and wave her arms to quieten them.

— 'Sorry, Smoke, couldn't resist. No, seriously, the venue will be The Harp in Covent Garden. You don't want to miss this because the first round is on me.'

Helene put her hands over her ears to stop herself being deafened by the roar that met this announcement as she made her way out of the auditorium.

~§~

Helene caught Harry as he walked along the corridor from the lecture theatre.

'My office. Now.'

She was clearly annoyed about something, and it appeared Harry was going to bear the brunt of her anger.

~§~

She sat behind her desk but didn't offer Harry a chair. He took one anyway.

'I thought I made it clear when you joined this team you were to follow orders; no freelancing.'

Harry remained silent.

'I've just had the post-mortem results for Charlie Palmer. He drowned all right, but he was also full of heroin, and had a foreign object lodged in his rectum. It turned out to be part of a broom handle. Not to mention the ligature marks around the neck and something carved between his toes. What can you tell me about it, Harry?'

Harry shrugged.

'Where did you go when you disappeared from the raid?'

'I've already told you. I went to St Katherine's.'

'Bullshit, Harry. That was already covered, and like I said before, no one there remembers seeing you. You were supposed to be at Palmer's house with your team.'

'A lot of people don't remember seeing me when I go somewhere. I'm good at being no one, remember? That's why you took me on, if I recall — '

'ENOUGH.'

Helene took a deep breath.

'I can't have you running your own agenda, Harry. You put the whole operation at risk if you keep going off and doing your own thing. We have to get it right, and you doing this could bring us all down.'

Harry said nothing but maintained eye contact with her.

'If I catch you doing this again, you are going down for the murders we already hold evidence for, as well as whatever it is you do next.'

'You won't.'

'I won't what? Lock you up?'

'Catch me.'

She knew he was right. She'd caught him once, but she'd been lucky. She wouldn't be that lucky again. Besides, she needed his skills if this team was going to work.

They'd set out to bring down a human trafficker and a bunch of murderers. They brought down another nasty piece of work into the bargain. Despite Harry not following orders, she knew she couldn't stay annoyed with him, and that worried her. He was a serial killer after all.

'I need you to be a team player. From what I can gather, and God knows that's little enough, you were an excellent team player. Maybe you can't be anymore. Maybe you have been on your own too long. Whatever the reason, I need to know I can rely on you, at all times.'

Harry lowered his head, seemingly staring at the floor.

Helene was startled when he looked up; he had tears in his eyes.

'I'm sorry. You're right, boss. I can't go off doing things on my own. I trained to be part of a team and that was taken away from me once. You gave me a second chance and I've let you down. I won't let you down again, you have my word on that.'

Helene searched his eyes, then smiled. He wouldn't let her down again.

'How did you know about the other boat?'

He held her gaze.

'A little flower told me.'

Helene frowned, then it dawned on her. She threw her head back and closed her eyes.

'Emma.'

'She's smart, boss. I told her to follow the money and she did. Traced a payment to some geyser and hey presto, up pops a boat. After that it was a matter of finding where it was moored. Had to be along the Thames for easy access. Go easy on her, boss. It was my fault.'

'I'm not going to give her a bollocking for a terrific piece of work like that. Anyway, back to you. Out of my office before I change my mind.'

Harry took the hint and made for the door.

'Oh, Harry.'

He popped his head back into the office, raising his eyebrows in enquiry.

'Well done.'

Helene winked at him.

'This is for you.'

He looked puzzled as she handed him an envelope.

'Open return for Hong Kong. I thought you might need some R&R. You will find an address in there too. Don't take too long. We need you back here. I've a feeling there is more of this to come. Oh, and Harry, save me the trouble of looking it up. Jb12:22?'

'He reveals the deep things of darkness and brings utter darkness into the light.'

~§~

Emma studied the screen. While searching the Dark Web during the investigation, she'd stumbled upon something which although not relevant to the investigation, had piqued her interest enough to make a note to come back to it when she had time. If this was what she thought it might be, it was dynamite. Before saying anything, she would have to be sure of her facts.

'I thought you'd be back in here.'

'Holy shit, boss. Will you stop doing that. I nearly had a heart attack.'

Helene looked at the screen then looked at Emma, eyebrows raised.

'Is that what I think it is?'

Emma nodded.

'I'm not sure whether it is legit yet, but seriously, I'm thinking it might be.'

Helene looked incredulous.

'Well as soon as you are sure, let me know. In the meantime, I want to pick up on something you said in Dubai.'

'What's that?'

'Remember when I mentioned I'd once met Sigourney Weaver, and you said, "Stop it. As if I'm not jealous enough"?'

'Yeah. Well, I am jealous.'

'Of what?'

Emma lowered her head to avoid looking at Helene.

'I think I'm just in awe. You're successful, confident, bloody gorgeous. It's like you are the personification of who I would like to be. Not only that, you make it all look so easy. You have no idea how out of place I felt in Dubai and Hong Kong. I didn't belong there, it's not who I am. I'm a little orphan girl from the East End. I live in a grotty flat. I'm not the sort of person that goes to five-star hotels and sips cocktails in the evening. I spend my time in darkened rooms and invade computer networks. That's my world.'

'Emma, you belong in all of those places. Just because you haven't been there before, doesn't mean you can't. Just because you grew up in a deprived area doesn't exclude you and don't you let anyone tell you otherwise. Everyone, no matter how they look, who they are or where they are from should ever feel a place is not for them. That leads to segregation and that is not the way the world should be going. Anyway, have you looked in the mirror recently young lady? And as for the success, that came after many years of trying and failing, then trying again. You seem to have that part wrapped up at an early age.

'I think you need to hear this. Without you, and to a degree Chris, we could well have lost Smoke, and that would be on my head, because I allowed him to go in alone, with no back-up inside. I was too focussed on the result to see the dangers. That was a mistake, and one I don't intend to repeat, but you saved me from having to explain to my bosses, and more importantly to Gypsy, why Smoke is no longer with us, and for that I will be forever grateful.

'Then to top it off, you both managed to solve the case. It's people like you that make people like me look so good, and don't you ever forget that, Emma.'

When Emma looked up again, she was crying.

'What's wrong.'

Through the sobs Emma managed to respond,

'I've never really been appreciated before. I'm not used to it; I really don't know what ...'

Helene wrapped her arms around her and pulled her close. The tears from Helene dripped onto the blonde head held close to her.

No one should ever feel that alone. No one.

CHAPTER TWENTY-EIGHT

Chung Xue's mind drifted as he watched the water passing by. The daily ferry trip between Kowloon and North Point on Hong Kong Island was the highlight of his day. Xue belonged here on the water, not stuck in an office entering data into a computer. He didn't even have a window in his tiny cubicle. To Xue, it was nothing more than a prison cell, a torture chamber even.

He stood at the starboard rail on the lower deck of the ferry, the fresh morning air filling his lungs. He was a creature of habit, always choosing to be on the starboard side of the boat. The view of Victoria Harbour opening up as they passed the point at Hung Hom always gave him a thrill first thing in the morning. Every day it would be different, the weather creating a never-ending change in the landscape. On the evening journey he would see the former Kai Tak airport, now being developed as a multipurpose site. Often, large ships would be moored at the new cruise terminal on the former threshold of runway 31. He wondered where they had come from and where they would go. Sometimes, he would imagine himself on board, preparing to get under way, perhaps as the captain, but he knew that would be forever out of his reach. His lot in life would be data entry.

This morning his eyes roamed over the surface of Kowloon Bay, not really focussing on anything; a vacant stare some would call it. Even the sparkling water reflecting the morning sun, did little to lift his spirits today. His eyes latched onto something barely showing above the surface of the water. As the ferry got closer, Chung realised he was looking at a body. Contrary to popular belief, very little remains above the water when a body floats. This he knew from watching American CSI programmes on the tiny TV in his apartment.

He shouted to attract the attention of a crew member.

'Over here. Look, Look! A person in the water.'

A gentle swell rocked the boat and slapped against the side. A slight easterly breeze brought relief from the unseasonably warm day as the HKPF marine officer leaned over the side of Patrol Boat 43. With a deft movement, borne of many years of fishing things out of the harbour, he snagged the body bobbing about face down in the water. Two crew members swiftly brought it aboard. This was only the second time the officer had recovered a corpse, most of the items recovered were not of the human kind.

One of the officers held up an identity card recovered from the wallet in the man's trouser pocket. Whatever Chen Li had done, he had clearly made enemies. Even though he was no expert, the missing fingers and toes suggested this was unlikely to be a suicide, and a good starting point for the murder investigation would be the inscription clearly carved into the man's forehead; 1J3:15.

~§~

1 John 3:15 Everyone who hates his brother is a murderer, and you know that no murderer has eternal life present in him.

*****

HUMAN TRAFFICKING – THE FACTS

Since 2003, the United Nations Office on Drugs and Crime (UNODC) has been collecting international statistics on detected victims of human trafficking. These show that human trafficking is a global issue occurring in every region of the world. Any country can be the origin, transit, or destination for victims, or any combination . The collected data provides information on victims who contacted the authorities and does not reflect the actual prevalence of the crime or the hidden number of victims, meaning the problem could be far worse.

The UNOC 2022 report on Trafficking in Persons[1] shows that in 2020 about 50,000 human trafficking victims were detected in 141 countries. Europe, the Middle East, North America and some countries in East Asia and the Pacific are destinations for trafficking victims. Sixty-five per cent of the victims detected in Western and Southern Europe were from overseas and trafficked from a wide variety of origin countries. Victims from East Asia and Sub-Saharan Africa were detected in almost every region of the world. Central and South-Eastern European victims were detected in large numbers but mainly in European destinations.

Human trafficking is carried out for many purposes; exploitation in the entertainment, hospitality and sex industries, domestic work or forced marriages. Victims can be forced to work on construction sites or in factories and in the agricultural sector, often without any or little remuneration. They often live in fear of violence and are kept in atrocious conditions. Some may fall victim to the human organ trade.

Children are forced to serve as soldiers or commit crimes for organised crime gangs.

In 2020 almost 39 per cent of victims were trafficked for sexual exploitation, the same percentage into forced labour, 10 per cent subjected to forced criminal activity, and another 10 per cent forced into marriage. The remainder were coerced into a variety of purposes such as begging and organ removal. The share of detected victims trafficked for forced labour has steadily increased for more than a decade.

One third of the victims detected is a child; girls mainly for sexual exploitation, boys for forced labour. The percentage of male victims has risen from around 10 per cent in 2003 to 40 per cent in 2020. These figures are only estimates and may vary from one organisation to another. The fact remains, Human Trafficking is a global[2] problem.

We need to be clear here, we are not talking about smuggling migrants, that is an entirely different matter altogether. These figures apply to *people trafficking*, treated as a commodity, the same as sugar, coffee, and drugs. To the traffickers they are not people, they are dollars in the bank.

Financial figures for illegal activities are obviously estimates; criminals are not known for declaring their incomes, but estimates show that the income from trafficking is in the region of $150 billion. Trafficking affects over 28 million victims, that is more than the entire population of Australia.

We simply cannot ignore this horrendous trade in people. Businesses need to do more, law enforcement needs to do more, WE need to do more.

If you suspect someone is the victim of human trafficking, tell the authorities. A false alarm with good intent is better than no alarm at all.

So how would you recognise that someone may have been trafficked? [3]

- •Living with employer.

- •Living in poor conditions.

- •Overcrowded living conditions.

- •Unable to speak without someone else present.

- •Scripted or rehearsed answers.

- •Employer withholding identity documents.

- •Signs of physical abuse.

- •Submissive or fearful.

- •Unpaid or paid very little.

- •Under 18 and in prostitution.

Clearly there are people who may be in some of these situations and not be trafficked, but these can certainly be a strong indication of someone who has been trafficked.

What can you do? The first thing to remember is you must not put yourself or anyone else in danger. If in doubt, report your suspicions to the authorities. Only ask these questions if you feel it is safe for all concerned

- •Can you leave your job if you want to?

- •Can you come and go as you please?

- •Has anyone threatened or hurt you if you try to leave?

- •Are there threats to your family?

•Are you forced to live with your employer?

•Where do you sleep and eat?

•Do you owe money to your employer?

•Do you have your passport/identification? Who has it?

If you suspect someone may be a victim of Human Trafficking, please, please, PLEASE report it to the authorities:

Argentina
Attorney Trafficking and Exploitation of People – PROTEX (Government of Argentina)
   •+54 37542921
Human Trafficking Hotline (Ministry of Justice and Human Rights)
   •145

Australia
Anti-Slavery Australia
(Non-governmental Organisation, NGO)
   •+61 2 9514 9660

Austria
Hotline for Human Trafficking (Austrian Criminal Intelligence Service and Government of Austria
   •+43-1-24836-985383

Brazil
Brazil Hotline for Human Rights (Government of Brazil)
   •100

Cambodia
Cambodian Human Rights and Development Association (ADHOC)
(NGO)
   •+855-23 218653 / 990554

Canada
Human Trafficking National Coordination Centre
(Canadian Police)
  •613-993-7267

Czech Republic
Caritas Operates Magdala, Charity Network
(NGO)
  •+420 296 243 330

Denmark
The Danish Centre Against Human Trafficking hotline
(National Board of Health and Welfare)
  •+45 70 20 25 50

Finland
National Assistance System for Victims of
Trafficking (Government of Finland)
  •+358 29 54 63 177

France
National Network for the Assistance and Protection of
Human Trafficking Victims
(Government of France)
  •+33 (0)4 92 15 10 51

Hungary
Hotline for victims of Trafficking
(Government Hungary, NGO)
  •06-80/20-55-20

India
Anti-Trafficking Helpline
(Ministry of Home Affairs)
  •1800 419 8588
Childline India
(Ministry of Women and Child Development, NGO)
  •1098

Ireland
Hotline for the Confidential Reporting of Suspicions of
Trafficking
(Department of Justice, Government of Ireland)
  •1800 666 111

Italy
National Hotline Against Trafficking
(Department for Equal Opportunities, Government of Italy)
  •800 290 290

Japan
Japan Network Against Trafficking in Persons (JNATIP)
(Government of Japan, NGO)
  •03 3207 7880

Kenya
Childline Kenya
(NGO, Government of Kenya)
  •116

Latvia
Hotline Against Trafficking
(Government of Latvia)
  •80002012

Laos
Sengsavang
(NGO)
●+856 41 260 276

Netherlands
CoMensha, Independent Coordination Center
(NGO)
●+31 33 4481186
Crime Stoppers Netherlands
(NGO)
●0800 70 00

Nigeria
National Agency for Prohibition of Trafficking in Persons
(Government of Nigeria)
●+234 7030000203

Malaysia
National Anti-Trafficking Hotline, Council for Anti-
Trafficking in Persons and Anti-Smuggling of Migrants
(Government of Malaysia)
●03-8000 8000

Poland
The National Consulting and Intervention Centre for the
Victims of Trafficking
(Government of Poland)
●+48 22 628 01 20

Qatar
The Qatar Foundation for Combating Human Trafficking
(QFCHT) Hotline
(NGO)
●+974 44912888

Romania
Hotline Against Trafficking
(Government of Romania)
    •0800 800 678

South Africa
South African National Human Trafficking Hotline
(Government of South Africa)
    •0800 222 777

Taiwan
Foreign Workers Consultation and Protection Hotline
(Ministry of Labour)
    •1955

Thailand
Safe Child Thailand Helpine
(NGO)
    •1387

United States of America
National Human Trafficking Hotline
(U.S. Department of State)
    •+1-888-373-7888
International TIP (Trafficking in Persons) Line
    •+1-802-872-6199

United Kingdom
Modern Slavery and Exploitation Helpline
Unseen UK (NGO)
    •08000 121 700
Gangmasters and Labour Abuse Authority
(Government of the UK)
    •0800 432 0804

References
(1) *The UNOC 2022 report on Trafficking in Persons.* (n.d.). [PDF]. UNOC. Retrieved 18 November 2023, from https://www.unodc.org/documents/data-and-analysis/glotip/2022/GLOTiP_2022_web.pdf

(2) *Polaris_AR-2022_Final-Web.pdf.* (n.d.). Retrieved 18 November 2023, from https://polarisproject.org/wp-content/uploads/2023/09/Polaris_AR-2022_Final-Web.pdf

(3) Identify and Assist a Trafficking Victim. (n.d.). *United States Department of State.* Retrieved 18 November 2023, from https://www.state.gov/identify-and-assist-a-trafficking-victim/

ABOUT THE AUTHOR

Glen R Stansfield likes to kill people – in stories – mostly! Crafting stories with a twist or two, and with strong female protagonists leading the way, he encourages his readers to examine contemporary social issues.

He has self-published two novels, *Fishing for Stones* and *Harry*, which is the prequel to the *Invidia* series.

Contributions to several print and online publications led to the release of a cookbook Around the World in Eighty Dishes. Now residing in Panama with his wife Jess, Glen is currently an ambassador for the Alliance of Independent Authors, encouraging authors worldwide.

You can connect with Glen at www.glenrstansfield.com

Cover created by Glen R Stansfield © 2024

<u>Licenced Images:</u>

Criminologists Couperfield/Shutterstock
Woodland Rob Hatton/Shutterstock
Girl Ariwasabi/Shutterstock
Face Butsaya/Shutterstock

* * *

9 780099 331 1 871